RESOLVE

RESOLVE

J. J. HENSLEY

THE PERMANENT PRESS
Sag Harbor, NY 11963

M

For information, address:
The Permanent Press
4170 Noyac Road
Sag Harbor, NY 11963
www.thepermanentpress.com

Library of Congress Cataloging-in-Publication Data

Hensley, J. J.—
    Resolve / J. J. Hensley.
        pages cm
    ISBN 978-1-57962-313-5
        1. Ex-police officers—Fiction. 2. Murder—Investigation—Fiction. 3. Marathon running—Fiction. 4. Pittsburgh (Pa.)—Fiction. 5. Mystery fiction. I. Title.

PS3608.E587R47 2013
813'.6—dc23   2013001133

Printed in the United States of America

For Kasia and Cassie

The truest of treasures

ACKNOWLEDGEMENTS

When I decided to take on the challenge of writing a novel, I envisioned a process that—like running—can be a very solitary endeavor. What I quickly discovered is how much personal and professional support one needs to finish such a project. I am blessed to know so many wonderful, intelligent people who were willing to assist me in this undertaking and believed in me throughout the journey. It is doubtless I will fail to mention everyone who I am indebted to, so I apologize in advance for any omissions.

Thanks to literary agent, Felice Gums and Idaliz Seymour at the About Words Agency, for believing in a first-time novelist when many others did not. Felice stuck it out with me until we were fortunate enough to discover Martin and Judith Shepard at The Permanent Press, who honor me every day by calling me one of "their" authors. I am also very grateful to Lon Kirschner who designed the book cover and assisted me with promotional materials. Additionally, Joslyn Pine's thorough copyediting corrected many of my grammatical and typographical errors.

When I was in the third grade, chance (and alphabetical order) led to me having what will be a lifelong friendship with Jeff Hartz. He and his wonderful wife, Gretchen, provided me with many suggestions, corrections, Web site assistance, as well as medical and educational insights that greatly improved this book. Truth be told, their young daughter, Abby, may have chimed in as well. Using the family name for a character in the novel is the least I could do to repay their hard work.

During the early portion of my life, I was surrounded by many caring people who dedicated themselves to educating the children of the Westmoreland community in Huntington, West Virginia. I would like to thank all the teachers I encountered in the Wayne County, West Virginia school system who always did the best they could with the resources available. Special thanks go out to Gary Norris, who helped teach me that persistence and dedication can trump natural ability and whose hatred of concrete basketball courts gave me the idea for the opening line of this book.

Throughout my career in law enforcement and the Federal government, I have run across too many remarkable people to possibly name them all here. The men and women I worked with in the Chesterfield County, Virginia Police Department will always be close to my heart. To this day, I am very thankful to have met people like Dave and Gina Shand who are incredible human beings. I was equally blessed to work with many great people during my time with the U.S. Secret Service. People like Brian Lambert and Treva Lawrence were just two of the many good friends I left behind when I transitioned out of law enforcement. My coworkers with the U.S. Office of Personnel Management— Federal Investigative Services inspire me every day. I am proud to work with people who rarely get the recognition they deserve. It is a particular honor to work with the staff of the agency's National Training Center.

Several people in the Pittsburgh community helped me out in writing this book. Thanks go out to William Stuart and Jim Vogel who helped me ensure some of the technical details regarding the Pittsburgh Police Department were correct. Any details that are incorrect are either intentional for purposes of the story, or are inadvertent mistakes on my part. I also need to mention the inspiration and assistance I have gained from the Pittsburgh running community, specifically Jenn Wohlgamuth and the staff at MoJo Running in Seven Fields, Pennsylvania.

Several people helped to proofread this novel. In addition to those mentioned above, Rick Kelly and Heather Brown spent countless hours reminding me my writing was far from perfect.

Usually, they did it in a nice way. My wife and chief editor—Kasia—and my mother—Kitty—tore through manuscripts and made invaluable suggestions. They were not always nice about it, but they love me.

Overall, the family support I have received throughout my life has been incredible. My brother—Brian Hensley—can be both my mirror image and my polar opposite. He and his wife—Julie—are wonderful people who I admire greatly. I will never be able to repay my parents, Jim and Kitty Hensley, for the support they have given me through the years. Not once in my life did either of them suggest I could not accomplish anything in life, and they always did everything in their power to help me along. They are tremendous parents and always have been. My grandmother, Dortha Hensley, has always been there for the family and never fails to give us her honest opinion on any topic, at any time, in any place, at any volume. We love you Dortha. I would also like to thank my relatives in Poland, my in-laws Jadwiga and Waclaw Lach. Thank you for being so kind to me and for raising an incredible daughter. Although I doubt they will ever read this novel, I should probably thank my dogs—Shockoe and Shiloh. They provided inspiration for the dog mentioned in the story.

I am most thankful to my wife, Kasia. For over a decade, she has been my best friend, confidant, and the love of my life. Her devotion, encouragement, and patience during this process have been indescribable. It was she who convinced me I should write a book, and who dared me to dream it could be published. While waiting for this book to be published, Kasia and I welcomed a little girl into the world. A tiny shout-out to Cassie, who can make a bad day vanish by showing me that heartwarming smile. Kasia and Cassie are my heart and my soul.

PROLOGUE

Concrete is harder than asphalt. Most people don't realize that.

Asphalt, blacktop, cinders—they are all more forgiving than concrete. You don't notice it much over short distances, but after a while the distinction will become as obvious to you as a mosquito bite when compared to a gunshot wound. So the rough, blackened, crater-pocked street that I'm on today may not be very appealing to most people, but this morning I'm over-joyed to see it.

This is my second favorite part of the entire journey.

My breath becomes visible for just a moment this early in the morning before the condensation dissipates into the breeze, and the bright colors draped over nervously bouncing bodies come back into focus. The anticipation of nearly 20,000 people standing shoulder to shoulder, front to back, back to front—all facing the same direction—is something to behold. About 4,500 of the runners will individually attempt the full 26.2 miles. The rest will compete in either the half-marathon or on relay teams.

The whole picture is surreal when you really think about it. It's like some LSD-laced zombie movie where thousands of vibrating forms wear ridiculously bright and skimpy outfits, stare at their wrists and prepare to press buttons that will start their watches, and then measure how long it takes to devour the city's unsuspecting population. Then there is a piercing gun-shot. Instead of scrambling back toward their sewer grates and manhole covers—like any respectable members of the undead— the demon spawn march in methodical unison, as if directed by some all-knowing evil entity. Everybody here, including me, should seek professional help.

What other large-scale athletic event has more participants than spectators? Where else do people huddle like emperor penguins at the starting point, spread out as the miles tick off, and then regroup to gulp down doughnuts and bananas at the end? Some of the day's onlookers will have had no idea what they were going to witness. They are accidental audience members who happened to step out their front doors and notice that Nike appears to have staged a breakout from an insane asylum. In urban races like this one, even the city's buildings seem to lord over the runners and look on in amazement as they congregate in one cramped and congested area. They seem to lean and sway to block out the rising sun as if to say, "Hurry, you ibuprofen-loaded ghouls! We can't protect you much longer."

The first time I ran this race, the distraction of the scenery carried me though the hours that I usually spend laboring to ignore the pain. People think I'm a little odd because of what I call *scenery*. The phrase *scenic Pittsburgh* would draw snickers from most people. A few years ago, before I moved to the area, I would have rolled my eyes dismissively too. But it turns out that the dirty, industrial image the city acquired really should have drifted away with the black soot and smoke over a decade ago. The brightly colored yellow bridges, blindingly reflective skyline, and unique neighborhoods are more interesting to me than any mountain, lake or beach. I think it's because the city shows progress. Maybe that's not the word. *Recovery*. Pittsburgh is *recovery*. It's the opposite reaction to the action of the previous century's industrialization. The balancing of the equation.

For the last two years, on the first Sunday in May, I've slinked my body out of bed at four o'clock in the morning and listened to my wife mumble something about me being insane while she drifted back into a peaceful slumber. Then, I have always grabbed my meticulously prepared running gear, eaten my bowl of warm oatmeal with one carefully measured teaspoon of sugar added, and headed downtown from our suburban home.

Each of those times I had already picked up my race bib the day before, checked and double-checked that I had my timing strip that would be wrapped around my shoe laces, and studied the course like a general surveying a battlefield. You know . . . in case the thousands of other people in the marathon don't know where they are going. I guess I *could* accidentally follow the half-marathon crowd if I were illiterate or blind and couldn't read the twenty large poster board signs hanging on light posts, buildings, and scaffolding at the point of divergence. The ten volunteers screaming at the top of their lungs, "Half to the left! Full to the right!" is a bit of a clue as well. So, getting lost on the course has never happened to me. Obviously because I study the course. I'm pretty smart like that.

The first time I ran the race, I crossed the finish line in 3 hours 43 minutes and 21 seconds. Last year, I really pushed it and knocked off a full 13 minutes, despite the terrible rain and humidity. Those times may not sound like much, but when the expedition to the finish is 26.2 miles away, *any* time is pretty good in my opinion.

People like me try to use a form of black humor to minimize the task at hand. We say unbelievably clever things like, "It's not the first 26 miles—it's the .2 that gets you." But the harsh, pavement-pounding reality of it is that 26.2 miles is a long freak'n way and there's no faking it if you want to finish. You can get lucky and run an impressive sprint. You can have an aberration of a 5K race. However, the brutal attrition of a long distance race is the best kind of truth serum there is.

After several miles, the ground beneath you seems to strike back. It punches into your feet with precise, focused blows and the impact that was initially being absorbed by your shoes migrates to the soles of your feet. From there the smoke signals of pain travel through your shins and into your knees. Your knees then convert the subtle puffs into high-speed internet signals that shoot up your spinal cord to produce pop-up ads in your brain that tell you that you're doing something unnatural and Darwin would not approve.

If you weren't completely honest with yourself in the months of training before a race, then you had better understand that the deception you allowed into your life is going to come back and kick you in the ass. No exceptions. That's how this sport is. I suppose that's how most things are.

Everybody in this race has a story. These things have it all. This is my sixth marathon and I've learned that when you really look, I mean *really* look, you can file people into neat little categories. Interwoven into the expected Type-A personalities you can find the former high-school star desperately trying to retrieve a little piece of forgotten glory, the former chain smoker, the ex-druggie, the new mother who wants to lose her pregnancy weight, the scorched divorcee with something to prove, the resilient cancer survivor, the nomadic retiree who abandoned an unfulfilled career, the clinically depressed man whose meds aren't working like they used to, the once hopeful who lost faith.

Recovery at every turn.

I trained hard, considering the circumstances. I didn't cheat myself at any point in my preparations. However, I don't have any illusions about setting any personal records this year. I'll line up next to the pace group led by the young and athletic-looking blonde woman whose ponytail sways back and forth like a silent pendulum over a sign on her back that reads, 3 HR 30 MIN 26.2 PACE GROUP. But after the first three miles, I know I won't see her or her Ben-Gay-slathered gaggle again.

During these pre-race moments, adrenaline usually makes me feel light and free. But the full gravity of comprehension is making me feel like the road and my shoes are magnets with opposing charges.

As the starting gun goes off and the tidal wave moves forward, I can't help but do the rough math in my head:

Out of the 4,500 people who start the marathon, many will not finish.

Over 200 will simply stop running, realizing that it just wasn't their day.

Another 100 or so will get injured and have to stop to get treatment.

And I know that 1 is about to be murdered.

I didn't come across this information by happenstance. I didn't inadvertently overhear it in some random conversation on the street. It didn't fall into my lap when I got copied on an email by mistake. There's no real mystery as to why I know this. I know a man is going to be murdered for one simple reason.

I'm going to kill him.

Mile 1

The initial surge of collective momentum always carries you through the start. It's strange that such a solitary sport starts this way. On these cool mornings, the crack of the starter's pistol is followed by the formation of a rainbow of old sweatshirts that are tossed aside to be picked up later for charity. Occasionally, one of these articles, which was meant to keep someone warm prior to the start, will land on your head as you try to negotiate the crowd. Fortunately, the packed-in throng of runners moves so slowly at this point that not much concentration is needed. Having someone's faded VOTE FOR GORE/ LIEBERMAN IN 2000 sweatshirt draped over your head could be a bit distracting at a faster pace. But at this point, the worst that could happen is you might be caught up in a crash comparable to a collision of lethargic snails.

A few spectators stand along Smallman Street, which pulls away from the downtown convention center. They are mostly family members and friends who can't believe they got up this early, but have come to lend moral support. It's not common knowledge that this city enjoys fewer sunny days than Seattle, but it's true. Our audience is trying to take advantage of a rare beautiful morning, and its members jockey for position in the warm sunlight.

After the runners pass the starting line, some of the devotees will spread out to various spots on the course hoping to catch a glimpse of their wife, husband, boyfriend, girlfriend, mother, son, or daughter. Others will visit the local markets before migrating one block west toward the overhang of the convention center where they wait for runners to start trickling past the finish line.

This stretch down Smallman Street runs parallel to the Allegheny River along the Strip District. The area is full of mostly old brick warehouses that contain markets, restaurants, and bars. The road here is a treacherous field of broken asphalt surrounded by manhole covers that jut out of the surrounding grey terrain fully intent on gripping an unsuspecting ankle. Like most western Pennsylvania roads, it is a layered patchwork of asphalt and concrete laid down with no regard to elevation or color. We have two seasons in this area: Winter and Construction.

When I look down, the only thing I can see in front of me is the next runner's heels kicking up and preventing me from seeing any potential hazards. I know they are there. It's just a matter of watching the people around me and preparing to react to the threat that I know is lying in wait for me. The whole thing is really kind of a paradox. You have to be comfortable and relaxed to run a good race. But the minute you get too comfortable, that's when the wheels come off, and the hard earth below your feet races up to meet your face.

━━━⟿⟿⟾━━━

The first few weeks after the students return from spring break are always frustrating. Most underclassmen leave their intellectual motivation on the beaches of Florida or South Carolina, and the seniors do little more than count down the days until graduation. Ironically, many come back with actual questions about the criminal justice system. Unfortunately, the questions are not derived from some deep epiphany acquired while reading Beccaria or Lombroso. Most questions are about getting records expunged for public intoxication, underage drinking, or public nudity. One time, I even had a slightly embarrassed, pimple-faced sophomore come up to me after a lecture and hesitantly ask me what the best course of action was in handling a charge related to the unlawful theft of, vandalism to, and unauthorized use of, an alpaca. You can't make this stuff up.

It was just a few weeks ago that I was grading papers in my office with Steven Thacker, my chronically miserable, and completely obnoxious, graduate assistant for the past two semesters. For the tenth time in as many minutes, he groaned, rolled his eyes, and began a rant that I was becoming all too familiar with.

"It's simple subject-verb agreement! And that goddamn spellcheck! Do they think it is going to catch Latin phrases?" He held up the paper where a red circle surrounded the misspelled Latin phrase.

Steven's hazel eyes narrowed and he used his pen-wielding hand to brush his shaggy blond hair away from them as he rambled on.

"Why won't they just proofread their papers one time? And *this* is supposed to be the future of the criminal justice system?"

He had scrawled the correct spelling under the student's error in big red letters. I squinted slightly to see from across my desk.

Without mentioning that Steven was only a couple of years older than most of the undergraduates, I reminded him, "A lot of them aren't Criminology majors. Even out of those who are, many will end up doing something else."

If ever there was a confluence of conflictions, Steven was it. He was an elitist from a poor family. He was quick to condemn others, but couldn't stand to be judged. He despised jocks, but was dutiful in his kickboxing training. And he hated anyone who was apprehensive about declaring his beliefs, yet he was still in the closet about his sexuality.

I happened to know about his sexual preference because while on a solitary run near campus one day, I saw him kissing another young man in the doorway of a townhouse. He saw me when he turned around, and later told me that he was in the closet because if his family knew he was gay, they would cut off all communication with him. That was about as close as I had ever come to having a heart-to-heart conversation with Steven. He could be horribly abrasive at times. Okay, actually he was pretty much an arrogant jackass, but I assumed that much of his animosity and abrasiveness must have come from his feeling like he had to hide from the world. I never liked Steven, but I still felt terrible that he thought he had to hide his true self from those around him. In this day and age, it must be torturous to feel as if you have to live in the shadows.

"Regardless of their major," Steven fired back without looking up, "they should realize by now that this isn't exactly high school. It's time for them to take a little pride in their work."

He cast a critical eye back on the paper. "Holy crap! It's *t-h-e-i-r*, not *t-h-e-r-e*!" Steven spat out with an air of disbelief.

He slammed down the notebook and wiped droplets of spit from his chin. In just a couple of months, he would be on his way to Florida State to work on his PhD. At this point, Florida didn't seem far enough away for my liking.

He was right that this wasn't *exactly* high school, but this wasn't *exactly* Harvard either. The Pittsburgh area is absolutely overflowing with colleges. In addition to the well-known schools like the University of Pittsburgh, Duquesne University, and Carnegie Mellon, smaller schools are sprinkled all along Interstate 79 and branch out from the Ohio, Allegheny, and Monongahela rivers. Some of the downtown schools are so close together that a wide-eyed, map-holding freshman could be walking through one campus and accidentally drift onto another.

For those outside the city, Pennsylvania has more unique ways to confuse the uninformed. We actually have universities named after people or towns that have the same names as other U.S. states. Imagine the bewilderment when an alumnus tells a prospective employer that they went to California University . . . of Pennsylvania. Or a proud parent proclaims, "My daughter got into Indiana University," and then has to add the requisite ". . . of Pennsylvania." It's all very odd. You never hear of other states advertising the "Pennsylvania University of Alabama" or some such nonsense.

Most colleges in the region do alright in the prestige department. If you were to put them on three tiers, I suppose Pitt, Carnegie Mellon, and the Penn State branch campuses get the most academic respect. A majority of the other schools in the area struggle to distinguish themselves from the crowd. Then there is my distinguished employer.

Three Rivers University lies just north of downtown and just south of respectable. Originally founded by the wealthy and highly deranged owner of a steel company, the university acquired a reputation for providing a slightly less-than-mediocre education at an affordable price.

As the story goes, by 1923, the founder—the late Henry Gadson Jr.—had been the mesmerizing leader of a nice little group of the upper-class citizenry in the Pittsburgh area. By today's standards, I suppose we would categorize Mr. Gadson's New Strength and Accordance Society as a cult. Inspired by the influx of eastern European laborers and their various beliefs, he and his circle of bored and wealthy associates strongly believed that by meeting in rooms full of candles, drinking prohibited spirits, covering their faces with a peculiar oil, and reciting passages from obscure religious and philosophical texts, they could bring about a new enlightenment during this period of exciting industrialization and unrelenting prohibition. To bring about this period of enlightenment, Gadson needed a platform.

So he used his resources to create the College of Casting Light and encouraged the Hungarian, Polish, and Czechoslovakian millworkers to learn English and improve their understanding of the world. Although the school was, and is to this day, very blue collar, it was a progressive undertaking that was unheard of in the era.

In spite of language barriers and cultural differences, by 1927 the college was doing pretty well. Finding people who could communicate in all of the necessary languages was certainly a major problem, but bit by bit the school helped some people improve their situations or, at least, learn a little bit of English. Then things started to head downhill for good ol' Henry. First, his cult disbanded and left Gadson without the moral support of his closest peers. Then came the stock market crash in 1929 in which Gadson lost a bundle. After traveling to New York to meet with his company's investors and accountants, Henry returned to Pittsburgh and took a walk into one of his mills. Standing on a walkway over a large vat of molten steel, Gadson decided to enlighten himself and forge a path into history by throwing his body headfirst into the white-hot abyss. Legend has it that his statue in the middle of campus was actually made from that very same tub of molten liquid, but that seems a little crazy even for this place.

The college's board members, fearful of the public scandal and tired of Gadson's eccentricities, understandably decided to create some distance between his legacy and the school. While the name change was an easy thing to do, the university is still basically a blue-collar, career-oriented entity with its share of oddball faculty members and trustees.

"Dr. Keller?"

Between being absorbed in the paper in front of me and Steven's weekly nervous breakdown, I hadn't heard the knock on the door. Steven had taken his gloomy presence away from my desk in order to retrieve another paper from the box in the corner of my office. His head was buried in the large cardboard box. He looked like an ostrich hiding from a cheetah.

"Hello, Lindsay. What can I help you with?"

Lindsay Behram was a senior in my CRIM 012—Victimology class. One of the benefits of working at a small college is that you get to know most of the students by name.

She looked hesitant. This was bad. This was going to go one of two ways. Either she was going to tell me that she was going to be late on an assignment and needed an extension, or—something I had been dreading for a while was coming.

"I was hope—hoping . . . I was wondering if I could ask you a question."

I swallowed hard and carefully constructed my next sentence in my head.

I get paid to talk for a living.

"Sure."

Yep. Brilliant as always.

"Do you . . . I mean . . . What's the university's policy about, you know . . . student-faculty . . . relationships?"

The rustle of papers in the corner caught her attention. The ostrich's head popped out of the hole and its normally unpleasant scowl had been transformed into subdued astonishment. Lindsay fixed her eyes on him in return.

Maybe this was a good thing. I had known this was a real possibility. Lindsay was a bubbly, outgoing, flirtatious student who had waited around to talk to me too many times when the other students left the classroom. Aside from that, she was a total knockout and she knew it. I'm talking about the type of girl who even the cockiest of male students doesn't dare approach until they load themselves up with three or four beers. She was tall and athletic looking, with the ability to shake her head and have every strand of her straight blonde hair fall magically into place. Men loved her. Women resented her. I just didn't want to deal with her.

Initially, I told myself that her lingering was legitimate and that her only interest was related to the course materials. Then the questions went from reasonable to basic. Then the questions weren't really questions, but rather complimentary observations about my presentation. Next, a quick brush on my arm while we talked. Then last week, a touch on the hand. And just yesterday, after all the other students had gone, she blatantly leaned across my desk, smiled, displayed major cleavage, and asked me if I wanted to grab dinner at her place to discuss the course. You know—because the effects of victim impact statements in church-based child molestation trials make for wonderful dinnertime conversation. She had actually boldly stroked my hand with her index finger when she asked me.

This had to stop. Being completely unprepared for her proposal at the time, I wasn't sure how to react. I simply pulled my hand away and told her I couldn't, while hurriedly gathering up my lecture notes. I left the room more numb with disbelief than anything else. Now I had collected my thoughts and I was more prepared to end this.

First off, I'm married and I plan on staying that way. Second, I don't think unemployment would agree with me. I get into trouble when I'm bored. And third, I'm thirty-nine years old. Granted, lots of men would ridicule me for not taking advantage of an eager twenty-two-year-old who wants to jump in the sack with a distinguished professor, but it's just not my thing. I have standards. If I'm going to nail some girl half my age, then I want to make sure I can hand her a wad of cash and send her back out on the street.

Just kidding.

"Lindsay, let me make something very clear." She and Steven were still staring at each other. She hadn't realized he was in the room.

"Any relationship between students and professors is strictly prohibited; and if I thought for one second that *anybody* was pursuing something like that, I would take the issue up with Dean Silo myself."

I can sound pretty authoritarian when I want to.

She was still looking at Steven.

"Hey! Do you understand me?"

She returned a confused gaze to me. I was actually glad that Steven was here to witness this. I needed him to back me up in case she made any crazy accusations later. The touching and flirting weren't overt enough for me to take action until yesterday's events, but now I had something tangible to point to. At least it was out in the open now.

"What . . . I . . . I'll talk to you later." She quickly vanished from the room and the heavy door swung closed.

Steven was still staring at the now vacant doorway. I was already feeling bad for her. I didn't know what kind of reaction to expect. Sadness? Fear? Maybe even anger? But she looked a little puzzled by my reaction. I knew I should have been clearer yesterday, but I was taken aback by her directness. Had I misled her in some way? I knew I was a charming bastard, but I really didn't think that I had led her on.

Well, whatever her intentions were, now she could move on to some quarterback or star pitcher closer to her age. Maybe she would go to law school next semester, entice some horny, parasitic ambulance chaser, and use what she learned in his class to drag him—and the school—into a messy sexual harassment lawsuit.

Maybe I'm too much of an optimist.

Mile 2

Things don't thin out much as we make the turn onto Penn Avenue and head in the opposite direction back toward the convention center. The annoyance builds on the hardening faces of some runners as they try to weave through the crowd. The pairs and groups of runners who run two or three wide on the street in order to maintain a conversation are like picket fences standing in the way of those who have their sights set on achieving a PR. That's a *personal record* in runners' lingo.

Store owners and street vendors cheer as we pass by. Burly guys carrying crates of vegetables stare in bewilderment at people who exert themselves for fun, not wages. In cities like this there is always the mandatory homeless guy who stumbles out of an alley in a haze and begins running with the crowd. He generally smiles and yells out a short phrase like, "Go Steelers! Whoop them Browns!" or some other expression that is guaranteed to elicit a cheer from the crowd. After about a half block, he gasps for air, steers himself toward the curb, and absorbs the applause from the onlookers with humility and grace, bowing out of the race like a true legend.

I know from reading the course map that two-thirds of the way down this straightaway are the first water and medical stations. They are generally in close proximity to each other. That's when the great mystery of how to drink water out of a paper cup while running will once again rear its ugly head. It's remarkably difficult to do this and manage not to either drown yourself or pour the water all over you. There are a few different approaches: the sip-and-hope, the chug-and-cough, or the popular funnel technique, where you bend the paper cup to create a channel of water flowing into your mouth, those are probably the top three. I usually attempt the funnel technique, with limited success. I've run in some races where they've used sturdy Styrofoam cups. You can pick out the funnel-loving rookie who can't figure out why his cup of water just exploded all over his face when he tried to bend it. It's funny when it doesn't happen to you.

———

"You know what the number one cause of divorce is, don't you?"

I bit my tongue, having heard Aaron tell this one before.

"Marriage!"

There was rhythmic laughter between footfalls.

"Randy, the point is that Debbie has been with me for over twenty years, so I don't think she's going to leave me now just because I bought another boat."

"I'm not saying she's going to leave you, Aaron. I'm just saying that you make things too hard on yourself. You know you're never going to hear the end of it."

"What about you? Don't you think a man has a right to buy a bigger bass boat regardless of what his wife says?" He had turned his head from Randy and was looking over at Jacob now.

There was the slightest tick on Aaron's face as he realized his mistake. Jacob was a widower who had lost his wife, Tabatha, to an undiagnosed heart condition a few months before. Everybody knew that their marriage had serious problems, but he still felt the loss immensely.

After a thoughtful pause, Jacob responded with a sly grin, "I suppose so. Just don't expect your pole to get any action anywhere but on that boat."

The crack alleviated the temporary tension.

That topic was still off-limits. During our frequent runs, pretty much anything was open for discussion: work, sports, politics, the economy—pretty much anything that distracted us from the run itself. Distraction is a friend on these runs in the first weeks of spring when the cold hangs on, only reluctantly loosening its grip. Talking about our relationships was commonplace until Tabatha's death. That spring, out of respect for Jacob, we mostly avoided the subject and he quietly appreciated our discretion.

We tried to run together every Monday, Wednesday, and Friday during the fall and spring semesters, at least when the cold and snow didn't hinder us. We scheduled Saturday as rest day because Sunday mornings were reserved for our individual long runs, which consisted of anywhere between ten to twenty miles depending on where we were in our respective training schedules.

While I liked running with those guys during the week, I came to appreciate the solitary nature of my Sunday runs. You can really think things through on those days when you have to stay in your own head and there isn't any chatter to distract you. It's also more of a challenge simply because of that—no distractions. You have to train your brain to ignore the fatigue and the pain all on its own.

Those days in late March were the initial ramp-up to the Pittsburgh Marathon for all of us, so that day's frigid eight-miler was more than enough. Well, at least it was enough for me. We had always done our best to find a common gap in our schedules to make sure that we had time for a six- or eight-mile run along the river trails or through the city streets. The other three established the ritual before I arrived at TRU. Jacob invited me to join the group after repeatedly seeing me running by myself. He'd been my running and professional mentor ever since.

Most of the sidewalks and paths are wide enough for only two or three people to run side by side; so as the junior member of the group, in both seniority and age, I typically trailed a few feet behind out of deference. That, and I didn't want Jacob to see me huffing and puffing at this pace.

The man didn't seem human. Despite being fifteen years older than me, Dr. Jacob Kasko could stick right with me for a marathon distance. By the day of the race, my conditioning should have improved to the point where I would be a minute or two faster than Jacob; but at that point in our training he was ahead of me.

"Cyprus, what are you doing?"

Jacob used the brief moment of levity to change the topic of conversation. I knew what he was asking me, but I worked up my best perplexed expression. I loved messing with him about this.

"Please tell me you are *not* eating that crap again," Jacob said in his playfully exasperated tone. "Out of all of us, you're the one who should be the most willing to submit to modern advances and not stick with eating habits from elementary school. I've told you a hundred times that Pop-Tarts are not proper running fuel."

Jacob pulled one of his beloved calorie-filled gel packs out of the pouch on his elastic running belt.

"You have to properly refuel or you'll keep fading down the stretch. If you want to finish strong, you have to refuel!"

At least once a week we went through this routine. Jacob heard me unzipping the small pouch on my waist belt, dig into a crumpled-up plastic baggie, and pull out pieces of a broken-up Pop-Tart. It drove him crazy, so I kept doing it. He bought the state-of-the-art silver gel packs that are full of carbohydrates, vitamins, protein, jet fuel, PCP, or some combination of substances that helped to replace some of the calories he burned during a long run. He converted Aaron and Randy long before I arrived on campus. On every one of our runs, they greedily squeezed the gooey red, blue, or brown ooze out of the packs and into their mouths every few miles. It's disgusting if you ask me.

"I guess I'm still a kid at heart. Besides, guys your age need all of the advantages you can get."

A collective moan came from the pack.

"Oh, here we go," Aaron chimed in. "We take the young Dr. Keller under our wings, accept him as one of our own, and he treats us with utter disdain."

Aaron Caferty was a professor in the School of Business; which is to say that he taught mostly real estate and basic marketing classes to the region's future slumlords and telemarketers.

Don't get me wrong. I liked Aaron. But he sometimes acted as if he were going to produce a modern-day Adam Smith, when he was more likely to produce the next Adam Sandler.

"Come on guys, leave Cyprus alone," said Randy Walker, my colleague in the Criminology department. "Obviously, any boy who carries the name of an island is bound to hold on to his independence. Besides, you can't expect a man from a non-academic background to trust a bunch of old intellectuals."

Ouch.

He liked to take these jabs at me. The fact that I looked ten years younger than I was had always meant that I'd fallen victim to labels like *boy* and *kid*. I'd gotten used to it over the years, so it didn't usually bother me. However, Randy's suggestion that I wasn't a *true* academic was his way of putting me in my place. Normally, I would have fired back some witty retort, but to be honest, I was pretty winded and the frosty air hitting my lungs was getting the best of me.

What he was referring to was the fact that after I finished my undergraduate work at the University of Maryland, I was a Baltimore city police officer for a while. After accumulating some hefty student loans while at U of M, I found out that Baltimore PD had a great student loan repayment program. All I had to do was work as a community police officer in some of Baltimore's more *troubled* areas for four years. Translation—*Send the skinny college boy into the hood. If he lives, we'll shell out some bucks.* So that's what I did. For four years and one day.

I fell in love with Criminology while at U of M. Everything was so neat and logical. There were rational theories for absolutely everything. I completely immersed myself in theories with cool names like *differential association, anomie*, and *hedonistic calculus*. It all made perfect sense. The inexplicable became understandable. Then I took that knowledge to the streets of Baltimore where I saw levels of depravity that books couldn't describe. I saw people who never had a chance and would never have a chance. In four years I was a changed man, and it wasn't for the better. I found myself on a treadmill of apathy and distrust that I couldn't escape. I had to try to identify some way of finding a glimmer of hope in the system and in humanity.

After the Baltimore experience, I decided to return to my hometown in southern West Virginia and become a probation officer. I had seen the worst of the worst and I suppose I was looking for some evidence that criminals could be rehabilitated. So I looked toward probation work as one way to help some people turn their lives around. I guess I had some successes, but in that poverty-stricken area surrounded by hopelessness, I soon found myself back on the treadmill and in a cycle of depression.

At first, I stopped socializing with my coworkers. Then I started finding reasons to avoid old friends. I followed that up with not exercising, taking sick days from work, reading two or three pages of a book and angrily tossing it aside. Movies—nope. Hikes into the woods—nothing. Relationships with women—infrequent and forgettable. Alcohol—more than I should have had, less than an alcoholic.

Some days I sat. Just sat in my apartment staring at a television I wasn't watching and that pumped out sounds I didn't register. Other days I went to work, went through the motions, moved a few papers around my desk, started getting short-tempered with clients, and departed no better off than I arrived.

I had no idea where my life was going and no idea where I wanted it to go. I was completely off course, and the worst part was that I didn't even know what course I was looking for.

"Cyprus, you keep eating your kid's food. Don't let anybody rob you of your childhood," Randy crooned with mock sympathy.

As our three-person running cabal turned past the green athletic fields toward the three-story recreation building where warm showers awaited us, I noticed a black sedan with a red bubble light on the dashboard parked in front of the main entrance. One of the student employees who usually checked university IDs at the front desk stood next to two men who were wearing dark slacks and dress shirts with subdued ties dangling from beneath somber jackets.

I wondered why city detectives were here instead of the usual campus security guards hired by the school. If there were a theft or an assault, campus security would respond and call the police only if they were needed. There should have been a TRU security patrol car there too.

As we approached the front sidewalk my question was answered when the student employee's eyes widened upon seeing the four of us and with a penetrating point aimed at my chest said, "That's him. That's Dr. Keller."

Mile 3

Having backtracked through the Strip District, the still continuous line of runners makes a hard right back across Smallman Street onto the 16th Street Bridge. This is the first of five bridge crossings that we'll make during the course of the race. I've already fallen back from the 3 hour 30 minute pace group, and I expect that I'll be seeing the 3 hour 45 minute group shortly. The elevation increases slightly as I work my way up the bridge, and it will drop off after the midway point. I can already detect hints of separation between the vibrantly colored shirts decorated with the dangling cords of iPods. It's usually this first hill when you see the gaps form and the seamless stream of durability starts to rip apart. It doesn't take much and it doesn't take long. This early in the contest it's more psychological than anything. The key is to keep your faith when things get difficult. You have to remember that even the smallest of climbs can shake your confidence to the core and cause you to question your resolve.

"Dr. Keller? Dr. Cyprus Keller?" said one of the detectives cautiously. He was expecting one of the older-looking men in the group to step forward.

Detectives are pretty easy to pick out if you're accustomed to seeing them. It doesn't take superhuman observation skills to key-in on the obviously unmarked car, cynical expressions, worn shoes, and unbuttoned coats with foreboding bulges near the hip. The fact that I saw detectives' badges displayed on their belts may have helped too.

"Please. It's just Cyprus." I answered.

Cops hate pompous titles. For that matter, so do I.

"What can I do for you detectives?" I asked.

Then, my thoughts raced to the point where they should have already been.

"Is my wife okay?"

The smaller of the two detectives, the one wearing the black leather jacket, said, "I'm sure your wife is fine. This isn't a family matter or anything like that. Do you have a minute?" He gestured to a picnic table that was away from my colleagues and any roaming ears.

My colleagues told me they would catch up with me later as I walked—slightly out of breath and covered with sweat—with the detectives over to the table. I'm used to being around cops, and as a rule they don't make me nervous, but I was certainly concerned about what they could have wanted from me.

None of us had bothered to sit when the detective began again.

"I'm Detective Shand," he announced, "and this is Detective Hartz." Shand gestured to his partner who dipped his head at me while pulling his coat tighter around him as a breeze shot by. "We need to ask you a few questions."

"Um . . . sure."

I get paid to talk for a living.

Shand was in his early thirties, shorter than me, and personified the city of his employment. His rivet neck looked like it belonged on the end of a socket wrench, and his torso was that of a man who enjoyed a good beer. He completely filled out a leather jacket that was just short enough for the bottom of a holster to be visible on his right side. His light complexion was characteristic of the area, and his squared-off hair screamed former military. His movements betrayed a hint of shrouded agility. The fact that he was home-grown was also abundantly clear after the first few words he spoke. His distinct Pittsburgh dialect leapt from his amplifying presence, and it was easy to imagine him throwing out a *yinz* in place of the more common *you all*.

He pulled out a small notepad and asked, "Do you know a student named Lindsay Behram?"

Son of a bitch.

She must have made some harebrained, outlandish accusation against me. In the back of my mind I was afraid she might accuse me of coming on to her or harassing her, but it never occurred to me that she would call the cops on me. What the hell for? She could have said anything. Sure, Steven was there when I shot her down, but she could say that something happened between us anywhere . . . anytime! How do you defend yourself against something like this?

I didn't allow my expression to betray my anger.

"Yes. She's a student in one of my classes."

Now it was Detective Hartz's turn. "Do you know her well?"

Did his tone carry just a touch of condescension?

Hartz was the older of the two and the polar opposite of his partner. Standing six feet five inches tall and weighing at least 230 pounds, his skin was dark brown and his voice baritone. His dark coffee-colored suede coat that he kept pulling around his massive shoulders by the lapels matched his experienced eyes. I noticed an enormous ring on his finger that prominently displayed a perfectly placed silver "Y" on top of a red stone. The word "National" arched above the garnet with "Champions" providing the cradle. I surmised that more than a quarter of a century prior he had played football at Youngstown State and made several quarterbacks pray for a quick death.

Determined not to react to any subtle insinuations, I calmly replied, "As well as you can know one out of twenty students in a class. I guess I've only known her for about three months."

It was Shand's turn now. They must have been partners for a while. They had a smooth back-and-forth tennis routine down.

"During those three months, have you . . . socialized with her? Seen her outside of class? Maybe become close with her?"

"Like I said, she is just a student in one of my classes. What's happened? What did she say?"

Ignoring my questions, Hartz asked, "Just one class?"

"Yes. Victimology," I answered a little too quickly.

"Victimology?" Shand bounced back to me even more rapidly.

The two detectives exchanged a quick glance. I understood they had a job to do, but I didn't like being the mouse batted around between two predatory cats. I especially didn't like having to wait for them to tell me what the accusation was when I could probably guess from a list of deviant forms of behavior. These two were not rookies, and I knew they weren't going to give me anything without some prompting. Show what you have to and keep the rest to yourself. That's the rule when you are questioning someone.

I was shivering uncomfortably from the rapidly cooling sweat trickling under the collar of my black and gold Pittsburgh Pirates sweatshirt. The glacial stiffening of my body contrasted with the incendiary activity smoldering in my mind.

My God! Was she accusing me of rape? I should have picked up on this the first time I thought that she might have been flirting with me. I should have taken precautions. I should have bolted out of the classroom after class. Carried a tape recorder. Something. Anything!

I wasn't going to play this game.

Letting them know that I caught the look they shared, I blurted out, "Is there a problem I should know about? What the hell is going on?"

Shand looked at me without the slightest trace of irritation. He calmly said, "It's nothing. It's just ironic considering the course name. She was killed last night."

Mile 4

As we come off the bridge, the street changes to Chestnut and carries us into the North Shore and East Allegheny neighborhoods. This residential area is where we'll see spectators sitting on their porches, drinking their morning coffee, and smiling at the production in front of them that has disrupted their usually monotonous Sunday morning routines. There is sporadic clapping from block to block, and we dash by the police cars that block intersections for us. Nobody is cold anymore. Fifty-seven degrees may seem chilly before the start, but after a few miles your body is warm enough. Anything warmer than the low sixties and you'd be shocked how the atmosphere can drain you.

In the 1982 Boston Marathon, Dick Beardsley and Alberto Salazar provided the most memorable finish in that race's history. Maybe the sport's history. The race has been immortalized as the "Duel in the Sun"; and one of the main storylines involves the ridiculously high temperature during the race and how it both mentally and physically depleted the runners. The way the meteorological conditions have been made part of the legend, you would think the heat of that April day would have been comparable to an August day in Savannah. The high temperature that day was only about seventy degrees.

I'm not tired at all, but I feel like throwing up. I'm thinking about the ancient maxim, "The fear of death is more to be dreaded than death itself." There's something to that, I suppose. I think if you know death is imminent then there may be a certain solace in that. It's inevitable. It's going to happen regardless of what actions you take. Just submit and accept. However, when the outcome is less than certain—even if all of the data tells you that death is highly likely, but not absolute—then the ambiguity of the outcome can overwhelm your senses and cause your psyche to overheat.

When you think about it, dying in this environment is fitting. Legend has it that the marathon's origins date back to 490 BC when a Greek soldier named Pheidippides ran from the battlefield of Marathon all the way to Athens to announce news of the Greek victory over the Persians. He did it. Then he dropped dead. He didn't even get a doughnut or a finisher's medal.

The left turn onto East Ohio Street is ahead, meaning the brigade of the insane will get corralled westward into a series of parks lined by townhouses and duplexes. I'm coming up on signs posted on the sides of the road that have a big red "4" staring down at me.

Rushing at me is the first of five points where it may happen. I shouldn't have come today, knowing what I know, but I can't hide from this. Whatever happens today is a result of my own actions. My hands are anything but clean.

I'm not moving that fast, but I'm feeling a little dizzy. I suddenly realize it's because I'm holding my breath. I've got to keep it together.

Got to see this through.

———⟡———

I've never been one who enjoys the rush of uncertainty. I really haven't had that sensation since I was drifting around in my professional life, trying to figure out who I wanted to be. Despite having done nothing wrong, the detectives' questions put me back on my heels. When you're used to being the authority figure in nearly every conversation you have, feeling defensive is pretty rare. But when it does happen, you feel your world's axis tilt just a little. Not enough to topple you over, but just enough to remind you that your perception of control is a tenuous illusion, and that you have spent a large part of your life talking yourself into believing your dominance is real.

It was obvious to me that the transition from a cop to a probation officer did not fix the underlying condition that caused my professional crisis of faith. It temporarily treated the symptoms, but then the disease came back with a paralyzing vengeance. I needed something to give meaning to my life and put me on track. I needed something to keep the millstone of my disillusionment from compressing me into psychological rubble. That's when I met Kaitlyn.

On the days I managed to shake off my anguish enough so that I could force myself into going to work, I spent most of my time interviewing, listening to, and re-arresting every type of criminal offender southern West Virginia had to offer. Culturally speaking, it was a different world down there. Criminally speaking, not so much. You could substitute "Baltimore crack dealer" for "West Virginia Oxycodone-pusher" and the story was basically the same in the end. Those who demanded the drug found those who could supply. Competition was eliminated by law enforcement activity, self-destruction, or rival conflicts. Black, white, Hispanic, male, female—it didn't matter. All of the players eventually got locked up or killed. The final tally for everyone in the chain was always zero. Nevertheless, the game would go on with replacements for the fallen; and when the courts decided that somebody was going to get a chance at redemption through the probation system, then I was there to show him how to avoid the stumbling blocks. Or, if he did happen to fall down, it was my job to throw him back into the jaws of the prison system. And everybody eventually falls. It's just a matter of degree.

I had all kinds of offenders on my client list. Most were involved with oxy or meth, but there was an assortment of others as well. I don't have a lot of positive memories about the job, but I did get one good thing out of it. Not every guy can say that the state correctional system helped him meet the love of his life.

Kaitlyn entered my life when the courts had ordered one of my stellar-citizen clients to attend one-on-one anger management counseling a couple of times a week. As part of a new community-friendly initiative, I was basically supposed to hold his hand while I took him to some office complex and introduced him to his counselor. I took Mr. Grumpy up to the fifth floor where I had been told the counselor's office was. After a few minutes in the waiting room, Kaitlyn Richards came out to meet me—I mean Mr. Grumpy—or whatever his name was.

She looked every bit the part of the consummate professional in her dark blue pants suit and a pair of low matching heels. Even in business attire, auburn hair pulled back into a ponytail, and wearing hardly any makeup, she couldn't hide her good looks. We shook hands and she introduced herself in a confident, but not arrogant manner. Her grip on my hand suggested to me that she would spend her days listening to the frustrations of others, and then take her own out on a heavy bag at a local gym. When our hands broke contact, I noted that even in her current attire a swimmer's physique was pleasantly noticeable.

She complemented all of this with a look of total alertness, and it was easy to assume that she was the type to work sixty hours a week and still never miss a workout. I was suddenly self-conscious that I hadn't shaved that day. She looked expectantly from me to Mr. Grumpy and back to me. After a few blinks, I realized what I was forgetting and I introduced her to my—and now her—client. Becoming somewhat professional and coherent again, I gave her my card, which she grabbed with a naked left hand, and I told her I would be calling to keep up on Mr. Grumpy's progress. I let an uncomfortable silence descend on us until she smiled, said goodbye, and took her new charge into her office.

Never one to shuck my responsibilities, I dutifully phoned her office the next day to see how the session went. I even shaved for the occasion. I introduced myself again and asked about the previous day's meeting.

Without divulging any confidential information, she told me that Mr. Grumpy was "still in compliance with the court-ordered counseling" and that everything was fine. Another awkward silence ensued, and I stroked my smooth chin, said my goodbyes and hung up.

I called her again a few days later to see how the latest session had gone. After all, I had to keep close tabs on Mr. Grumpy. This five-foot-six, 140-pound miscreant had been in a five-second bar fight in downtown Huntington. He had nearly broken another guy's skin before passing out drunk in mid-punch. He had a terrifying prior criminal record for public urination outside of a monster truck show. The man was obviously a menace. The hard-core drug dealers, burglars, and other felons assigned to me would just have to learn to share my attention. Mr. Grumpy needed me.

Again, Dr. Richards informed me that Mr. Grumpy was "still in compliance with the court-ordered counseling" and that everything was fine.

Good to know.

This time I let the stillness build until she actually asked me if I was still there. Flustered, I told her that my cell must have lost the signal momentarily, and I asked her to repeat what she'd said. She did, and I gave my thanks before hanging up. I made a mental note to buy a cell phone.

When I called again the next week to ask about Grumpy's progress, I made it as far as, "Hi, it's Cyprus Ke—" before she impatiently snapped, "Why don't you just ask me out already?"

I suddenly wasn't sure I could be with a woman who was this direct. I'm an old-fashioned guy. Besides, there was Mr. Grumpy to consider. This would create a conflict of interest and I would have to pass him off to one of my colleagues. What would he do without me? And who did this lady think she was? I decided right then and there that I was going to quickly back away from this situation. Maybe after we had dinner one time.

We had a private ceremony three months later. I asked the judge to take some wedding photos of us with my new cell phone.

Back when we started dating, it hadn't taken us long to figure out we were going to be together. We just had to work out a few details. Last names, for instance. I wanted her to take my last name, but she wanted to keep hers. So we made a deal. She would keep her last name and in exchange I would have to be fine with that.

Psychologists are very skilled in the art of compromise.

I have to admit, I was never sure I was the marrying type, but married life definitely agreed with me. For a few months I didn't even mind the part of my job that involved being lied to a thousand times a day, or getting a call from the jail telling me one of my projects had held up a Stop-and-Rob gas station while wearing a work uniform with his name patch on it, or spending my afternoons collecting warm plastic cups of urine so loaded with THC that it refused to even slosh around. Kaitlyn made everything better, and things started coming into focus for me.

My new bride even tried to get me to understand myself better. But, of course, I blew off her so-called constructive criticism because why would I listen to an expert in human behavior who also happens to be my best friend and wife? No, sir. I was way too smart for that.

But overall, things did improve. I started experiencing a feeling that was completely new to me: ambition. For the first time in a long time, I began to think that there was more I could do with my life. Not that what I was doing wasn't important, but I needed something more. Something different. Something to shake things up.

Detective Shand's words echoed in my head. I was still a little lightheaded and out of breath from the run, and I struggled to wrap my mind around what he was saying.

I finally responded to the news in the same stupid, dumbfounded way that people had reacted to my words when I was in his shoes.

"Killed? Lindsay Behram?"

Through puffs of cold breath, Hartz went straight to the point and said, "We're tracking her movements from yesterday. When was the last time you saw Lindsay?"

Tracking her movements? This was no car accident. This was not "a drunken student falls down a set of stairs and hits her head"-type deal. When Shand said *killed* he meant *murdered*. These guys were investigating a homicide.

I immediately replied, "I saw her around three o'clock yesterday afternoon."

Not a flicker of heightened curiosity on either of their faces. Of course. They knew I saw her. Why else would they be looking for a professor she had for only one class.

Shand returned to me with a quick tennis forehand, "What did you two discuss?"

I knew from my years in law enforcement that the two worst things an innocent person could do in this situation were to either lie, or omit a portion of the whole truth. There was no way I was going to conceal anything, even if it could create an appearance of impropriety down the road. Cops become cynical by nature. It just happens. If I were to get caught in a lie, I would be putting the crosshairs on my own forehead. Besides, nothing ever happened between the two of us, and Steven was there to witness my glorious moment of righteous indignation.

I shyly batted my answer back, "I think she had a thing for me. Kind of a crush, I suppose. But I made it very clear that nothing was ever going to happen between us."

Uh, oh. I had already gotten the sense that these guys were good at hiding their emotions behind stoic expressions. Real good. And what I just saw flash on each of their faces was brief. Just a quick peek. A quick pulse of heat lightning that didn't make the slightest sound, but opened up the surrounding scenery to further examination for a brief moment in time. I had figured they might not have been prepared for my response, but this was something more. It was the last thing I expected and certainly not what I wanted. Each of their faces betrayed a look that summarized what I had felt all too often when I had questioned a suspect at a crime scene and had heard a single fact that unexpectedly fit. They had simply been toying around with the dial on the front of the safe and the tumbler had accidently, and remarkably, clicked into place. One number in the combination . . . down.

For the first time, the two detectives spoke almost simultaneously. Hartz, suddenly looking less concerned with the cold breeze, won the brief verbal tug-of-war and reasoned, "So you did know her a little more than your other students?"

"I suppose I know . . . I knew her a little better because she tended to stop me after class and ask me questions. She was flirtatious, but that was it. I swear, nothing ever happened between us. I did not return her implied pronouncements of affection at any point. I was very clear about it yesterday!"

Implied pronouncements of affection? Way to not sound pompous, Dr. Dumbass. And when a person being questioned says, *I swear*, that's what is called a qualifier. Usually, it means that the person is lying through his teeth. This was sure going well.

Now, it was Shand coming at me with a backhand this time, "Yesterday in your office." A statement. Not a question.

I hadn't said she came by my office.

"Yes. My graduate assistant, Steven Thacker, was there with me in my office until three-thirty. He witnessed the entire exchange where I made it completely clear to her that there could be no relationship between us," I exclaimed as my irritation started to rise again. Continuing in a labored breath, "I explained that university policy forbids it and that it was simply not going to happen."

"How old is Mr. Thacker?" asked Hartz, without letting a second pass.

What a strange question to ask. If I were interrogating some pompous professor at a second-rate university who openly admitted a recently-made-dead student was hitting on him, I certainly wouldn't focus on some grad student's age.

I managed to breathe out, "I guess he's around twenty-five or so. He's scheduled to graduate this May."

It occurred to me that I better start asking some questions of my own before it began to look as if I were not asking because I already knew most of the answers.

"Wait a second. You're asking a lot of questions that make it sound like this wasn't an accident. What happened to Lind . . . Ms. Behram?"

Nice job idiot. First name basis with the deceased.

The fact that I have always tried to be on a first name basis with *all* of my students, and that it is actually possible at a small school like this where everybody seems to know each other, is probably not something the detectives wanted to hear at this point. Maybe I could also dazzle them with my knowledge of adult learning theory and the benefits of informal interaction in the classroom while I'm at it. Genius.

Hartz's turn to swing the racquet. They were falling back in line with their routine.

"She was found strangled in the Hill District. You know the area?"

"I know of it, but I don't go up there. No reason to, of course."

Of course. Because *of course* I didn't have a reason to go to a high-crime, drug-infested area, detectives. I was an upstanding pillar of the community in one of the country's most-respected institutions of higher education. Well . . . at least I was a well-liked fellow at a barely accredited college. The point was, didn't they know that I had written journal articles that probably had been read by two or three pairs of people?

What the hell was Lindsay doing there anyway? I didn't take her for a druggy, but I could see her as a party girl. I guess if she was naïve enough to go up there to buy some Ecstasy or weed, then that might explain some of this. However, in all of my time on the street I never, ever saw a drug-buy-gone-bad end in strangulation. It just doesn't happen. Gunshot? Sure. Stabbing? No problem. Beaten to death, run over by a car, set on fire, drowned in the gutter . . . why not? But not strangled. I knew it didn't make sense and so did the men standing in front of me. Strangulation is often a crime of passion committed by someone the victim knows. Someone the victim knows intimately. It's usually a personal crime. Or, in some cases, a crime of blind rage.

"You teach Criminology courses, right? So I'm sure you know what the next question is," Shand said in his best rapport-building tone.

"I was in my office grading papers until seven, and then I stopped by the Silesian Deli over on East Ohio Street for a few minutes and ate a sandwich. I left there and walked back to the assembly hall to catch an eight o'clock lecture. I was there until around ten."

"And then?" Hartz prompted.

"Then I went home. I was there all night. And no, I was not alone. My wife was home."

Hartz raised an eyebrow and did not wait for his counterpart to ask the obvious follow-up.

"And your wife will confirm you were there all night, I suppose."

"Absolutely. She was in bed, but still awake when I got there."

Shand scribbled and spoke. "What kind of lecture, Dr. Keller?"

"Cyprus," I corrected again as another ice cube dropped from the back of my head to my neckline. "It was about how some studies have indicated positive associations between cognitive reasoning ability, auditory stimuli, and sexual virility in apes. So I brought a book of Sudoku puzzles and Barry White CDs up to the bedroom when I got home. My wife told me later that the studies must be flawed."

I seriously need to pick better times for sarcasm and self-deprecating humor.

I expected a sliver of displeasure, but to my relief a slight grin actually crossed Shand's face.

Seizing the opportunity I asked, "Can you guys tell me what the T.O.D. was? Maybe I can put your minds at ease."

I was referring to the *time of death*. Building rapport through the use of a common language is Interviewing 101. Dr. Pompous needed to leave this stage and former Officer Keller, Baltimore PD needed to make an appearance. This was my way of saying, *See detectives! I know what T.O.D. stands for! I'm not some perverted, coed-chasing, cold-blooded murderer who leaves some poor girl's body decomposing in gang territory. No sir. I'm one of you! Now let's go down a beer and have a bunch of laughs about responding to suicide attempts gone terribly wrong, or dealing with skanky 300-pound barflies who offer us sexual favors if we don't arrest them for walking through the bar's parking lot wearing nothing but a toothless grin. Next round is on me!*

Besides, the chances were good that my whereabouts could be accounted for at whatever time the murder actually occurred, but I wanted to make sure. I was at my office with Steven, then I used my credit card at the deli, then I sat in a lecture hall with seventy-five other people. I was feeling pretty good about my story, which just happened to be true.

Shand's demeanor had lightened considerably as he disclosed, "The coroner places T.O.D. at approximately nine-thirty P.M. Who at the lecture could confirm that you were there?"

That's why he had lightened up. The T.O.D. put me in the clear—assuming my alibi checked out. And what kind of idiot gives a bogus alibi that is easy to check?

"I sat in the back by myself," I explained, "but there was a lady who had to scan my university ID into a portable card reader in order for me to get into the event for free. There was a line for university employees on one side of the lobby, and another line on the opposite side for everybody else because they had to have a ticket. You'll find my ID was scanned around eight P.M."

"Just out of curiosity, why did you sit by yourself? Didn't you know anybody? It's kind of a small school," Hartz inquired as he again pulled his coat tight.

"Not very well," I said, choosing to answer his second question. "The lecture wasn't completely in my field, so most of the faculty members there were from other departments." Then I added, "And I'm still pretty new here."

Hartz continued with another question. "Where were you before coming to Three Rivers?"

Perfect. Time to fully introduce myself as one of the brotherhood.

"I was a probation officer in West Virginia. Baltimore PD before that," I said with false dismissiveness and a slight wave of my hand.

Shand nodded with some level of appreciation and said, "Well, you know we'll have to check your alibi. We have to follow up on everything. You know how this works since you were one of us. The D.A.'s office and the press . . . well . . . it's a pretty college girl found dead in drug land. You understand."

I nodded sympathetically as he went on.

"You said that the lecture wasn't completely in your field. If you ask me, it sounds way out in left field for someone in your occupation."

"It dealt with brain functioning, sexual behavior, and touched on aggressiveness. I've done some research on sexual predators. I thought there might be something useful for me there."

"Was there?"

"Apparently an alibi."

With a silent laugh he forged ahead with the next basic questions. "Do you know of anybody who would want to hurt Ms. Behram? Was she having any problems with anybody that you were aware of?"

"No, but I truly didn't know much about her. Seemed like a sweet girl, and she may have been just a little misguided in her intentions when it came to me," I asserted more calmly than before. I was still cold but I was starting to relax.

I took advantage of another short pause in the interview while Shand scribbled my response into his notepad. Hartz looked up at an obstinate tree struggling to produce buds. "By the way, how did you know she came to my office?" I asked as if I had just thought of the question.

Returning his focus to ground level, Hartz answered, "The victim's roommate told us she had wanted to go clothes shopping with her, but Ms. Behram said that she needed to see if you were in your office, that she had to talk to you about something. Her roommate also mentioned that she thought Ms. Behram was seeing an older man, but she was secretive about it. The victim apparently made references to her "older boy-toy" when talking to her friends."

He let that sink in.

"You understand how this could look, so I need you to be completely honest with us. Are you sure there wasn't something more between you and the victim? Something more than a student-professor relationship?"

I could envision suspects looking up at this composed colossus and spilling their guts for no other reason than wanting to pacify the god of reckonings who was looming over them.

"Not in any way," I vowed, while wiping my sleeve across my damp forehead. "If she was referring to me, and I don't think she could have been, then she was very much mistaken. But Ms. Behram didn't strike me as the kind of person to make a leap like that. I don't think she was talking about me."

Shand asked, "When she left your office, what was her state of mind?"

I stopped in my mental tracks as it occurred to me what had just happened. Unbelievable. I was finding it hard to believe that I taught this stuff for a living. It's like a spider showing other spiders how to hunt for prey, but then he goes for a short eight-legged run and gets gobbled up by a bird.

Damn, I liked these guys!

They got me to lower my guard with subtle grins and by giving me some facts about the case. Just a small demonstration of how I was being trusted with information because I had an alibi. They implicitly acknowledged our bond of the badge and then they serve up a question like that. Beautiful work.

If I said that I have no idea what her state of mind was, then I would have appeared evasive, indicating that I'm probably hiding something. After all, what kind of former cop can't read a twenty-two-year-old girl who's infatuated with him? If I claimed that I *knew* her state of mind, then it could appear that I either knew her very well; or perhaps I had talked to her about the meeting later that evening and thus knew exactly what she was thinking at the time. Clever, clever. It was a no-win question, and the detective wanted to see how I would handle it.

I took a breath and addressed both of them.

"Detectives, all I can tell you is that I made it abundantly clear that there was no relationship between us and never would be. I can't be certain of what was going through her mind, partly because after she had started asking me about the possibility of a relationship, she noticed Steven in the room. At that point, she looked more surprised, and probably embarrassed, than anything else. Then she said she would talk to me later and simply left the room. I never saw her again."

My frustration was back now. Not at the detectives, but the fact that I had let my guard down. These guys played me beautifully and I had fallen for it. Hell, the T.O.D. may not have even been real. They may have gotten me focusing on a particular time frame only to see if I would get lazy with the rest of the timeline for my personal alibi. I was tired. I was cold. I was mad at myself. Truth be told, I was probably mad at Lindsay for putting me in this position. And then I was getting mad for letting myself get mad at a poor dead girl who probably had a very bright future ahead of her.

"You said Steven was about twenty-five years old." Hartz's words jarred me back from my internal version of corporal mortification.

"I did."

"Did he know the victim?" Hartz prodded.

"A little, I guess. He helps out with the Victimology class, so he knows her from that."

"Did he know her outside of class?" Hartz had something on his mind and took control of the questioning.

"I don't know. I don't think so. What are you getting at, Detective?"

"Twenty-five *is* older than twenty-two."

"You're barking up the wrong tree. They weren't romantically involved."

"Thacker is a faculty member since he's a graduate assistant, right? I would guess that he teaches some low-level classes?"

"Technically . . . I suppose he is. And he does. What difference does that make?"

"The roommate also mentioned that she thought the victim's boyfriend worked for the university," Hartz said, with some added emphasis on the word *boyfriend*.

As angry as I felt, I still hadn't really raised my voice, but the knob on my volume control was definitely beginning to turn.

"Look. I wasn't seeing her. Steven wasn't seeing her. If she was seeing somebody who was a faculty member, then I sure don't know who it was!"

Shand calmly turned the page of his notepad, raised his eyes and interjected with, "If Mr. Thacker was seeing her, and he thought that you wouldn't approve of a relationship between them, then it makes perfect sense that he would hide that fact from you, doesn't it?"

"No. He wasn't seeing her. I'm certain."

Hartz shot back, "You can't know everything about everyone. You were a cop. You know that."

"You're off base here."

Shand added, "Maybe he was afraid you would turn him in if he told you. Maybe Ms. Behram was actually there to talk to you about her relationship with *him*."

"No."

The voice from Hartz's direction exclaimed, "That's true! You said she was taken aback when she saw him in the room. Then she left without argument."

"No. That's not what I meant."

Volume knob turned a millimeter more.

The two voices battering me were indistinguishable now.

"Dr. Keller, does Steven have a girlfriend?"

"No!"

"Well, there you go. Maybe she was his girlfriend."

"No!"

"They may have been seeing each other right under your nose. You shouldn't be embarrassed. People hide all sorts of things, Doc."

"It's Cyprus."

"Maybe she actually used you to make Steven jealous. Maybe he got *really* jealous."

"No!"

I was colder. More tired. More frustrated. Getting hungry. My head was starting to hurt and my shoulders ached. Too many thoughts raced through my head. This had to stop.

The rapid fire continued and I heard, "You have to admit, her sleeping with some twenty-five-year-old grad student makes more sense. And she was a hottie! I'm sure Steven would have jumped at that."

"He didn't!"

Volume knob a half-inch louder.

"You can't know that."

"He was probably seeing her for a while. You couldn't have known."

Shaking my head, "He wasn't!"

An excited voice, "You can't be sure. How could you know?"

"BECAUSE STEVEN THACKER IS GAY!"

Volume knob broken off—lying on the floor.

The sudden silence after the detective's machine-gun repartee was jolting. I couldn't hear a sound around me. Then it slowly came back into focus. Traffic in the distance. The harsh breeze scraping off the corner of the recreation building behind me.

Then the soft mumbling.

The footsteps behind me resuming.

The pairs and trios of students walking into and out of the building.

The pace of the steps picking up. They had important things to do now.

They had to go tell the story about how a professor at this small school where everybody seems to know each other, just "outed" a closet homosexual by screaming it at the top of his lungs in the middle of campus.

If there was a vat of molten steel around to dive into, I would have been putting on my best swim trunks.

Mile 5

Asharp burst of noise breaks the cadenced sounds of shuffling feet and measured breaths. My shoulders and arms involuntarily tense up and the muscles contracting in my neck wage a battle with my reflexive compulsion to look in the direction of the shot. In milliseconds, the sound waves ricochet off the surrounding residences, the statues and monuments in the park, sending countless panicked pigeons skyward. Torsos attempt to twist left while legs do their best to maintain an unswerving path. My throat closes and my legs lose some strength as the audible shockwave penetrates my chest. If I didn't know any better I would swear that I can feel my pupils expanding into giant pools of tar. Anybody here who is wearing a heart rate monitor will surely notice a spike in an otherwise dependable pattern.

More loud bangs follow with the sound of clashing metal. A pattern of beats emerge and then I scold myself for my nervousness. A high school band in heavy blue uniforms is lined up on the left side of the road. The abrupt outburst of snare drums and symbol crashes serve the dual purpose of scaring the hell out of me and pulling off a razor sharp introduction to "Eye of the Tiger." My edginess has made me hypersensitive to stimuli that, under normal circumstances, wouldn't alarm me. As my body's adrenaline production subsides to respectable levels, I reorient myself to my location and its significance.

I see a crowd gathering about 200 yards past the water and first aid stations on the right. A young girl, about twelve years old, hands me a paper cup of cold water when it's my turn to pass. The waxed surface of the cup feels slick against my sweaty fingers and my hand still trembles from the stun of noise. This has to be the first time in my life that I wished a band would have been playing a Rick Astley tune. The water station girl was trying to be nice by filling the cup to the rim, but the predictable result is that most of the water spills out as soon as I take it from her hand. I try to slow down to stop the spillage and to focus my eyes on the circle of concerned faces in the approaching distance. Somebody nudges me in the back. A silent request to speed up and drift toward the middle of the road, or get out of the way. I take a couple of sips of water, toss the cup to my right into a cemetery of its relatives, increase my momentum and merge back into the flow of foot traffic.

I see medical personnel up ahead carrying large red nylon bags. The EMTs are trotting over to the anxious group. The uniformed responders struggle to navigate the throng of onlookers, and when I pull even with them, I can easily decipher the frustration on their faces. It's taking them way too long to reach somebody. They aren't far off the road, so everyone has become a motorist rubbernecking at the scene of an accident. A few runners bump into each other in front of me and exchange apologies. I pass by just as the EMTs arrive, and the downward-looking crowd parts just enough to allow them access and to afford me a view. The man in his forties is red-faced, breathing heavily and sitting up. His green New Balance tank top heaves rapidly along with his chest, and his eyes are glassy and unfocused.

I can feel the curtain of strain being pulled back. I know it's just temporary and there is a lot more road ahead of me. The man being treated on the sidewalk wasn't targeted by another person. He was simply victimized by exhaustion. He doesn't realize it, but he's lucky in comparison.

—◦◦◦—

"You okay there, *kiddo*?" Randy asked, and insulted, when I walked into the locker room.

They all had showered and were in the process of getting dressed in the steamy air. Randy stood shirtless in the corner, finger probing the inside of a belly button that, for a distance runner, was surrounded by an impressive amount of pale blubber. Jacob was pulling on a sock while sitting on the bench that bisected the white tile floor. He wore a look of genuine concern. He was probably wondering if the police visit had something to do with Kaitlyn and thoughts of him losing his own wife had to have flashed in front of him. Aaron stood on a scale and nodded with satisfaction as it rattled out a number.

"I'm fine," I answered. "I'm afraid a student in one of my classes was killed last night."

Randy never looked up as he nonchalantly withdrew his index finger, gave the digit a visual inspection and said, "Oh, yeah. Who?"

"Lindsay Behram."

Randy's eyes sharply shot my way as the name seemed to register.

"She took several Criminology classes. You probably knew her," I added sadly.

Turning his attention to finding a shirt in his locker, "The name is familiar, but I can't put a face with it."

"I think I remember her. Real pretty girl?" asked Aaron, stepping down and releasing the scale from its duty.

Having no reason to downplay her looks, I answered, "The guys in class were always mesmerized by her. She was memorable."

"Damn. I think she was in my Marketing 100 class last semester. That's a real shame." Aaron paused respectfully, and then reached up to the top shelf of his assigned locker for his fake Rolex.

Jacob, finished with his socks, stood and pulled on a crisp white Brooks Brothers shirt. "How was she killed? Car accident?"

"No. The police said she was murdered. Her body was found somewhere in the Hill district. She'd been strangled."

Jacob shook his head in disgust. "Been a while since we've lost one that way. Murdered, I mean. It's probably been ten years or so. If memory serves, that was some kind of stabbing over at Station Square. Some boy got jealous over his girlfriend dancing with someone else; and the next thing you know, the jealous boyfriend was on his way to jail and the other kid was off to the morgue. Very sad."

Randy moved to the large wall mirror at the end of the row, threw on a fifteen-dollar, paper thin cream-collared shirt, and pawed at the buttons while asking, "Was she in any of your Psych classes?"

"No. At least not that I remember. And I don't forget many of my students," Jacob responded as he smoothly adjusted the cuff links on his shirt. After a moment of contemplation, he turned to me. "Why are the police talking to you about it?"

"She came by my office yesterday. They were just following her movements throughout the day. Looking for leads. I'm sure they'll talk to a lot of people."

I sure hoped that was true. The detectives had ended the interview by getting all of my contact information and asking if I would be available if they needed anything cleared up. Truth be told, I think they were sharing some of my discomfort after I bellowed out a student's personal secret for all to hear. Their automatic reflex was to distance themselves from the leper— and at that moment I had declared myself the king of the leper colony.

"Are you alibied?" Randy snickered as he struggled to button the top button on his shirt, eventually giving up. "Are we going to be interviewed on the news and saying things like 'He was such a nice man. We never imagined he could be violent!'—or one of those catch phrases the neighbors of serial killers always say?" The mock interview continued with, "'We had no idea he was choking out college hussies and—'"

"Nice," Aaron broke in, bringing Randy to a record-scratching halt. "Very classy, Dr. Walker. What if she was your daughter? Try to show an ounce of respect. Don't mind him, Cyprus." Aaron's eyes showed signs of real anger.

I made a note to myself that if Aaron Caferty, the area's most proficient propagator of slumlords and crooked insurance salesmen, ever became my moral compass, then I should use a shotgun cartridge as a piece of chewing gum.

"Oh, the kid knows I'm just playing around. And I'm sorry the girl is dead," Randy strung out the word "sorry" with his hands held up in mock surrender.

Randy had been studying Criminology and the criminal justice system for his entire adult life. In fact, teaching and researching the subject was the only job he'd ever had. From the beginning, he never really hid the fact that he looked down on me due to me cutting my teeth in the "real world." Academia has to be the only line of work where you get looked down upon for having actually performed the tasks that the profession teaches. How much sense does that make?

Not wanting to appear as if I was avoiding Randy's original question, I finally replied, "Yes, I have an alibi. The detectives said that she was killed around nine thirty. I was at the assembly hall attending a lecture. Besides, I'm sure I'm not a suspect. They were just covering their bases. I would have done the same thing in their position."

"Pffttt," Randy half-snarled and half-spat, "the cops will go around chasing shadows and taking coffee breaks until some dirtbag brags to some other dirtbag, and the case gets handed to them on a silver platter. They would have better odds of actually solving the case if they just let things play out. They should just go write some tickets, work on their G.E.D.s, and wait for the killer to screw up."

Why this man chose this profession is beyond me.

"Ohhh, I don't know 'bout that, Randy." I threw out my best West Virginia accent. I had lost it years ago, but I could still summon it on occasion. "I was talk'n to those two boys out 'er and they seemed the right sort to clean up dis mess. Some cops got some smarts these days, ya know. I hear that some of 'em can even talk on that CB radio thang and drive at da same time! Yesiree."

Aaron laughed as Randy's face became a cherry lollipop. Jacob stood expressionless, facing his locker. Without moving his head, his eyes moved slightly as he looked sideways toward Dr. Dickhead to gauge his reaction.

"I . . . I don't mean you, Cyprus. Or any of the Criminology students here for that matter. I was just making a generalization," Randy grumbled as he resumed his battle with the top button on his shirt. Either he'd gained weight over the winter or bought a shirt that was far too small.

I said nothing and stripped off my sweatshirt which was now soaked from both my sweat and the steam lingering in the locker room. At this rate, I was going to catch pneumonia.

Randy fumbled his way back toward his locker and away from the mirror, as Aaron took his place in order to put a tie on. The sides of the mirror were clearly visible on each side of Aaron's tall, thin body. In his moderately fashionable beige-colored suit and brown Kenneth Cole shoes, he looked every bit the reputable college professor. However, when put under a tad more scrutiny, the overabundance of hair gel and potato chip thin mustache muttered "used car salesman." You couldn't help but like Aaron's personality and you wouldn't hesitate to take his hand in friendship, but you couldn't shake the feeling that when you gave him one hand, your other one should be on your wallet.

Randy once again gave up on the button and haphazardly wound a tie decorated with miniscule horses around his neck. He didn't bother to check his progress in the mirror. He hastily stuffed his dirty clothes into a plastic bag, which he then put into another, thicker plastic bag—which he tied off with the utmost care. Then, satisfied that his sweat-soaked laundry was subdued, he threw the entire crinkly bundle into his gym bag. It was the same routine every time. How a man could be such a slob and yet display such obvious obsessive-compulsive tendencies is beyond me.

Jacob, almost completely dressed and looking very Charlton Heston-ish, started organizing items in his locker. Each of us had one assigned locker plus an additional one we all shared. Technically, we weren't supposed to get an extra one; but Aaron had thrown out his best sales pitch to someone on the recreation building staff, and secured us an extra locker that we would use for storing our gel packs, Pop-Tarts, extra shoelaces, running belts, hats, and other supplies. The four of us managed to completely pack the two small shelves of the locker in no time.

The shared locker had a few hooks deep inside where we could hang our Velcro runner's identification bands or medical information bracelets. The identification bands had become common in recent years, and Kaitlyn had insisted I get one. The thinking behind the invention was that if you were out by yourself on a run and suffered from heat stroke, got hit by a car, fell down a ravine, got struck by a comet, or Wile E. Coyote dropped an Acme safe on your head, the hospital would be able to identify you and call the emergency contact number printed on the tag that the band was strung through. Randy and I had ID bands that could be strapped around our ankles, while Jacob and Aaron had medical bracelets that warned of a severe allergy to penicillin and debilitating migraine headaches, respectively.

I usually prepared my running belt right before we ran. Unless I was running early the next morning and would be pressured for time, I never saw any reason to start breaking up Pop-Tarts the day before. Aaron and Randy would simply grab a few gel packs out of the shared locker and stow them in their running belts as we were on our way out the door. But not Jacob.

Jacob had his post-run routine down to a science. He owned an expensive running belt that exhibited a series of elastic pouches that were perfectly sized for his gel packs. That way, Jacob could pull out particular flavors of mushy calories at the specific points his cyborg brain had computed that his body would need the energy. Whenever we went on training runs, he popped out those gel packs one at a time, going straight down his neatly planned-out row. After every run, the first thing he did, once we returned to the locker room—even before showering—was to prepare his running belt for the next run by reloading the silver carbohydrate bullets vertically into the pockets. The ceremony resembled a legendary hunter getting ready to go out on a safari the next day. He carefully calculated at what points he would squeeze the calories into his system and stuck with it religiously. Calories replaced verses calories burned.

In spite of my smart-ass urges, I never gave him a hard time about his obsessive preparation. Jacob was all business when it came to preparation and I had to respect his ritual, if for no other reason than I got the feeling that it would be like teasing General Sherman about playing with matches. He knew exactly what he was doing and it was probably best if you didn't get in his way.

Randy was the first one to finish up, and he grumbled a good-bye to all of us as he carried his damaged demeanor out of the locker room. Aaron soon followed, allowing enough time so he wouldn't have to walk out with Randy, and he mumbled something about running off to teach a *useless* business ethics class.

Jacob had made his way over to the mirror and adjusted a Windsor knot in a silk tie. "Are you just going to stand there half-naked or are you going to hit the showers?" he asked while eyeing me in the mirror.

Taking his age and life's work into account, Jacob was the unquestionable star of our running group in terms of both stamina and academic reputation. He served as the senior faculty member in the Psychology department; and because of his track record in obtaining huge research grants and his close friendship with Clyde Silo, the Dean of Academic Affairs, he was undoubtedly the most powerful professor at Three Rivers. That explained why the Department of Psychology somehow thrived at a school that was more oriented toward specific vocations.

Every time I was in here with Jacob, I felt a ridiculous discomfort—like a boy standing in a locker room full of men. My physical conditioning certainly wasn't the reason for this feeling. I'm not embarrassed to walk around shirtless. Other than a long scar on my right forearm from a homeless guy's box cutter, I look to be in good shape. I mean I'm not going to be on the cover of *Men's Health* or anything, but as far as college professors go, I'm above the mean. And I'm not shy about what's below the waist. I mean I'm not going to be on the cover of—well, you get the picture.

Of all the silly things, I feel weird about my tattoo. I have the scales of justice tattooed on my left shoulder with the word JUSTICE in block letters below the base of the scales. When I was twenty-two and trying to feel tough while working the Front Street area of Baltimore, getting some symbolic ink seemed like a fine idea. It was a reminder that regardless of what evils I encountered, I still needed to pursue the ideal. The ideal what? I'm not sure. The ideal system? Outcome? Cause?

Regardless, I have always felt idiotic when talking to Jacob and having the scales sitting there in plain view. The scene has always brought to mind images of Cooter from *The Dukes of Hazard* trying to have a conversation with Gregory Peck. You wouldn't even be able to follow the conversation, because you would just want them to return to their normal environments so everyone could feel comfortable again.

Wishing I hadn't taken my shirt off, I told Jacob, "I've got a problem. I messed up and word is going to get around real quick."

Jacob turned from his reflection and uttered in his best conspiratorial tone, "I really hope you're not going to confess to murder, my boy. I may be able to give you tips on building an insanity defense, but I can't make any promises."

I thought he was serious until one side of his mouth started to curl up.

"No, of course not. But my talk with the detectives didn't go well."

Jacob waited stone-faced for me to continue.

The locker room door behind me swung open, and we both remained silent until a student passed by on his way to the urinals. The pause gave Jacob a moment to think of something else, and once the visitor was out of earshot he broke the silence.

"You didn't . . . I mean you weren't . . . Cyprus, did you . . . do something with that girl? Like . . . sexually?"

His face was the picture of concern and I was taken aback by it. Surely he knew that Kaitlyn meant everything to me and that I meant everything to her. He had met her on several occasions, and he and Tabatha had had us over for dinner more than once. Since his wife's death we hadn't visited him, but that was to be expected. I instantly forgave his suspicions because I supposed that at his age he had seen plenty of men screw up their marriages for three minutes of pleasure. I mean thirty minutes. If it were me, of course.

"No. Nothing like that." I chose not to tell him about her interest in me. "But they started asking me about Lindsay possibly having a relationship with Steven Thacker."

"The graduate assistant you can't stand?"

I thought about arguing about my level of dislike for Steven, but I quashed the thought, remembering how many times I had bitched about him to Jacob.

I nodded in affirmation.

"So? Was he seeing her?"

"No."

"Are you sure?"

"Positive . . ." I tried to continue but Jacob beat me to the punch.

"Because you know you never really know a person. He could have been hiding it from you. He is a graduate assistant after all, and the university policy . . ."

I couldn't go through this again.

Keeping my voice to a loud whisper, "He's gay, Jacob. He wasn't seeing Lindsay. I'm sure. One hundred percent—no doubt about it—would bet my house on it—certain."

Jacob raised his eyebrows and gave a slight nod. His expression then became quizzical.

"Well then, what's the problem? You weren't involved with her and neither was your grad assistant."

There was a flush, and we waited while the relieved student passed by our aisle and left the locker room. He didn't wash his hands. I hate that.

I explained how Steven was not openly gay and how I had managed to broadcast his sexual preference on a Goodyear blimp. Jacob sat on the nearest bench, looking down at the tiles contemplatively. I could tell that he was playing out multiple scenarios in his head.

"It's going to get around, you know. This university isn't as sensitive to political correctness as most, but this could cause big trouble for you. Especially if Steven makes a formal complaint against you."

"I know. I was thinking about trying to get in front of this thing."

"Absolutely." Jacob agreed. "You may as well be open and contrite now. You made a mistake, but this isn't the end of the world. You need to take this up the chain and explain the circumstances."

"You're forgetting that I'm not exactly considered the golden child over at Castle Silo."

I was referring to the impressive-looking Whitlock Building that housed the Office of Academic Affairs. Dean Silo had never been a fan of mine and the feeling was mutual. The university's unique regulations allowed the individual academic departments to hire and fire their own faculty members, and Silo was relegated to only making recommendations. During my employee orientation, I had met with him and immediately picked up on some feelings of animosity. Subsequently, I would run into him at various faculty functions and the negative vibes only worsened. So I spent most of the first few months at the school slightly curious as to why I rubbed the dean the wrong way, but it honestly didn't bother me too much.

At some point I made some offhand remark about the dean's lack of affection for me to Jacob, who I knew was close with Silo.

Jacob confided in me that Silo had been pushing for one of his close personal friends—a very well-known professor at Duke—to get the position that I eventually obtained. Despite having achieved a pretty good reputation for my PhD work, on paper alone, I wouldn't have stood a chance against this guy.

We were both interviewed for the job, and the Criminology staff felt my competitor brought with him the attitude that he was going to come up to the Steel City and show the local, small-time professors how things were really supposed to be done. The man from North Carolina carried on for forty-five minutes about "fixing" the department, while sharing his vision of producing the state's best legal scholars and topnotch law students. He cited numerous studies he had conducted and books he had written. At one point, without any prompting, he actually got up and handed the panel autographed copies of his latest book—about the Social Threat Theory. This prompted another twenty-minute speech in which he condescended to his audience, while elaborating on a theory that any second-year Criminology undergraduate student would have grasped immediately.

Jacob couldn't help but laugh when he recalled the rest of the story as it was told to him. According to Jacob, one of the members of the selection committee, who happened to have been a rather serious-looking former Secret Service agent named Brent, waited for the lecturer to lose steam, and then asked the interviewee one question. He inquired if the renowned professor was familiar with the Proximity Pummeling Theory. The professor cocked his head so far that his glasses slipped down his nose. After a moment's thought, he replied that he had not heard of it. Brent then stood up, leaned forward, his hands tightly seizing the oak table in front of him, and told the prospective employee that if he didn't get his ass out of that room and back down I-79 he was going to become an ideal case study on the topic.

As the enraged academic piloted a silver BMW through unapologetic Pennsylvania hills, I pulled onto the campus in my used Jeep Wrangler. I took my turn with the committee and was amazed that my down-to-earth disposition struck a chord with them. I think the job offer was cemented when the man I would come to know as Brent Lancaster looked slyly at his fellow committee members, and asked me if I had heard of the Proximity Pummeling Theory. I responded by telling him that I was once bitten on the neck by a coked-up auto mechanic during an arrest. I had been trying to cuff the guy when I unexpectedly found myself wrestling with him in a tiny closet inside a moldy apartment. That's when he decided to go Pac-Man on me. I explained to Brent that I had practical experience in testing the theory in a controlled environment, and that I found the theory to be useful if applied properly.

Jacob put on his suit jacket and started for the door. "Don't worry about Silo. I'll have a word with him before you head over there. Today's Friday, and he's usually tied up in the afternoons. I'll speak to him this weekend, and then you should make an appointment to see him on Monday."

I agreed and Jacob secured his locker before heading out the door.

The steam in the locker room had vanished and a rush of uncomfortably cool air from the hallway had rushed past Jacob on his way out. I realized that as naked as I felt now, Monday would probably be worse.

After I showered and dressed, I headed back to my office and tried to get some work done. I had a stack of essays to read from my Introduction to Criminology class. I feigned interest and picked up a stapled grouping of white sheets. This course, and the Victimology class, kept me more than busy since I typically required students to submit research papers and essays rather than simply giving them multiple choice exams. I gave up after my fifth attempt at reading some freshman's essay on the disparities between the prison sentences of white collar criminals and typical street offenders.

The fact that some CEO can steal a quarter of a million dollars and get a few months in a minimum security facility, while a guy who takes two hundred bucks from a convenience store register gets several years in the state pen, is inexcusable. But regardless of the topic, I couldn't focus on the words and I soon lost interest.

Kaitlyn was going to be home this afternoon, so I decided to call it an early day. She had managed to set up a pretty successful private practice near our home in Wexford, and she met with patients in a modest office that was only five minutes away. If she didn't have any appointments scheduled, she could simply work from home with her assistant, a brown beagle mix named Sigmund.

Being a workaholic, it was always a safe bet that Kaitlyn was being productive regardless of her environment. Even on weekends, she volunteered at the local children's hospital counseling terminally-ill kids and their families. The hospital staff absolutely loved her, and she managed to draw billboard-sized smiles out of sick children and desperate parents with ease. On a few occasions, I had accompanied her to the hospital and personally witnessed her rock star status in action. To watch her cast her spell was intoxicating in itself. On this day, she would need to brew a very special potion to lighten my darkening mood.

After a quick fifteen-minute drive, I pulled into our subdivision glad that our two-story home was far from the highway. The west end of the development was where the houses had some room to inhale. It was nice being close to a city and all of its urban amenities, yet still spot the occasional deer walking past the yard. Sigmund was a huge fan of the arrangement since our backyard—enclosed by a natural wood picket fence—allowed him to see the wildlife and unleash his devastating beagle bark on Mother Nature whenever he saw fit. As I pulled into the driveway, I saw a floppy-eared head pop up in the front window like a prairie dog searching the horizon for activity. When my key hit the front door, I could already hear toenails tapping in rapid succession on the hardwood floor. I entered the house and was immediately attacked by two front paws and a wet nose. Unfortunately, due to Sigmund's height, when he lunges at me his paws and nose tend to strike me in the id, ego, and superego. In this instance, I turned away sharply and narrowly avoided several minutes of being doubled over in pain.

I knew where Kaitlyn would be, so I headed in that direction being closely trailed by panting and tail-wagging. She inhaled sharply and swiveled her chair in my direction when she sensed someone entering her den. She had been engrossed in some psychology journal displayed on her computer monitor. A CD playing Brahms had drowned out my footsteps and Sigmund's tap dancing.

"You scared me! I didn't hear you come in."

Sigmund was still attached to me, investigating my pant leg to make sure I hadn't been unfaithful with some other dog.

"I decided to come home and get an early start on the weekend."

I walked over and my wife raised her head enough for me to give her a peck on the lips. Her form-fitting jeans and low-cut top told me that she didn't have any appointments this afternoon. It was already three o'clock and she rarely saw patients after five.

"I should be finished here in about an hour or so. I was thinking we could go grab some dinner at Garcia's tonight. If we go early, we shouldn't have trouble getting a table."

Normally, I would never have passed up a trip to my favorite restaurant.

"I don't know. I thought we might stay in. How about we try going there tomorrow?" I leaned over and scratched Sigmund behind an ear.

"*You* don't want to go to Garcia's? Something's wrong. Want to talk about it?" Pointing to the monitor, she added, "This can wait, I'll make the time." She gestured toward another chair in the room as if it were a couch set aside for her patients.

I love Kaitlyn with all my heart, but I should have been drawn and quartered for marrying a psychologist.

"It's okay. Just a rough day. I'll tell you about it later."

"Seriously, I've got the time. Have a seat."

"Later."

I walked out of the room and down the hallway to the kitchen. Sigmund apparently didn't want to be analyzed either and joined me in my act of civil disobedience. I grabbed a Yuengling from the refrigerator, stood at the island in the center of the kitchen, and cracked open the beer. I tossed the cap down on the island and the metallic rattling sound caused Sigmund's head to snap up and tilt to one side.

I took a couple of sips of the beer, and walked out onto the deck at the rear of the house. We chose this house because it backed up to a completely wooded area on the outskirts of the development, and the perceived isolation was blissful. The yard ran downhill from the house, which made mowing the lawn a brutal task; but the view that opened up over the small gully was worth it. Sigmund took off down the stairs of the deck in pursuit of some imaginary squirrel or groundhog. The clouds that blanketed the day had left town and abducted the cold wind in the process. The temperature had reached the mid-fifties, and the afternoon was as pleasant for a March day as could be expected in this region.

"How long have we been married?"

It was Kaitlyn's turn to catch me off-guard. Her feet were bare and I didn't hear any footsteps.

"About a decade. But every day with you is a honeymoon."

I could still get away with cheesy comments like that. She's always had the remarkable ability to not lose her temper with me even when I deserve it—which is pretty often.

She smiled and walked toward me as I leaned on the rail of the deck and continued, "And would you say that you know me pretty well at this point?"

I nodded.

"And has there ever been anything, anything at all, even the slightest hint in my behavior that would lead you to believe that I would let you stew in silence when something is bothering you?"

I smiled back.

"No, ma'am."

"Then start talking. And just be grateful that I'm not charging you my standard fee."

I took another sip of beer and told her the entire story, including what I didn't tell Jacob. He didn't need to know about

Lindsay's advances toward me, but I couldn't keep that from Kaitlyn. Full disclosure is the only way to have a real marriage. I told her about Lindsay's office visit, the interview with the police, their suspicions about Steven, and my carelessness in revealing his secret. She listened patiently, didn't interrupt once, and carried the perfect look of empathy on her face.

I started to wrap things up by telling her about my plans to see Dean Silo on Monday, and how Jacob was going to try to soften him up before the meeting. I finished my account of the last two days along with my beer.

Kaitlyn slowly paced the deck as she worked through the details in her mind—the psychologist debating with the wife, trying to agree on what responses to give. A minute passed and then she finalized organizing her rolodex of thoughts on the matter.

"I assume if Steven files a complaint, the university will be concerned about liability."

"Yep."

"And if liability is an issue for an organization, the organization will have to demonstrate that it has taken steps to correct the cause of the liability."

"Yep."

"And you are the cause."

"Yep."

With a roll of her eyes she asked, "Don't you get paid to talk to people for a living?"

"Yep."

Another minute passed as she wore out the boards under our feet.

"And this girl, Lindsay—how old was she?"

"About twenty-two, I guess."

"And how old are you?"

"Thirty-nine going on twenty-five."

"Was she good looking?"

"Yep."

"Why would she be hitting on you?"

I simulated Sigmund's head tilt.

"Thanks, sweetie."

"Nothing personal, baby, you're good looking and all, but a girl like that usually has an agenda. Girls who chase after older guys are usually . . . troubled."

"I don't know," I said, as I looked out into the yard and watched the dog sniff a particularly interesting blade of grass. "She was a good student. I can't imagine how she would have benefited. Other than the obvious." I flamboyantly formed my right arm into an "L" shape and flexed a bicep.

The jab in my diaphragm turned the "L" into a backwards "7" and I found myself thankful that she was taller than Sigmund.

"Stop it. This is serious." She stepped up to the rail beside me, and we watched Sigmund make himself comfortable on a part of the hill warmed by the sun. "Silo already hates you. And we're okay with money, but not to the point that you can be unemployed long."

I noticed that a small yellow bird had landed on a tree branch just outside of the fence line. I wondered if it was a finch and made a mental note to go online later to look it up.

"It will be alright," I said unconvincingly. "I'll talk to Silo on Monday and, if necessary, throw myself on the mercy of the court."

"And don't be a smart ass."

"Yes, dear."

"And don't insult him in any subtle way. Don't even imply."

"Don't worry. If I insult him I'll be perfectly up-front about it."

The bird flew away, probably sensing the stare of death being sent in my direction.

"I'm kidding. I'll be good. Besides, maybe Steven won't make a formal complaint. Maybe he won't even be that upset. Hell, I could luck out and he won't even hear about it."

And maybe Sigmund would get nominated to the Supreme Court.

Mile 6

To make sure people don't take shortcuts during the race, electronic timing mats are strategically placed on different parts of the course. We crossed one at the beginning of the race and the timing strips attached to our shoes allowed a computer to start the clock on each of us. The second mat is stretched out across Brighton Road as we make our exit out of West Park. A computer records the times of those of us still running. Our participation will be electronically accounted for in this perspiring roll call to guarantee the integrity of the race.

Just past the mat, three scaffolds are erected in the middle of the street. On the scaffolds stand the official race photographers. They take still shots with machine-gun speed and make sure to get a photo of every runner. In a few days, the photos will be posted on a website with the word SAMPLE emblazoned across it. People will be able to buy the unscarred photos for a hefty price. I weave around one of the towers and nod to a sniping photographer.

After being scanned like items at a grocery store and photographed like mafia dons under FBI surveillance, we move past a children's museum and make a turn toward the Andy Warhol Museum which sits in front of a bridge also named for the famous artist. I have to tick off mile markers and landmarks in this way. If you start thinking about the fact that you have twenty miles to go, the concept is too overwhelming mentally and you'll never finish.

Mental, physical, environmental—all of the challenges you face in a marathon can be put into one of those three categories. You can train to overcome the physical. You can do your best to dress right for the environmental. But, conquering the mental aspect is tricky for most people. For some reason it clicked with me from the beginning. The systematic and disciplined way you have to envision things on long runs appealed to me immediately when I took up this hobby. Which is strange considering *systematic and disciplined* was nowhere in the room when this madness was conceived.

———〜✺〜———

In a short amount of time, Kaitlyn had vastly improved my life. We bought a small house and quickly adjusted to living together. Both of us felt we were a perfect fit for each other, and for once I loved going home after work. Going to work, on the other hand, still made my stomach tighten; and while I didn't take any more sick days, I was still looking for a profound idea to present itself.

One night I was attending an informal group counseling session at a local bar with one of my coworkers (I had started socializing with people again). We were deep into a highly intellectual conversation with our career consultant, Mr. Johnnie Walker Red, when one of us noticed a running shoe commercial on the TV over the bar. There were people jogging—young people, old people, black, white, tall, short. They all looked weirdly happy as they bounced around, bounded over park benches, and laughed while their happy dogs trailed behind.

One of us, I don't remember who, slurred, "Wee should start wunning!"

A voice replied, "Are you kidding? I bet yourr couldn't wwun a mile!"

And then a voice lisped, "I . . . I'aam gonna run a marathon! Am you're gonna do it wit me."

I'm pretty sure Johnny W. must have said that last thing.

I wasn't anything close to being a runner at the time. I mean I had run when I had to at the police academy or in pursuit of a suspect, but mostly for me it was all about hitting the weights or the heavy bag a few times a week. Running long distances? That was what cars were invented to prevent. However, the idea of facing a new challenge somehow resonated with me.

I started my training over the next few weeks. First, I began by doing what I'd always done with anything new to me. I studied it to death. I mean I studied *everything* I could about distance running. I gulped down everything on the internet. I gorged on every relevant book in the library. I inhaled every running magazine I could find. I became bilingual: in addition to speaking "Human," I learned to speak "Runner."

I became educated on all of the technical terms and acronyms for every injury and treatment I might possibly encounter. Iliotibial band syndrome = ITBS. Chronic exertional compartment syndrome = CECS. Plantar fasciitis = PF. Non-steroidal anti-inflammatory drugs, a.k.a. Ibuprophen = NSAIDs. Rest, Ice, Compression, Elevation = RICE. So if you are hoping to set a PR and have ITBS, CECS, or PF and they can't be treated with NSAIDs and RICE, then you're SOL. Got it?

My coworker had long given up by the time I signed up to run the Marshall University Marathon. I affixed a spreadsheet to the refrigerator and Kaitlyn watched in disbelief as I chalked up my weekly mileage. Each week I added two or three miles to my weekly total. Before I knew it, I was knocking out six-mile runs on my *easy* days.

I can't say exactly why, but this undertaking made absolute sense to me. It was so simple, yet challenging. You move forward, tick off another mile, move forward some more, repeat, repeat, repeat. It changed everything.

From that point on, when I was handed a thick stack of folders representing new probationers, I found myself thinking, *No problem. I can run ten miles. I can handle this.* I exhausted myself during the days and slept like a sedated narcoleptic at night. I started to eat better. I drank less alcohol. In short, I became a better man. My body transformed from bulky to lean. Even on the days I didn't run I lifted weights and crunched my abs into submission.

The MU race offered me views of the West Virginia portion of the Ohio River Valley along with a mixture of city streets and inviting parks. The major selling point of this small marathon was finishing inside of the university's football stadium while carrying a football for the last hundred yards. For a first-time marathoner, having your name announced over the stadium speakers and seeing yourself on the jumbo-sized video board in the end zone is well worth the registration fee. Who am I kidding? I would still think it was cool if it were my fiftieth marathon.

I clocked in at just over four hours, and Kaitlyn was there at the finish line to support me. She handed me a Gatorade and, in her typically cuddly manner, asked me why I didn't finish with a better time. We exchanged smiles, and then I threw up right next to her feet.

True love is something you can't hold in.

"Dean Silo will see you now," announced the gargoyle perched at the desk outside the Office of Academic Affairs.

Ms. Beatrice Holbrook was a cliché, wrapped around a banality, and boxed up into an ugly stereotype. The administrative assistant was the cagey, uptight gatekeeper for Dean Clyde Silo. If it was the dean's intention to use her to filter out the more trifling problems of staff members and students, the sixty-five-year-old jagged splinter of a woman was perfect for the job. Even if a visitor could possibly withstand her scouring stare, flattened nose, and alien ears, her medieval torture device of a personality was sure to make the strongest of constitutions burst into flames and scatter like a pile of dry ashes.

The hard wooden chair in the waiting area groaned with appreciation as I got up from it. As uncomfortable as that chair had been for the past half-hour, it seemed a better prospect than having to walk past Beatrice's desk on my way to Silo's office. I smoothed out my sport coat and made my way past her lair.

"Don't be too long in there. He's a very busy man and cannot be bothered with frivolities. You understand?"

I really didn't have any say in how long this would take, but I was not going to argue the point. And had she just called me a frivolity?

"I'll do my best," I said in my most courteous tone. "How are you today?"

"See that you do," she hissed without responding to my question.

I felt the sudden urge to get a tetanus shot.

I grabbed the unwieldy iron knob on Silo's door and passed through the portal. Glancing above the frame as I entered, I half expected to see the words ABANDON ALL HOPE, YE WHO ENTER HERE scorched atop the passageway.

After telling Kaitlyn everything the previous Friday, I busied myself through the weekend on household jobs I had been putting off. It helped my productivity level that watching television wasn't an option. I made a few attempts at turning on the TV but Lindsay's murder was on every newscast. Every station was using some file photo the university must have given them. The same photo was in the newspapers as well, only in black and white. She looked a couple of years younger, and her hair was dark brown with a red streak down the left side. She looked more innocent, but there was a hint of rebellion in her eyes. I guessed that the photo was probably from her freshman year when she had it taken for her student ID. She must have decided later that Lindsay—the college woman—was going to be a blonde.

To take my mind off of everything, and to avoid the temptation to run on my rest day, Sigmund and I spent all of Saturday putting shelves up in the basement and fixing a broken electrical outlet. Kaitlyn worked on potting a bunch of plants, or herbs, or something else, that would eventually be put into her garden.

An eleven-mile run on Sunday morning made me feel docile, so I shocked my wife by volunteering to go to IKEA with her to look at some furniture for our guest bedroom. I truly hate that place. It's a maze of random furnishings and knickknacks that sit under large blue signs promising to show you a shortcut out of there. But the shortcuts are nothing more than subterfuges that guide the mice down another path, where two dollar ultra-modern shoe horns are on display next to house slippers that look like cartoon frogs. My personal cheese at the end of the corporate labyrinth is in the form of their giant cinnamon rolls that are sold next to the checkout lines. But, even with that incentive, getting me to go into the place usually takes an act of divine intervention. I figured the angrier I got at navigating the maze, and the more I wanted a cinnamon roll, the less I would think about facing the consequences of my error.

Silo was sitting behind his oversized desk, thumbing through a pile of printouts covered with numbers and littered with Post-it notes. When I released the office door to let it close behind me, the latch produced a violent scrape and agitating clicking noise when it returned to its original position. My shoes double-tapped across the unexpressive walnut floor as my heels and toes held muted, but audible conversations. Ignoring the noises, the head of the Academic Affairs department didn't look up from the papers until I was standing in front of his desk.

"Have a seat, Dr. Keller."

"Please, it's Cyprus," I corrected him while falling into an oversized leather chair that made me feel like a child sinking into a cardboard box packed with Styrofoam peanuts.

The dean hadn't bothered to stand or attempt a handshake. I think it made him self-conscious. He was a diminutive, unattractive man, who didn't do himself any favors by wearing suits much too big for him. Today's suit looked like something he was either married in decades ago, or that someone else had been buried in. His puppet-like hands peeked out of wrinkled sleeves. Luckily, some attention was drawn away from his elfish stature by the way he attempted to cover a formidable bald spot by combing over a few wisps of hair that were the shade of dirty snow.

Silo was partially a product of the already screwed-up mentality of the school and his office was legendary for a singular reason. It was in that very room where, just prior to the crash of '29, the incident occurred when several members of Henry Gadson's little cult decided to hold an impromptu ceremony in the founder's office while the school's founder was out of town. Apparently, one of the more robust ladies involved had been well lubricated by both spirits and a special body oil when she began leaning toward and staring into one of the surrounding candles, while reciting some words originally spoken by some guy named Parmenides. It turned out that the ceremonial oil had a disturbing reaction to flames. To their credit, the rest of the nutbag battalion tried to put the poor woman out. But, with their hands and faces besmeared with the same oil, the result was predictable. Nobody actually died during the bonfire of the idiots, but the cult members had seen the light, so to speak, and permanently retreated to their mansions to heal their egos and numerous second-degree burns.

"Dr. Kasko has filled me in on what transpired last week. I can't say I'm happy about the situation. You do realize that we cannot have members of our faculty revealing the personal aspects of our students' lives? Regardless of how you feel about the young man's sexual orientation, discussing it in public is totally unacceptable."

The way *I feel* about his sexuality? Silo's words almost shuffled past me in the crowd of verbiage because of the distracting way he spoke. He had the annoying habit of creating a part-slurping and part-smacking sound with his lips and tongue between each sentence. The first time I met him, I wasn't ready for this maddening tendency, and I instinctively wanted to shield my irises from the piece of gum that was sure to fly out.

"Wait a second. There seems to be some misunderstanding. I don't *feel* any particular way about Steven's sexual orientation. In fact, if I have any *feeling* about it whatsoever, it's in a supportive way. He has the right to be with whomever he chooses as far as I'm concerned."

The dean pushed a pair of bifocals up and further exposed an accusing nose.

Twisting side to side while trying to sit up in my flimsy throne, I explained myself further. "What happened was a complete accident and I was trying to help Steven. The police had the wrong idea about him and Ms. Behram. I certainly didn't have any malicious intent."

"That's not really the point is it, Dr. Keller?"

"It's Cyp—" I was cut off by the preamble of a sucking click on his lips.

"You have put the university in an unfortunate position. As faculty members, we have a solemn responsibility to uphold the absolute highest standards of personal and professional conduct. Three Rivers University has always prided itself on being able to provide a first-class education and consistently attract the best professors and students. Being a part of the TRU family means putting aside your personal feelings regarding the lifestyles of others and accepting everyone for who they are. I have to say that I'm disappointed in your narrow-mindedness."

I reached up to check if blood was coming out of my ears. Maybe I had suffered a stroke when I had to deal with the Queen of Darkness in the waiting area. If there was an upside to his insulting me, it was that it prevented tears of laughter from forming in my eyes after his acid-trip description of TRU.

Remembering Kaitlyn's counsel to be on my best behavior, I unclenched my jaw and stated slowly, "Dean Silo, I don't think you're hearing me. I don't care about Steven being gay. I wouldn't care if he were straight. I wouldn't care if he were a bisexual hermaphrodite nymphomaniac who enjoys cross-dressing and singing 'Careless Whisper' on Tuesday nights." I managed to move myself to the front of the absurd chair and grip the ends of the arms. "I made an error in the heat of the moment and I'll be happy to apologize to him." Then I recalled that this entire exercise might be a moot point.

"Has Steven filed a complaint? Has he even heard about this?"

Silo leaned back smugly, and crossed one leg over the other.

He said, "Not yet. But as you know this is a small campus with a close-knit student body. I cannot imagine that this will remain quiet."

Putting both feet back on the floor, he leaned forward and picked up a silver pen from his desk. Pointing to some marks in a small appointment book in front of him he explained, "In fact, rather than wait on anything official, I've spoken to Mr. Thacker and asked him to come here this afternoon. I will explain to him what happened, inform him of his options regarding filing an official grievance against you, and allow him time to choose a course of action." The left lens of his glasses rose slightly along with that corner of his mouth. "If Mr. Thacker feels that there is some way the university can address this issue to his satisfaction, then of course I will have to take that into consideration."

The translation was easy. Silo was going to make sure that Steven would say that he would pursue legal action against the school unless I was fired. He was going to portray me as a loud-mouthed homophobe who had it in for Steven. Then, the dean could convince the Criminology department's faculty members that they had no choice but to let me go. Silo would be rid of me, all consciences would be clear, and all involved could take credit for saving the university from being dragged through courtrooms for years to come. I was even willing to bet Silo would find some way to reward Steven for his understanding and cooperation. Perfect.

"Of course, I will let you know the outcome of my meeting with Mr. Thacker. In the meantime, I would advise you to refrain from having any contact with him. I believe your next Victimology class is not until late morning tomorrow, correct? So, I'll be sure to call you or send you an email by the end of business today." Silo said all of this while scrutinizing a loose thread that protruded from one of the buttons on his suit jacket.

"You can't be serious about this. If I can just talk to Steven, I—"

"You are to have no contact with Mr. Thacker!" The lip smacking became deafening. "You have put the university in enough peril and you have proven that you cannot be prudent with your words, Dr. Keller."

"Cyprus."

"Stay away from Mr. Thacker and let the university handle this. This is not some back alley in Boston where you can try to strong-arm some witness into changing his testimony!"

"Baltimore."

"I tried to warn the hiring panel when you first showed up on our radar. The top professionals in academia do not cut their teeth by writing speeding tickets and flying informants."

"Running informants."

"Whatever. You never had the pedigree or temperament for academia, and unfortunately for you it has finally come to light."

Silo twirled the pen in his hand and his gaze fell to his calendar book. "Now, if you will excuse me, I have another meeting to attend to—*Cyprus*." He pronounced my first name like it was an infection.

I slowly rose to leave.

"It's Dr. Keller. And fuck you."

Walking toward my office, I weighed my options. I could resign and try to cut my losses, but there were too many questions left unanswered. Had Steven heard about what I had done? Was he the vindictive type? I mean, I didn't think he was ever going to want to be my best friend or anything, but I never felt as if he particularly disliked me. Would Steven let himself be manipulated by the dean? I could easily see Steven telling Silo to go stick it once he realized he was being used as a pawn.

No. I couldn't quit. Not with this many uncertainties. The prospect of not having a paycheck was daunting as well. Kaitlyn and I do pretty well, but not *that* well. And sitting around and waiting was never my thing. A preemptive strike was in order, so I picked up my pace and made a beeline for my office door. As soon as I made it to my desk, I reached for my Blackberry. By my Blackberry I mean my desk drawer full of scraps of paper. Due to my exceptionally well-designed organizational system, in a matter of minutes I was able to find a handwritten note that had Steven's name and phone number on it. As I stabbed the numbers on the phone's keypad, I read the rest of what was on the piece of paper, and allowed myself an inner cheer for still having a valid coupon for the oil change and transmission place in the North Hills area.

If I could catch Steven before his meeting with Silo, then at least I could explain the situation. The Criminology faculty members didn't exactly love Silo, so if he wanted to get me fired for disobeying his orders and contacting Steven, then he would have a tough climb.

The phone rang several times until a machine picked up. Steven's voice told me to leave a message and he would call me back. I pressed down on the protruding square where the handset had been sitting and dialed the number again. Same number of rings, same result. Hanging up the phone, I sat atop my desk pondering my next move. Remembering that I had scheduled office hours starting in a few minutes, I jumped up, grabbed a blank sheet of paper from my printer tray and used a black marker to write a message announcing my office hours had been canceled. I snatched a roll of tape from the top of a cabinet, hung the sign up on the hallway side, then closed and locked my door.

The next ten minutes in my office were about as productive as my first five. I sat at my computer and searched the university's phone directory hoping to find a cell phone number for Steven. No luck there. Eventually, I scrolled down the page and found that he had an apartment listed in the Mt. Washington neighborhood that overlooked the city. I jotted down the address on the same coupon with his phone number and stuffed it in my pocket. Determined not to stand around idly and watch my career become road kill, I propelled myself out of the office.

By the time I had walked to my car in the campus parking garage, beads of sweat had formed on my forehead. I stripped off my sport coat, threw it over the backseat of the dark green Jeep, and within seconds was winding my way down Ohio River Boulevard and eyeing the climb onto Mt. Washington. The Wrangler groaned as it pushed its way up onto the platform that presented an incredible panoramic view of most of the city. I cracked a window to let the early spring air dry my face, and thought about how I would explain things to Steven.

The apartment was set back from the edge of the ascent, and was concealed by a series of overrated and expensive restaurants that capitalized on the view. Steven's building was a faded light blue, four-story structure that looked like a haven for wannabe artists and musicians. It was easy to see why a graduate student would choose to live here. Steven was listed as the occupant of apartment 2G, so I passed by, trying to eyeball the second floor. Each apartment had a door opening up onto a walkway that was visible from the street.

On my second trip around the block, I found a parking space on the street. As I evened my rear bumper with the car positioned in front of the open space and shifted into reverse, I swiveled my body in order to parallel park. My foot had started to release the brake and move toward the gas pedal when I caught sight of them. The two men were standing on the second floor outside an apartment. Hartz was knocking on the door while Shand stood watch. The detectives were positioned on either side of the door and didn't appear to be engaged in any unnecessary chatter. Any decent police academy hammers those two things into your brain when it comes to approaching a residence: 1) never stand directly in front of a door in case someone starts blowing holes in it; and 2) shut the hell up so you might hear what is going on inside.

Hartz knocked two more times, and the frustrated-looking detectives exchanged glances before walking toward an exterior stairwell. Deciding that I didn't want to stick around and shoot the breeze with them again, I shifted the car back into drive and slowly pulled away. Not being a big believer in coincidence, I didn't think it was too much of a stretch to conclude that they were looking for Steven and had come up empty. There was no way that they had let the entire weekend pass without trying to interview him. Not with a high-profile case like this one. They either hadn't been able to find him during the past two days, or they were attempting a follow-up interview for some reason.

Regardless, I realized it was highly unlikely I'd be able to speak with Steven prior to his meeting with the dean.

Back on campus, I pulled into my designated parking spot and sat listening to the radio. As I pondered my situation, Tom Petty was singing "Breakdown" in the background. I could wait outside the Whitlock Building in hopes of catching Steven on his way in, but I didn't even know what time the meeting was. Silo said the meeting was scheduled for the afternoon, but I couldn't make out a time in his appointment book.

Looking at my watch, I was surprised to see it was almost noon. I was supposed to meet the guys for our usual Monday run in half an hour. I initially dismissed the idea, finding a seven-mile run trivial at the moment; but considering my limited choices, I got out of the vehicle and started the trek over to the recreation building. A hard run usually clears my head, and at this point I had clutter piled up in every corner.

We met in our usual spot in front of the recreation building, and stretched our hamstrings, quads, and calves. The skies were clear and the thermometers were supposed to tease us today with a high of around sixty. Randy's extreme exuberance for the unusually nice weather was evidenced by his wearing shorts and a T-shirt he had picked up at some 5K race a few years ago. He looked as if the weekend had recharged him: he was bouncing up and down on the balls of his feet doing his best Rocky Balboa imitation. I hated it when he was in a good mood—it made him unbearable when he got on a roll. He had a temporary moment of panic when he noticed a small streak of dirt on his ankle that he must have gotten while stretching before I had come outside. The panic subsided when he brushed it off easily. If the man could run in a plastic bubble, I think he would. I could just see him rolling down the Boulevard of the Allies like a giant runaway hamster.

Aaron was more apprehensively attired in a long-sleeved shirt—made of something no human can pronounce, and similarly constructed long pants. He was wearing his Brooks. Wednesday, it would be his Adidas. He rotated shoes so the muscles in his feet and legs wouldn't get used to the exact same movements. I know, it sounds crazy; but according to the modern literature on the subject, he was right to do so. The things we do to gain the tiniest advantage.

Jacob had a thick, plush-looking, purple hooded sweatshirt cloaking his torso. For some reason the comfortable sight of it made me want to take a nap. His black cotton shorts had the letters TRU printed on the left side and carried a small depiction of the school mascot on the right—"The Railer." This made-up term, and the accompanying logo, were intended to represent a railroad worker pounding a steel spike into the ground with a ferocious-looking sledgehammer. I actually thought it more closely resembled a man in the middle of a backswing with a golf club preparing to strike a slightly misshapen penis.

The four of us made small talk as we finished warming up.

"No, no, no . . . Cimitrex is going to get bought out; it's just a matter of time," Randy rambled about his latest stock tip.

"I never invest heavily in tech stocks," said Aaron. "Sure, I missed out on a lot during the early nineties, but when the bubble burst, I stayed nice and dry."

"Cyprus, did you take my advice on that mutual fund?" Aaron asked as he paid extra attention to a troublesome calf muscle.

I distractedly told him that I hadn't, but I would look into it.

Randy and Aaron continued ranting about the market, while Jacob and I continued limbering up.

Jacob spoke quietly, "How did things go with Silo?"

"I'll tell you later."

Aaron and Randy weren't listening, but I didn't want to get into it with them around. It seemed that word of my blowup during the police interview hadn't reached them yet.

Changing the subject, I asked, "Aren't you supposed to have a meeting this week with the federal guys about some grant money?"

"Spent two hours with them at WVU this morning. I just got back here on campus. It's looking pretty good, but there is still some finagling to do."

I slipped into the bitchy cynicism that cops have sometimes. "So they made you spend ninety minutes driving to Morgantown for a two-hour meeting, just so you could turn around and drive ninety minutes back? How courteous of them."

Shrugging it off, Jacob said, "They have the money for research and TRU wants me to do the research. That's the way the game is played."

I didn't care about any of this. I was just trying to act normal. Trying to *feel* normal. I started feeling foolish for engaging in what Jacob had to know was a weak effort at self-distraction.

I got quiet and pulled a leg back behind me to loosen a quad muscle.

"You don't look well, my friend. You have to relax. Even if Steven does find out about it, perhaps he won't be upset." Jacob consoled.

"Steven is just part of it," I admitted. "I don't think I told you, the murdered girl had come to my office on the day she was killed."

I had a short inward debate about telling Jacob about why she had come to see me, and opted to keep that information to myself.

I changed course with, "I'm no stranger to seeing death, but it's never easy to see somebody alive one minute and know they were gone a short while later."

Jacob nodded his understanding.

"I've been here a long time, Cyprus. Unfortunately, this happens from time to time. Usually it's an accident—a car crash or overdose—but it's always hard to take when it happens to a student you had in class. For most of the city, it's just some blonde girl who had a future snuffed out like the flame on a candle. But for anybody who was in the classroom with her, they'll be stuck with an empty seat to remind them of the loss. I know it's weird. Even when you don't know your students well, you still feel responsible for them. It's like their parents, whom you never met, entrusted their child to you. You illogically think it is your job to protect them, but you can't."

The four of us finished stretching, ran out of small talk, and set out southward toward the Allegheny River. Lindsay's murder didn't come up in conversation until the third mile, and even then it mostly consisted of typically empathetic comments about how the parents must be devastated and how young she was. The only one who didn't seem to have gotten the memo on appropriate emotional responses after a death was Randy. He chugged away in front of me, and tried to move us away from the subject of Lindsay's death by talking about how too many people were going to be allowed to enter the Pittsburgh Marathon this year, and what a travesty it was that the route was changed. I actually agreed with him on both points, but we were barely halfway through March and May was still weeks away. There would be plenty of time to bitch about it when a coed hadn't been murdered the previous Friday.

We raced down a trail that parallels the river, to the sounds of barges hauling coal and traffic creeping over the multitude of bridges. Pittsburgh has more bridges than Venice, which is great for scenery, but lousy for traffic. By the time we reached our turnaround point at Washington's Landing, Randy was less hyper than when we began and his face was showing signs of impatience.

"The paper said she was from Clearview," Aaron puffed while moving to the left side of the path to avoid a protective looking goose standing watch over her goslings.

Or is it geeslings? Or ganders? I would have to look that up along with the finch thing.

"I think it was Clarion," Jacob corrected. "And she was planning on becoming a journalist, according to the story."

I had avoided the news, so I was a little behind.

I inquired, "Was that what her degree would have been in?"

Aaron responded, "Yep. Scheduled to graduate this spring. Heather Braun over in the Journalism department told me that the girl seemed a little wild, but she was anything but flighty. She was actually very focused during class. Coming from Braun, that's high praise."

"Gentlemen, can we move on?" Randy's dam finally cracked. "You act as if you're shocked that this stuff happens!" His pace picked up to compete with his anger. "Most of us have been in this business for at least twenty years and you know that students die sometimes! You know this! Let's not make a saint out of the girl!"

Randy paused as a cyclist passed by.

Throwing a quick look my way, he continued, "Hearing this level of naiveté from *the sapling* is one thing, but you two ought to be a little more seasoned at this point in your careers, don't you think? Let's not all be children."

"Stop." I grabbed the back of Randy's shirt and pulled back. The entire group halted as if I had yanked on the reins of a horse. Spinning Randy around, I kept my voice even as I chose the words to drill into him.

"If you enter a room and see pieces of a burnt-up Brillo pad and an empty Coke can, what's been going on in there?"

I once responded to a disturbance call where I found a teenage boy standing in his bedroom, naked, with the exception of a football helmet. He had a rose tied around his little railroad spike and was rubbing a vibrating cell phone on his testicles. The look I had on my face when I entered the room must have been similar to the expression Randy was now giving me.

He managed to fumble out, "I . . . I . . . wha-what?"

"Someone's been smoking crack and using the steel wool as a screen and the Coke can as a pipe." I poked a finger into his sweaty shirt. "That's a tough one. Let's try again. You know those pens with the ink that turns a different color when it comes in contact with counterfeit money? Why does the ink turn a different color?"

"Look here, I'm not . . ."

"Wrong answer. The ink contains iodine that reacts to the starch that is contained in normal paper. Real money is made from a special cotton and linen blend that doesn't react the same way."

Jacob started to step in. "Cyprus you've made your . . ."

"Here, Randy. I'll toss you a softball. When police officers make a traffic stop, they usually touch the back of the car they are approaching. What's that all about?"

Randy was wide-eyed and his mouth was open, but nothing was exiting the tunnel. He had been hit by the one-two punch of not expecting me to go off like this and not having a clue as to what I was talking about.

"It's to make sure that the trunk or hatch is secure and nobody will get behind them when they walk toward the front of the car, Randy. And it has the added bonus of putting finger-prints on the car in case some psycho guns down the officer when he reaches the driver's side window! That way there is at least some sort of evidence on the car and the son of a bitch might get convicted!"

I poked hard with each of the last three words.

"But you don't know any of that, do you, Randy? You can talk about general deterrence versus specific deterrence or social disorganization theory until you're blue in the face, but the truth is that you are an idiot when it comes to putting theory into practice! So you can talk down to me all you like and call me kid, or kiddo, or junior, but the sad truth is that you are a pathetic fraud who wouldn't be able to hack it on the street for five minutes! Try walking into a death-trap of an apartment and seeing a three-year-old dead on the floor while the mother sits on the couch getting high! Take a shot at getting a schizo-phrenic fifteen-year-old the help she needs, only to find out later she cut off her own ears to silence the voices after Daddy sold her meds on the street. Or how about you watch helplessly as some of your coworkers disappear from roll call because some crackhead didn't want to give up his stash, or some maniac thought trying to avoid three months in the city jail for simple assault was worth a cop's life! Is that not the kind of resume you're looking for, Randy?"

Silence.

I knew running was cathartic, but Jesus! All three of my col-leagues, if I could still call them that, were triangulated around me and each had backed up a half step at some point. Where the hell did that come from?

Eventually, it was the salesman of the group who felt obligated to fill the empty space.

In his most diplomatic voice, Aaron choked, "Well . . . we still have a little more than three miles to go. We should probably get moving." He gave a nervous twitch of his mustache and added, "We're like brothers, right? And brothers fight now and then."

Randy appeared to be absent. He stared at me and then his head turned toward Aaron and then Jacob. I could tell he was as embarrassed about not knowing what to say as he was about what I had actually said.

Eventually Randy gulped, "I'm going to take a different route back. I'll see you guys later."

Randy wandered off into an industrial complex, probably not realizing that he was supposed to be running rather than walking.

Aaron looked blankly at Jacob, and then over to me with disbelief and perhaps a trace of resentment. He mumbled, "I better go with him."

Jacob and I nodded our agreement.

When Randy and Aaron were out of sight, Jacob said, "I don't have class until three thirty. What do you say we call this an easy day and walk back?"

I didn't answer, but started retracing our steps slowly on the gravel path.

"So, I'm guessing your meeting with Clyde did not go well?" Jacob asked while looking up at the Duquesne Incline in the distance.

The Incline is basically a short rail system that runs from the point where the Ohio and Monongahela rivers converge. It scales a steep hill, where the Duquesne Heights neighborhood sits. People can hop in these things that look like shrunken trolley cars and move up and down the slope with the assistance of cables. My own gaze was fixed on the station at the top that was adjacent to the Mt. Washington neighborhood I had visited just a short time before.

"You could say that. Silo's gunning for me and he's going to try to get Steven to insist that I get terminated. He's supposed to be meeting with Steven at some point this afternoon."

"He's talked to Steven?"

"At least enough to get him on the schedule. It didn't sound as if they had gone into any details as of this morning." I eyed one of the trolley cars levitating up the rise. From this distance it looked like part of the set for "Mr. Rogers' Neighborhood." Now that I think of it, he had a trolley too. But I don't recall college girls being strangled in his neck of the woods.

Jacob watched his shoestrings and listened to the gravel crunch under his weight. After a few seconds, he said, "When I spoke to him this weekend, he gave me the impression that he would be fair."

"He gave you the wrong impression."

"I'll keep working on him. You didn't give him any ammunition, did you?"

"Like?"

"Like, you were professional the entire time. Like, you didn't melt down and engage in a verbal blitzkrieg that would make Patton weak at the knees? Like, you did not insult his entire person and question his qualifications? Like, you didn't poke him in the chest and question his manhood and his intellectual abilities at the same time?"

"That doesn't sound like me."

I could feel the two laser sights centering on the side of my head.

"It wasn't that bad," I lied. "I held it together pretty well, all things considered."

"That's why I like you, Cyprus. Always the perfect portrait of discretion."

Mile 7

While turning south and crossing the Warhol Bridge, a few gusts of wind press against my chest and the right side of my body. Disrobed from the North Shore buildings, I tilt my head down to lessen the wind resistance caused by the moving air along the Allegheny. This part of the race is quiet. The bridge is just wide enough to accommodate all of the runners. No bands on the side. No spectators. Just the PPG buildings with their reflective black surfaces and cathedral inspired rooftops, approaching at my two o'clock position. I unzip my running belt and chew a few shattered pieces of my snack right before my feet hit the shore at the end of the span.

Coming off the bridge onto Duquesne Boulevard, thunder erupts. Runners are exiting the bridge, making a hard right turn, and then duplicating the maneuver to hop onto the Roberto Clemente Bridge. The spectators who were at the starting line and in the Strip District have gravitated over to this choke point to catch a quick glimpse of the athletes before they head back to the North Shore. After the eruption of sound, glimmer of digital cameras, and flourish of homemade signs, the commotion is gone and thousands of feet push back across the river toward PNC Park. As far as baseball stadiums go, it's first rate. One of the best in the country. The satisfying seats and low ticket prices console a fan base that hasn't seen a winning team take the field in over fifteen years.

I never thought I would be going to Pirates games. I never envisioned living here at all, much less teaching at a college. It's funny how one decision leads to the next. Sometimes it's the small strides that lead to major life changes.

After running my first marathon, I was absolutely hooked. I ran two or three a year, and in between those races I kept up my training by running shorter races at faster speeds. 5K races are 3.1 miles. I used those for speed work. 10Ks are 6.2 miles. Those were for speed and endurance. The 13.1 mile half-marathons were for tuning things up just a few weeks before a full marathon.

I ran locally and I traveled to other states. I spent money on gear, hotel rooms, entry fees, and protein bars, just so I could punish my body on new roads and trails. I felt like a missile. I felt sharp and confident like never before, and it carried over to all aspects of my life. I started taking graduate evening classes at the local university. I willed myself through textbooks and journals the way I did up mountain roads. When I thought I had reached the top of the mountain, instead of standing there in triumph, I sought out others to climb.

Kaitlyn's practice was doing well enough so that after I finished my master's degree we decided I could pursue my doctorate full time. I turned in my badge and gun and picked up a new laptop and briefcase. I let my hair grow out and tried to lose the haircut that screamed *cop*. Before long, I had established a formidable reputation as a researcher and writer, but I really found my second calling in the classroom. The students seemed to appreciate hearing from a doctoral candidate who wasn't on parole from an ivy tower, and they helped me get back to chasing the ideal.

I found that the Criminology students I taught didn't have the same level of optimism as I did when I was an undergrad. The world had changed. They didn't believe that things would get better. They didn't believe that the battle for civilization was going to be won by the good guys. They had watched as jihadists crashed planes into buildings and genocides went unnoticed in faraway lands. Videos of beheadings peppered the internet. New illnesses like SARS and H1N1 flu were popping up for unknown reasons. Our American flags were all made in China. The students thought we were going to lose the war, and that inspired me more than anything. When you stand before an army that thinks defeat is inevitable, but its soldiers keep showing up to sharpen their bayonets, how can you not stand a little taller?

It took me only a few minutes to get cleaned up in the locker room. Aaron and Randy must have beaten us back and had already vacated the area. I dressed in silence, not even bothering to put my tie back on. Jacob went about his program, prepared his gear for the next run, and assured me that he would make another attempt at tranquilizing Silo. Walking out of there, I felt a tinge of guilt for unloading on Randy, and probably insulting Jacob and Aaron and their academic backgrounds in the process, but I felt better overall.

With my shoulders feeling a little lighter, I tried to accept the fact that my fate was out of my hands, and decided to head back to my office. If I wasn't suspended when tomorrow came, then I would need to go to class and have my material ready. The sun on my face felt good as I crossed the campus and emptied my mind of Lindsay, Steven, Silo, and the police.

I had forgotten to remove the hastily made sign from my door before I took off in search of Steven. The clear tape left a sticky silhouette on the door when I pulled it off. Walking over to the small CD player on a table in the corner, I hit the power button and pushed play. Mozart is always good to listen to when you're working. I'm not sure the CD player in my office has ever held music created by another composer. The only time I listen to classical is when I'm working—or reading at home—and even then I can only handle Brahms or Mozart. Eventually, I'll get a stereo that plays digital downloads and my CDs will go the way of the cassette tapes stacked up in my basement.

Feasting on protein bars that were stashed in a desk drawer and sipping on a sports drink I kept in my tiny refrigerator, I tore into ungraded assignments and future lesson plans. Like a possessed professor, I marked up paper after paper and made notations for myself regarding what points I needed to stress more and what topics I could move away from. I doubted any of my students could actually read my handwriting, but I inked comment after comment with zeal. If I was going out, at least I would go out competently.

I didn't want to leave TRU. For all of its faults, there were benefits. I chose to work here for two main reasons. First, the university pays me surprisingly well. Secondly, the people here don't really bother me about how much research I do or how often I get published. I'm left alone to be a real *teaching* professor. I suppose I could really solidify my status at Three Rivers if I pulled in some major grant money, but that's just not me.

Only when I had to turn on my desk lamp did I realize it was dark outside. I had completely lost track of time in my flurry of productivity. Even with the clock on my desk reading 7:30, I found it hard to believe how time had slipped by. I typed a quick email to Kaitlyn, telling her that I would be home in a little while, and I sorted all the paperwork into proper piles.

The old sodium vapor lamps lining the campus streets gave off a yellowish hue and low hum. Most of the students had retreated back to their dorms, apartments, or parents' homes and, while not abandoned, the school property was far from bustling. Over the top of the library, I could see the glow from the lights at PNC Park. Opening day wouldn't be for another ten days, but preparations for another long season were underway. I'm a big fan of baseball. It's a game of patience and anticipation trying to survive in an ADHD world. Maybe someday I'll move to a city where the team can actually make the playoffs.

The yellow tint of the air turned to off-white as I entered the parking garage. The first two levels were reserved for faculty and only four cars remained in sight of my Jeep. Reaching over with my keys to unlock the driver's side door, I found myself thinking about the way my dad used to talk about traveling to see the Cincinnati Reds play games at old Crosley Field.

It was just a slight change of color.

A portion of the dark green paint on the Wrangler turned black and then back to green. I instinctively tightened up and brought my right arm up near my head in a defensive position and spun to my right. Something smashed into the outside of my shoulder and sent a jolt across my shoulder blades. The pain was excruciating. Tunnel vision took effect and all I saw was the tire iron being raised by an unfriendly right hand. Not being able to move back because of the car, I stepped forward toward the figure that was starting to come into focus. I quickly struck out with my left and landed a solid punch center-mass on the blur. The tire iron missed its mark and the shadow stepped back.

Now I could see my attacker. Under the black hood of a torn sweatshirt, Steven tried to regain his breath after I had slammed his diaphragm.

"What the hell are you doing?" I yelled.

Steven's response was to move forward in a kickboxer's fighting stance, with left foot and hand forward, and re-engage me. Catching me watching the tire iron still being held in his right hand, he snapped his left leg up and landed a vicious side-kick to my face. I bounced back against the Jeep as he once again closed in on me. Fully coming to the realization that the tire iron had been meant for my head, and Steven had intended to make me a homicide statistic, I charged forward into the storm.

People skilled at kickboxing and karate generally don't feel very comfortable when an opponent is on them chest-to-chest. They want to have space to put force behind focused punches and directed kicks. Extremely close combat is unfamiliar to them and throws them off their game. Most law enforcement defensive tactics training is based on holds, arm bars, wrestling, and judo techniques. You have to use your opponent's momentum against them and strike only when an opening in their defenses becomes clear.

The collision with Steven put us right up against each other, and I felt him moving backwards with the force of my body. His legs were neutralized as weapons as soon as he was off-balance and struggling not to fall backwards. When he finally got a leg firmly planted behind him to stop his migration across the parking garage floor, I delivered a crushing blow to his nose with my forehead. The crack of bone breaking preceded a guttural groan. The gush of blood was instantaneous.

Undaunted, he pushed forward, so I pulled sharply on his sweatshirt and executed a decent shoulder toss. I should have kept my grip on his shirt and slammed him flat on the ground, but I released him in midair. I expected him to land on his back and either go unconscious or submit, but some part of his kickboxing training must have taught him the correct way to roll out of a fall. He tucked his chin into his chest and minimized the damage by curving his back and rolling onto his right hip. I couldn't believe it. The tire iron was still in his right hand. He was back on his feet in an instant.

We danced in a circle near the front wall of the garage, both panting.

"Steven. Get a hold of yourself. You don't want to do this."

I thought about how absurd this was.

"I know I outed you, but this is a little extreme, don't you think?"

Without a word from his face that was dripping with crimson, he came right at me.

Having plenty of room to maneuver, he had the advantage. I took a left jab to the chin, a kick to the stomach, and another left to the side of the face. I tasted his rage as it dripped down the back of my throat. He feigned like he was going to finally unleash the hand choking the metal rod, and then he delivered a low kick to my left knee. Before I knew it, I was kneeling with my victimized knee down and my healthy one up. The shoulder that had taken the initial blow felt like it had spent the night in a trash compactor. When I had thrown Steven, I felt a tingling sensation all the way down to my right wrist. If the injured limb stopped working, I was going to have an even bigger problem. I had a good idea what was coming next, and I was going to need that arm for one last task.

Steven stood above me, unrecognizable with the flattened nose and accompanying fountain of color. I tried one last time to reason with him. If ever there were an overreaction, this was it.

"You have to stop," I spat red. "This can be fixed. It's not the end of the world." I held my left knee, intentionally communicating that it was useless.

He edged closer and wiped blood away from his mouth with a sleeve.

"Steven! Think, for God's sake! You're not a killer!"

It was when his sleeve pulled away. It was right there on his face. That's when I knew that I had miscalculated everything up to that point.

"Sorry, Cyprus. Can't take the chance."

He raised the tire iron above his head, wound his hips up, and let the corkscrew unwind in order to deliver the fatal blow.

Pushing off my right foot, I leapt back and the weapon slashed diagonally past my face. My right arm was hanging across my body as I held my damaged but still-functioning left knee, and I said a silent prayer as I prepared it for battle. Steven had shifted all of his weight forward with the powerful swing and he was leaning slightly to his left after the follow through. I brought my right forearm across the right side of his neck with all the force I could muster, by turning my torso and slingshotting my arm while stepping forward.

The result was predictable, to a point. The quake caused by the impact on the side of his neck was enough to cause a hiccup in his carotid artery. The blood simply stopped flowing to the brain just long enough to cause disorientation, or even a momentary loss of consciousness. The overly aggressive slash with the tire iron was the opening in his defenses I was waiting for. The blow landed precisely as I had hoped and Steven's internal CPU went into standby mode. The problem was, he was nearly toppling over before I struck him. When I unleashed all of my strength into his neck, his feet left terra firma and his head cartwheeled toward it.

Mile 8

North Shore Drive runs behind both the baseball and football stadiums and winds past the downtown casino. This time of year, Heinz Field serves only as a taunting reminder to the Steeler-crazed city that football season is still a lifetime away. During the season, I've seen fans tailgating at eight in the morning for a four o'clock game. You can't drive two blocks in western Pennsylvania without seeing a Steelers car magnet, license plate frame, bumper sticker, or window flag. I've seen scores of vans, pickup trucks, and sedans that are painted black and gold and look like Terry Bradshaw vomited memorabilia all over the interior.

But for now, the stadium is just a landmark for distance. Last May, this street wasn't on the route, but this year it takes us on the stadium tour that concludes with a long ramp onto the West End Bridge. The climb isn't really that bad. The fact that you can see it coming for several blocks is what settles into your conscious and subconscious thoughts, and nags at you with every step.

No crowd here. I easily hit a water station before making the climb. It's a sidewalk oasis in an otherwise unpopulated area. This is the extreme western part of the course. The smart fans will stay downtown near the local businesses that serve hot coffee and breakfast pastries. No reason to claw your way to a remote outpost just to see a madman or crazy woman streak by. No. Stay close to base. Stay centered. If you start trying to see all of the things, you end up missing everything.

Concrete is harder than asphalt. Most people don't realize that. I doubt that Steven knew it.

The sound when his head hit the concrete bumper at the front of the parking space we were occupying was sickening. It was like a hammer hitting a stone under ten feet of water. The released tire iron competed with it by producing an ugly tune, but even it couldn't drown out that horrible sound. Not exactly a crack. Not exactly a thud.

Knowingly, I knelt down and put two fingers on his neck, exactly where I had struck him. I sat down on a neighboring concrete bumper and stared at a blue light bulb hovering over the emergency phone on the far wall of the structure. When picked up, it rang directly to campus security. They could be here in three minutes—but to save Steven they would have to have gotten here two minutes before I sat down.

Another minute passed and I had gathered myself enough to make the call, but I never made it to the phone. As I stood up and started walking toward the blue light, the sound of sirens filled the campus. Security vehicles screeched into the parking lot from each end, triangulating me in their headlights and spot-lighting Steven's lifeless form behind me.

I'm not a fan of lawyers. It's not that I despise them. That would be illogical. They serve a certain purpose and they are an essential part of our legal system. Understood. Kierkegaard seemed to understand, and be in awe of, Abraham's willingness to kill Isaac, but he was terrified by the acts that could be justi-fied by blind faith. Lawyers have the tendency to declare that the ends justify the means more than most people. They seek out loopholes and absurd mitigating circumstances and smile when an animal is set loose on the public—to hell with the detritus left behind. It was for the greater good. The system. I'm in awe of that. But do not confuse that with admiration.

So I sat in the small interviewing room at the Zone 1 Police Station on Brighton Road. They used to call these things interrogation rooms. But, then again, they used to call the areas around them precincts. Now they were interviewing rooms inside of zones. I would wait and not ask for an attorney unless they put the cuffs on me.

My cell phone had survived the battle royale and I had been permitted to call Kaitlyn. I told her that I had been attacked, that I was okay, and that I had killed the attacker. She was mortified and insisted on coming to me right away. I told her where the station was and told her that I would be giving a statement for a while. I could almost hear her hands shaking when she hung up.

Once campus security had arrived at the parking garage, a hailstorm of activity had taken place. The two security patrol cars were followed by two Pittsburgh PD cars. Then two more. Then the ambulance. Unmarked Crown Vics with detachable bubble-lights found their way through the logjam that had formed. I knew eventually the medical examiner, or coroner, or whatever they called it here, would make an appearance.

I answered some cursory questions thrown at me by the officers. Yes—I was attacked. Yes—I defended myself. No—I did not use a weapon. Yes—I knew the . . . victim. The EMTs from the ambulance treated me, and told me they wanted to take me to Allegheny General for x-rays and a CAT scan. I gingerly rotated my injured shoulder and politely declined. They shook their heads as I signed a waiver confirming my stupidity.

A detective from one of the unmarkeds approached to have me relive the scene again. He smelled of cigarettes. Knowing where this would eventually go, I told him to reach out to detectives Shand and Hartz. I mentioned that they were working a case that involved me and the . . . and Steven Thacker. I figured that even if the duo didn't pick up the chatter on the scanner, they would certainly hear about this soon enough. The man from one of the Crown Vics suggested that they take my full statement at the station. I started walking toward his car to avoid being put in a marked cruiser. I dreaded the next few hours. Two people were dead. I was a common denominator.

So I sat in the little room. I sat and waited.

When the detectives who were already familiar to me entered the room, they were cordial and concerned. Shand and Hartz took seats opposite me, with a beat-up metal table occupying the space between us. They told me they were sorry that we had to see each other again under these circumstances.

Build rapport every chance you get.

They told me that I looked awful. I had checked myself in the two-way mirror on the wall when I had first arrived. Awful was a compliment. If there was ever going to be a sequel to "Fight Club," I'd be a hit at the casting call. My pants and sport coat were in shambles. My white shirt was streaked and spattered with a mixture of B-positive and whatever Steven was. I didn't know what my shoulder and upper arm looked like, but I envisioned an abstract artist's rendition of an old British flag. My knee seemed fine—at least I had *that* going for me.

Detective Hartz started the interview with the greatest question of all. It's the question that investigators all over the world often forget to ask, yet it can be the most insightful interrogatory of them all.

He asked, "What happened?"

I recounted the night's events starting with my walk to the Jeep. The crush of the tire iron. The fight. The swipe at my head. The arm against his neck. The end.

They listened patiently and quietly. Shand was taking a few notes, but not many. I guessed a camera was running on the other side of the mirror. When I finished, Hartz asked me if I needed anything. A glass of water? Coffee? Then Shand told me that he was sorry that I had to go through that attack. It must have been an awful experience. Was I sure that I didn't need medical attention?

Express empathy toward the subject.

Hartz leaned over and lowered his voice. He said, "Look, we need your help understanding all of this. Obviously, you did what you had to do. Steven attacked you. He had a weapon. You fought back. We know this. Some students were getting ready to head up to a car on the third tier and they saw you two fighting, and they said . . ." He looked to Shand who flipped back a page in his notepad.

"That freaky guy in the sweatshirt had a lead pipe and was try'n to decapitate that old dude."

Old dude? I still get carded at the liquor store! Kids can be cruel.

"One of them used a cell to call campus security, but the response was too late."

Hartz continued, "So, Thacker came at you, and nobody would blame you one bit if you somehow got that tire iron away from him and had to use it against him."

Divert blame away from the subject. Provide a justification.

"I never had the tire iron. He had it in his right hand until . . . until the very end."

Scratching of pen on paper came from Shand's direction.

"Okay. We can go with that. But the *why* of the whole thing is what we can't go with. Why would he attack you like that? You two worked together."

While I was waiting for the detectives, I had thought a lot about the *why*. It didn't make sense. Steven was wound tight, but to snap, go off the deep end, and become homicidal over someone exposing the fact he was a homosexual was beyond my comprehension. I could see him filing a complaint. Maybe even confronting me verbally. But looking for a speedy way to remove lug nuts from my brain? Come on! There was only one other reason I could think of why Steven would come after me, but I couldn't make myself believe it.

"I think he knew that I told you guys he was gay. More importantly, that I had told you in public and people overheard us."

By *us*, I meant *me*.

"He wasn't open about being a homosexual, and I'm sure he would have been angry about the information getting out there." I waved my hand toward a wall which apparently represented *out there*.

Pointing a thumb in Shand's direction and squinting slightly, Hartz said, "We were both there. It wasn't the most delicate way to yank somebody out of the closet, but do you really think Thacker would find it worth *killing* you for?"

No.

"I don't know. Maybe. He wasn't a laidback kind of guy."

Shand chimed in with, "You're assuming that the gossip mill was working overtime and he'd heard what had happened."

I moved my head up and down in agreement and felt my tendons and muscles declare a state of emergency. Blood found its way into my mouth again.

"He was supposed to have a meeting with the Dean of Academic Affairs this afternoon. I had told a colleague about my mistake and he said he would talk to the dean about it over the weekend."

"So you could get in front of it," Hartz stated. Not a question.

"Right. So I met with the dean this morning, and Steven was going to meet with him in the afternoon. The dean was going to inform Steven of my error, if he didn't already know about it, and see if he wanted to file a formal grievance against me."

Shand looked up incredulously and acted as if he hadn't heard me right. In a half-amused tone he asked, "Wait a second. The dean . . . what's his name?"

"Silo."

"Dean Silo. He was going to dime you out and explain to Thacker that he had a legitimate option to make a complaint against you?" He leaned back and looked to see if his partner reflected his sentiment. "That's cold, man," he concluded.

Learning my anatomy lesson well the last time, I didn't nod.

Hartz wore a thoughtful expression and fiddled with his college ring. He chose his words carefully. "Silo must have spoken to Thacker in order to set up the meeting, right?"

"Either he did or his assistant did."

"When did that happen?"

"I have no idea. Before I met with him in the morning."

Something had struck a nerve.

"Had you talked to Thacker since our conversation last Friday?"

"No. I admit I tried to call him to explain things, but I just got his machine."

"What number?"

I thought I still had the coupon with his number on it in one of my pockets, but I didn't want to pull it out and show them that I also had his home address. One of the patrol officers had searched me as a matter of procedure, and finding the paper harmless, put it back in my pocket. Or did he take it with him?

I wanted to avoid giving off a crazy stalker vibe if at all possible. I had just killed the guy, so being outside his apartment and looking for him would not have looked good. Being upfront and honest with these guys was starting to become difficult.

"His home number, I think. I looked it up in the school's directory. I don't know if he carried a cell phone."

The two detectives looked at each other and somehow communicated that they needed to have a private conversation. Hartz told me that they would be back in a few minutes, and the investigators left me sitting there with my wounds.

About five minutes had passed and they came back into the small box. I could see from their faces that something had been decided. Some agreement had been reached or understanding met. They took their chairs and the metal legs scraped the hard floor.

Shand spoke first and I noticed the notebook was nowhere in sight.

"Dr. Keller, we think you may have been wrong about some things."

No kidding. I said nothing.

"Are you certain that Thacker was gay?"

"Considering I saw him kissing a man once, and that he later admitted to me he was gay, I feel reasonably sure about it."

"We're thinking either he had you fooled, or he was bisexual," Shand countered.

This was leading up to the other reason I thought might have prompted the attack.

Hartz added, "You see, we've been looking for Thacker . . . Steven for a couple of days. We needed to confirm your story and see if he knew Ms. Behram."

Shand put two calloused hands on the table and continued, "But this afternoon, we became aware of some images that were captured with an elevated camera in the Hill District. We didn't even notice it was there until we re-canvassed the neighborhood to look for witnesses. We asked around about it and we were told it's a traffic camera, but between you and me, traffic isn't the problem up there. The brass just forgot to tell us we had eyes in that area."

I understood and told him so.

He looked at me like I was the biggest sucker in the world. The former cop who had lost all his instincts. Sad. Pathetic.

"A car registered to Thacker was caught on video one block from where the body was found. Right around the T.O.D. and not long before her corpse was discovered. We actually got a pretty good shot at the driver's face. It was Thacker."

Something didn't add up.

"You got a good picture of his face at nine thirty at night? In the dark?"

Hesitation. Delay.

Hartz admitted, "We may not have been completely straight about that. It was closer to seven o'clock."

The recent leap forward from daylight savings time meant there was just enough sunlight at that time to get a decent image.

"So I blew a perfectly good lecture alibi."

They both smiled.

Hartz said, "Actually, it turned out that there was no record of you being at the lecture." He waived a hand dismissively. "We checked out of curiosity and your name wasn't on the list of scanned IDs. Probably a technical glitch. But don't worry, we have your credit card being used at the deli and the manager there remembers you. He told us that you come in a couple of times a week."

That was the first good news I had heard in a while. Good ol' Lenny. Or Lintle? The deli guy.

"We just checked with the medical examiner who picked up Thacker's body. He has some serious scratch marks down one of his arms."

Reflexively, I looked at my hands.

"Do you remember scratching him?"

"No, but I could have."

"Well, we'll have an evidence tech come in and take some scrapings from under your nails, but I *know* we have skin under Lindsay Behram's nails. We got skin from three nails and Thacker has three deep marks down his arm."

I stayed quiet.

Hartz tried to console me.

"It looks like you just got caught in the middle of two people in a bad relationship. You were in the wrong place at the wrong time, and the girl made the mistake of coming to see you when Thacker was there. You said it yourself, he was about to go off and work on his PhD. He had a bright future ahead of him. For whatever reason, Lindsay decided to crash his party and expose their relationship. You can't blame yourself. The guy was twisted."

Shand was recalling something.

He said, "We were executing a search warrant on his apartment when we got the call that he had attacked you. There was some pretty messed-up stuff in there. Bondage, S and M, and all that. Men, women, group sex—the whole gamut." He shook his large head. "Thacker was a troubled guy. You're lucky to be alive. Go home and sleep well. If we need anything, we know where to find you."

Troubled. That's the tactful way Baltimore PD described their ghettos. That's how Kaitlyn had described Lindsay. I decided, right then and there, to hate that word.

Some lady in a uniform came into the room and took scrapings from under my nails. On her way out the door, she shared a look with the detectives which told them that at first glance there didn't appear to be any skin present. Tests would have to be run to confirm that fact.

Hartz stood and opened the door. I walked out into a lobby I hadn't seen before. I had been brought in through a rusty back door. Kaitlyn was pacing back and forth biting a nail. When she saw me she did a double-take. I had forgotten about my face. I should have had the detectives warn her.

She ran up to me and I saw tears forming in her eyes. There was something on the tip of my tongue I was going to say to her, right before the blinding pain of her embrace wiped the slate clean. Whatever it was vanished. I said the only words that came to mind.

"Come on. Take me home."

Mile 9

The sloping ramp onto the West End Bridge takes us over a minute to overcome. I lean forward and have no problems conquering the ramp, because on the bridge—or maybe just past it—is the second place it might happen. The knee that got kicked by Steven sends me a few warning signals on the ascent, but never fails. A lot of people train hard and put in all of the miles, but they don't account for hills. You can spot those people, stopped and wasted, at the halfway point of the bridge. Just a short distance to the south is where all three rivers converge and the wind is swirling here. I keep my head on a swivel because I want to see it coming. I need to see it. How can there be true closure if you don't face the consequences head on?

When you reach the point where the bridge flattens out, you can turn your head to the left, look down the Allegheny and see a snapshot of the city, its history, its future. Modern sport boats and fiberglass kayaks take care to avoid rusty barges that haul coal up and down the river past exasperated brown and slate factories. Vehicular traffic runs along the shores of the river and the downtown streets. Trains rumble in all directions, on tracks that rest under skies that loan space to passing airliners. Old architecture blends with the new, and steel intertwines with brick. International technology corporations tower over plumbing supply stores.

Most days I would appreciate all of this. Most days. This morning, I scan the area for signs of distress. I see plenty of victims. No shortage of them here. On both sides of the bridge, I see lone individuals regurgitating breakfast. The climb got to them.

Several are wearing paper bibs for the half-marathon, some for the full distance. Those who are participating in the relay fly by, wondering what the big deal is. Of course, most of them have just begun their portion of the journey and don't understand what lies ahead of them over the next six to eight miles.

The wreckage is massive this year, and the sweat in my eyes makes it hard for me to sort through the sick and injured. The long ramp wipes out scores of competitors who move to the sides of the huge yellow bridge. Some will return to the course, some will hobble back to their cars. But I'm only looking for one person. Just one. I have to find him sometime over the next eighteen miles.

I have to find him, because he has to answer for what he has done.

I have to see his face when he comes to the realization that it was me.

I have to know that he knows—I beat him in the end.

———⁓⁓⁓———

There had been another assailant waiting for me at the house upon my return. When I came into the front hallway, Sigmund caught me off-guard and plunged head-first into my groin. I was shocked to find that my body could still bend over in pain. Before I had time to appreciate that small victory, my nemesis took advantage of my new position and landed a two-pawed blow to my head.

Man's best friend, my ass.

Kaitlyn waited patiently downstairs while I showered, dabbed my cuts and scrapes with hydrogen peroxide, and swallowed a couple of painkillers. When I ached my way to the living room, I gave my wife a replay of the assault, leaving out any mention of blood spurting and bone breaking. In the car, I had told her that Steven was the attacker, and the questions that came back at me were too much for me to handle. She saw that I needed to decompress and backed off to give me time. Sometimes being married to a psychologist is wonderful.

Kaitlyn had calmed down during the ride and she teetered between sympathy for me and rage against Steven, neither of which was useful. I was sorry that Steven was dead, but he *did* try to kill me. *That* action deserved an unmistakable reaction. Even if exposing his private life had set him off—and I had my doubts about that—trying to give me tenure at the Afterlife Community College was taking things too far. As for her rage against Steven . . . well, the guy was on a slab. There was nothing more that could be done to him.

When I told Kaitlyn what the detectives had shared with me about Steven's involvement with Lindsay's death, she wasn't surprised. She reminded me that the man was obviously *troubled*, evidenced by his attack on me, and I couldn't discount the possibility that I was wrong about them not having a relationship. Not wanting to debate the issue, and noticing that the pain pills were about as effective as breath mints, I let it go.

While Kaitlyn prepared for bed, I sent an email to my department head stating that I would be taking a sick day. I followed that up with an email to my colleague, Brent Lancaster, the former Secret Service agent, asking him to put up a note in each of my classrooms that the lecture was cancelled for the day, and no, my graduate assistant would not be available to take care of that. I guessed that after the news got out, he would never ask me about the Proximity Pummeling Theory again.

We went to bed a short while later, but I was too worked up to sleep. Around two, I slid out of bed, threw on a pair of sweat pants and headed downstairs. It's drilled into police officers, firefighters, and other first responders: after a traumatic incident, you don't want to use anything that will bring you down or pick you up. No caffeine, and absolutely, *positively* no alcohol. So I grabbed myself a tall scotch and went into a guest bedroom we had converted into my home office.

I tried. I really tried to accept it. I had been out of the game for a couple of years. But I had spent well over ten years of my life learning to read people. To anticipate their actions. To see the warning signs and intervene at the most opportune time. The fact that Steven attacked me wasn't what was occupying my thoughts. You can never truly know what a man is capable of when he feels cornered or betrayed. I don't know, maybe I wouldn't have believed it before he came after me, but I knew differently now.

It was when I had told him that he wasn't a killer and he moved his arm away from his face. I saw it as clear as anything I've seen in my life. I was dead wrong. He was a killer and he had killed. He had killed Lindsay, and I had been a witness to the precipitating event. When she walked into my office, it was a foregone conclusion. Her life was over.

So I drank my scotch, listened to Sigmund snore, tolerated the stinging sensation on my lips, and tried to accept a new reality. Steven was guilty and the DNA test would prove it. I had no doubt. Maybe he was dating Lindsay and he was the older boyfriend the roommate mentioned. Maybe she was going to report the relationship and that's why he killed her. And yes, maybe he was furious at me for obvious reasons and he figured, 'Hey, since I'm out killing people this week anyway, I'll just head over to TRU and whack Cyprus while I'm at it!'

No.

What was it he said when he was standing over me? *Sorry, Cyprus. Can't take the chance.* What chance? If word had gotten around that he was gay, then that genie was already out of the bottle. Killing me accomplished nothing. In fact, he would have been the obvious suspect.

The chance that I had figured out that he and Lindsay had a thing? Perhaps. She had said she would talk to me later before bolting from my office. So he was willing to commit two murders to avoid getting . . . what? A letter of reprimand?

Technically, graduate assistants were de facto faculty members and weren't supposed to have relationships with undergrads, but who were we kidding? It happened all the time, and nobody was going to try to enforce a rule that was put on the books simply so the university could be covered in a lawsuit. It was a joke and Steven had to have known that. In fact, he was arrogant enough to violate the policy and dare the administration to come after him!

Wrong. This was just wrong.

It was something else. Something else entirely. The police had their killer and I had tied things up neatly for them when I lowered his heart rate to zero. High profile case—closed. Backs patted, badges polished, a city saved from a killer. I knew how it worked. I had seen it before. Fade to black, roll the credits.

My scotch was empty and my multicolored shoulder felt better. I thought about what to do next and I knew what the right answer was. I knew what Kaitlyn would say. I would go back to work, be thankful that I'm not in a casket, and move on with my life. I would make amends with Randy, Aaron, and Jacob, and finish up the semester. Final exams and paper submissions were right around the corner. I had some good ideas for a research project that I could start over the summer and I would throw myself into my work. I really needed to get published more often. That's what professors love, right? So many things to do. So many ways to occupy my mind. As for my spare time, weightlifting was on hold, but my legs still functioned, so I could still train for, and run in, the upcoming marathon. Everything would work itself out.

I finished off my scotch and went back to bed. The last thing I remember before I drifted off into a deep sleep was thinking how remarkable it was that extreme circumstances could turn anyone into a driven killer.

Mile 10

The eastbound turn onto East Carson Street represents the commencement of the closest thing to a straight-away on the course. The Monongahela River dictates the contours of the road we are on. Old industry sits on this shoreline, refusing to give ground without a fight. Point State Park juts out into the water, marking the division of the three rivers, while ducks and geese surround its prominent fountain. The crowd is reappearing. As we approach Station Square, the shouts of inspiration and paperboard signs rematerialize. One reads, GO DANA! YOU CAN DO IT! Another screams, GO DADDY WE LOVE YOU! I have to smile when I see one imprinted with dry wit. It simply states, GO . . . YOU. Every little bit of motivation helps, I guess.

I'm still running strong. Fatigue hasn't set in yet and the legs aren't wobbly. It's this pace. It's slower than my usual pace. I have to come at him from behind—not obvious, but not looking like I'm watching for him.

Hide in plain sight.

Seek him out.

Confirm the kill.

He'll be somewhere between point A (the starting line) and point B (the finish).

He'll never see it coming if all goes according to plan.

～∞～

Having persuaded myself that this ugly chapter in my life was over and it was time to reinvest myself in my work, I woke up the next day feeling battered but more relaxed. I had slumbered until ten o'clock when Sigmund had finally had enough of my insolence and woke me up with a healthy dose of doggie breath in my face.

In the kitchen, I found a note from Kaitlyn informing me that she had gone into the office and would call me later to see how I was feeling. My stomach roared and reminded me that an assortment of protein bars had served as the previous evening's meal. I made myself an omelet, held back on the hot sauce out of respect for the cuts in my mouth, and annihilated it along with a bowl of cereal. Grabbing a large cup of coffee, I headed to the computer to check my work email.

I had two new messages. One was from Brent, who was characteristically courteous but to the point. He would take care of notifying my students that class was canceled; he had heard about the incident and hoped that I was unharmed. No questions, no undue sentiment. I appreciated his succinctness.

The second message wasn't as pleasing. Silo was informing me that, pending an internal investigation by the university, I was suspended. He cited the vaguest of reasons, *inappropriate conduct*, and explained that the department heads and the university's president would review the facts of the case in full. They would construct an official report that would be forwarded to the Criminology department. I would be contacted if a statement from me was desired.

No, 'Gee, I'm glad you're still upright' or 'Get well soon, we miss you.' The email also stated that the investigation should only take a few weeks and I would receive an official notice of the outcome. In the meantime, a substitute would be found to instruct my classes, and I would be provided with that individual's contact information in a subsequent email so I could get the lucky winner up to speed. I would continue to receive my salary during the inquiry.

I stared at the email and picked it apart. After the third reading, I slumped back in my chair and played the whole thing out in my mind. I would be fine. The inappropriate conduct he was referring to was the coming out party I hosted for Steven. I didn't know if he had officially filed a complaint, but I seriously doubted he would come back to life and press the issue. I would be cleared. This was just Silo playing petty games with me. I shouldn't have expected anything different. I had crushed a student's skull in a campus parking lot. I wasn't expecting to get an engraved invitation to speak at commencement.

So work was on hold for the time being.

For all intents and purposes, I was unemployed.

Not good. I get into trouble when I'm bored.

About an hour later, I received a call from the graduate assistant who was assigned to teach my classes while I was gone.

"Uh, Dr. Keller?"

"Yes."

"I'm Brian An . . . An . . . Andrews. I'm s-supposed to be covering for you—I mean—not covering, but . . . your classes. I'm taking over . . . not taking over, but helping you with your classes. Not that you need help. It's just . . ."

The poor kid was so nervous he could barely put a sentence together. It wasn't an awkward nervousness, it was much worse than that. Apparently killing a graduate assistant with my bare hands was having an adverse effect on my ability to communicate with people.

I interrupted his stammering with, "I suppose you need to know where to pick up in my classes, right?"

"Uh, yeah. That would be great. Mr. Killer. I mean Dr. Killer. I mean . . . Keller."

I'm pretty sure I heard him slap himself in the head, so I waited and gave the poor bastard a chance to catch his breath. I briefed him on where I was in my lectures, and told him he could find the materials I had graded in my office. He sounded unsure, but hung up quickly.

I busied myself for the next few days with every home improvement project imaginable. I fixed things. I broke things by trying to fix them. I decided the ceiling fans were a little too noisy. The toilets didn't flush quite right. Had the icemaker always vibrated like that?

I made daily trips to the Home Depot and filled my cart with hex nuts, degreasers, electric screwdrivers, work lights, and wire cutters. It wasn't until one morning when I found myself standing around the store with some severe-looking retirees at a birdhouse building class that I decided I had gone too far and hung up my tape measure.

Even Sigmund got sick of me. His naps were continuously interrupted by me doing *him* a favor by walking him a few times a day. Kaitlyn was now working mostly from her office and I suspected it was by choice. I went running every morning and tried to rehab my shoulder every evening.

Eventually, I ran out of things to do, and my legs could only handle so many miles. I tried reading a book about the Unabomber, but never even made it to his days as a professor at Cal-Berkeley, which was before he cracked up. Lindsay and Steven intruded on my thoughts again. The case was closed. The news told me so. The DNA tests on the scratches were conclusive. They found her hair in his car. Over and done with.

Sorry, Cyprus. Can't take the chance.

The emotional side of me struggled with the fact that Lindsay may have died because of her conversation with me. If true, not only did I serve as the audience to her demise, but I actually chastised her for coming to me. Could I live with not knowing for sure? That side of me said *no.* My logical side told me to build a birdhouse. I hate birdhouses.

From my computer, I accessed the school directory by entering my username and password. I looked up Lindsay's address. It was still listed. I wrote it down and flashed back to writing Steven's address on the old coupon. The morning after the attack, I had checked the pockets of the bloody coat and found the scrap of paper. I threw it away along with the tainted coat. I pulled up a mapping program on the computer and entered Lindsay's old address. I printed out the route that would hopefully guide me to some answers.

Frightening Sigmund into thinking it was time for another walk, I grabbed my keys and headed for the driveway. The day after the attack, Kaitlyn had called a friend to drive her to campus so she could retrieve my vehicle. I had offered to go with her to spare her friend the trip, but she thought returning to the scene and seeing the pools of dried blood would have a negative effect on my mental health. Sometimes being married to a psychologist sucks.

As if on cue, Bob Seger sang for me to "Turn the Page" as soon as I powered up the Jeep. The engine protested and I felt a pang of anxiety at the idea of needing a new car. With rush hour over a couple of hours before, the trip to the Oakland neighborhood took me less than twenty-five minutes. The directions on the passenger seat told me the apartment was in a complex off Forbes Avenue. I found a parking spot a block away in front of an art supply store and squeezed into it on the first try.

I really had no idea what I would say to Lindsay's roommate. I wasn't even sure if she would be home. If she was a student at one of the local universities, then there was a chance she would be in class. Even if she were home, if she knew that Lindsay died because she showed up at my office, she might slam the door in my face. Who could blame her?

The apartment building was the type where you need a code to get into the foyer or someone has to buzz you in. Wanting to avoid an awkward introduction over an intercom speaker, I waited for a resident to leave through the glass door. In my jeans and brown suede jacket, I looked more like a student than a professor. A tardy student carrying a computer programming text barely gave me a glance as he rushed out of the building. I slipped in through the closing door and found the nearest stairwell. Apartment 301 was at the end of a hallway that reeked of stale beer and staler pizza. A fluorescent bulb flickered over a doormat that framed an image of a marijuana leaf.

I knocked on the door and heard footsteps approaching.

A female voice asked, "Who is it?"

I started to speak and then realized that she couldn't see me through the peephole. I was unconsciously standing to the side of the door.

Moving into her line of sight, I announced myself. "My name is Cyprus Keller. I'm a professor at . . ."

A deadbolt turned and the door opened. The girl was no more than five-feet-two and weighed as much as a helium feather. She had dark purple hair that was twisted into pigtails. One side of her nose was decorated with a gold stud and a small parrot tattoo protruded from under her shirt collar. She wasn't the type that anyone would call pretty, but she probably had detonated on many occasions when unthinking young men called her *cute*.

"Why are you here?" Not hostile. Real curiosity.

I kept my tone soft and respectful as I said, "I was hoping to speak to you about Lindsay. Would you mind?"

She turned and walked to a small living room area where three mismatched sofas and a tan beanbag chair surrounded an old chest that doubled as a coffee table. Despite the lack of coordination in the furnishings, the apartment was immaculate. Magazines on current affairs were neatly stacked on the chest, books were alphabetized by author on a bookshelf in the corner, and old newspapers were neatly kept in a wicker basket beside a narrow stand displaying photos of the roommates in different settings. Even the half-used joint perched in the ashtray on the fireplace mantle was perfectly centered.

Not sure my introduction had been heard, I repeated, "Like I was saying, I'm Cyprus. I knew Lindsay from class."

"I'm V."

I looked at her, hoping for an explanation.

"It's really Virginia, but I just go by V."

"Virginia's not so bad."

"My last name is Richmond."

Her voice didn't match her appearance. This girl wasn't tough. She was just trying to find an identity.

"Virginia Richmond?" I smiled. "Parents can try to be too clever sometimes."

She smiled and between perfect white teeth, said, "I agree."

"V it is, then. Are you a student?"

"Yeah. Poli Sci at Pitt."

The interest in political science explained the magazines and newspapers. Young people usually go for more mindless periodicals.

"I'm very sorry about Lindsay," I said. "Would you mind if I asked you a few questions about her?"

"Why?"

"Because I'm trying to make sense of what happened to her."

She shrugged her consent.

"Were the two of you close?"

"We lived together for the last two years. We were opposites, but we were the best of friends. People always thought she was kind of a ditz, but she was deeper than that." Tears welled up in her eyes. "She was kind of a Barbie doll, but she knew it. She even made fun of herself for it. But she was smarter than people gave her credit for."

She used her shirt collar to wipe her eyes.

"It's unreal. I'm calling her the Barbie doll when I'm the one who was out shopping for clothes all evening while she's getting killed."

"I'm sorry. I didn't know her well, but she seemed nice." I didn't mention the flirting and seductive behavior. "The man who killed her," I saw tears starting to fall into her lap. "Steven Thacker. Do you know how long she was seeing him?"

Her pigtails swung back and forth, "I didn't even know his name. Actually, I thought it was somebody else. I guess I still don't completely believe it."

"What do you mean?"

"I had the impression that it was somebody much older who was taking advantage of her. I tried to tell her it was trouble. When I saw the picture of the man they say did it in the paper, I thought there was some mistake. That guy didn't look old. And he was a grad student, right?"

"Why did you think it was somebody older?"

"Just the stuff she said. It sounded like he had a house and money. She said he talked about them traveling around Europe after she graduated." She shook her head and got angry with herself. "I shouldn't have assumed. He was probably lying to her. He didn't have any money, he was just stringing her along."

She looked at me sheepishly.

"The paper said that you killed him."

"Yes."

"So you think he did it then?"

"Yes."

I tried to keep her relatively calm while not talking down to her. "I need you to think back for me, okay? Was there anything else that she said about the guy she was dating?"

"Like what?"

"Maybe about other people he was seeing? Or people he saw in the past?"

She was lost. I had to be careful with this.

I tried again. "Do you know if this type of relationship was new to him? Or—maybe if there was anything different about their relationship? Anything unusual? Something she was uncomfortable with."

Still lost.

Last try. I made an effort with, "Did she ever mention if her boyfriend was into seeing other women? Or even men? Maybe experimenting a little?"

V fired back, "What are you talking about? Lindsay wasn't into anything like that. Whenever she started dating a guy she demanded total monogamy. Total!" Her tears were still there, but they covered eyes that were becoming determined. "If she thought there was anything going on behind her back, she would have ended it right then and there."

"I'm sorry. I didn't mean to upset you. I'm just trying to get a handle on this."

She sighed and came back down. "It's okay. I just got used to defending her. People thought she was shallow because she was so popular. They didn't know her the way I did. Believe it or not, I used to tease her about being so old-fashioned."

"Do you know how long she had been seeing this guy?"

"This Steven guy?"

I didn't answer.

She thought back and said, "Only for a few months, but she was crazy about him. I could see how excited she was when she would go off to see him."

"Where did they go?"

"I don't know. She didn't give me details after I started giving her a hard time about seeing him. I knew I shouldn't have been so suspicious," she looked down at the carpet as she added, "but I guess I was right to be."

I leaned forward and made eye contact.

"I'll leave you alone now, but I do need to know one more thing."

"Okay."

"What is it you aren't telling me? What is it that you didn't tell the cops?"

Eyes dart side to side, ever so slight. Arms contract and start to cross. Just three inches.

A tremor from her throat told me something when she said, "Nothing."

Leaning forward a little closer, I asked, "That's not exactly true, is it?"

Her right hand started pulling imaginary fuzz off the sleeve of her sweater. She didn't even pretend to make eye contact anymore.

"That's all I know." She wiped her eyes and started to stand up.

I put a hand up and she stayed seated.

"You knew who he was. You knew who she was seeing, and I don't think it was Steven Thacker."

Silence. Two seconds. Three.

"I told you, I don't . . ."

"You did know! You knew and you didn't tell the cops. Why?"

"I didn't know anything!"

"You did. And you do!"

"You should leave."

"You were her best friend! She's dead and you really don't give a damn!"

"I do!"

"If you did, you wouldn't be lying to me now!"

The eyes came back to me.

"What's wrong with you? Why are you doing this? Why don't you believe me?"

"Because you know I work at Three Rivers. Because you know she came to see me on the day she died. Because you just admitted that you thought the guy Lindsay was seeing was older than Steven. Because all of that should give you every reason to suspect that I might have been the boyfriend! Because you had every reason to tell the cops that I might be the guy and you didn't. Because you let me in here even though you *should* think it's possible that I'm the older man who was taking advantage of your best friend. Because you *know* it wasn't me who was seeing her, because you *know* who it was!"

Her panicked response was, "No, I swear! I didn't know. I never knew his name!"

"You had to, because you knew it wasn't me! You know who it was. You didn't tell the police and now you're protecting someone. Why else would you let me in here?"

"Stop it!"

"Tell me."

"People will think she deserved it."

"How did you know it wasn't me?"

She cried out, "Because she said you were one of the good ones!"

Mile 11

The half-marathoners split off near Station Square and the rest of us continue down East Carson Street. The road slowly pulls back from the water and enters the city's South Side. Once again the streets that were lined with spectators are replaced by people coming into work and making deliveries. The neighborhood is lined with bars and tattoo parlors that were packed to their rooftops just a few hours before.

I check my pace and try to determine if I'm on target. The digital readout on my wrist tells me that I'm on pace. The running watch is the last important part of a runner's equipment checklist. I wear one I got for free with a subscription to a running magazine. All it does is act as a stopwatch. I don't even know how to set the time on it. It doesn't have any fancy features, but its huge numbers are easy to read when buckets of sweat pour into my eyes. At one time or another, I was subjected to hearing about each of my running partners' watches. Aaron and his black watch containing a heart rate monitor. Randy and some dark blue gizmo that records the times of your last 100 runs. And Jacob with some grotesque, lime green microcomputer that has GPS capability, measures changes in elevation, and can shoot laser beams. Well, maybe not laser beams.

According to my orange hunk of plastic, I can stand to drop back a little. I can afford to fall a little behind, but I can't risk getting too close. Not if this is to go down the right way. I chew another piece of a decimated Pop-Tart and slow down through a water station. Lots of people slow down to drink their water. Nothing unusual here. After I'm sure a few seconds have piled onto my pace, I toss the cup aside and resume the pursuit. I'm not even nervous about this anymore. I'm excited. I'm excited, and that makes me nervous.

She regretted it as soon as she said it. The words hung out there and taunted her.

I waited a few ticks and returned to a normal tone, "What do you mean . . . *one of the good ones?*"

She asked me if she could get a glass of water. She actually *asked* me. I can sound pretty authoritarian when I want to.

When she returned to her sofa with a plastic Steelers cup (of course), she looked ready to come clean.

She sniffed, "I just didn't tell you because that's the way she would have wanted it."

I waited.

Let her fill the void.

"I told her it was risky, but she felt it was going to do some good—both for her career, and in general."

I didn't move.

"I honestly don't know who she was seeing. Maybe it was this Steven guy. But you're right, I know it wasn't you."

I provided just a little push with, "Tell me about the whole thing. How was she working it?" I had no earthly idea what I was talking about, but that's never stopped me before.

"She just made the approaches and recorded the information. If a professor bit, she documented it, but that was all. She never, ever followed through with it."

Let her fill the void.

"After she came on to a professor, and he made it clear that he was willing to either go on a date with her or sleep with her, she would tell him she couldn't go through with it and call it off."

So Lindsay was baiting professors. Damn. I hated it when Kaitlyn was right.

"Why?" I asked as I leaned back again, giving her words some room. Another *why*.

"It's a whole group of them. Four or five girls. Different schools. All over the country. She said it was going to be huge. They were going to create a website, put it all on there, get some attention and expose a bunch of college professors in the process. She called it her *independent study* course because she knew she couldn't do it for real—I mean, actually use it for a class. She saw some journalism students get a bunch of attention for the RISE thing and she thought this would be even better. She wanted to be a reporter more than anything and saw this as a way to get her name out there."

I remembered reading about the RISE controversy. A bunch of journalism students in Chicago had gone undercover and volunteered to work for the community organization and uncovered a system of bribery and tax evasion. For a few weeks after the story broke, the students were interviewed on all of the networks and made their rounds on the cable news shows. I also remember how the students recorded their investigation.

"Was Lindsay recording conversations with professors?"

V nodded and took a hard swallow of water.

"And you say that other girls were doing this?"

"Yeah. They met on some blog for journalism students. They were all at different universities, but basically doing the same thing."

I thought about the seriousness of what I had just learned.

"You said that I was one of the good ones. Does that mean she found some *bad* ones?"

Again, a nod.

She followed with, "A bunch. She was trying to get professors from different departments. But she said that you wouldn't budge. She told me that she was giving you the full-court press and all you did was get uncomfortable. I think she really respected you."

"Did you know why she came to my office on the day she was killed?"

The tears were drying up now. Her breathing was less shallow.

"She said she was finishing up the story and wanted a recording of a professor actually stating what the student-faculty relationship policy was. She wanted you to say it, because you were one of the few who turned her away. It was her idea of being fair and demonstrating that not all professors were jerks. The whole thing was supposed to be about exposing hypocrisy in higher education, or some crap like that. She couldn't ask any of the profs who actually took her up on her . . . her suggestions. They would have gotten suspicious and thought she was up to something. She just wanted some audio from you so she could show that faculty members did know that relationships with students were off-limits."

She recorded the whole thing.

I asked, "Why didn't you just tell the police all this? It could have been important."

"You really didn't know her well, did you?"

"No."

"Well, her dad is a big time Methodist minister around her hometown. Her mom runs a school for kids with special needs. Do you think I want them to know that Lindsay was throwing herself at male professors at the school? If she broke her so-called story and made it big, then so be it. She could tell her parents that it was for the greater good and declare her moral superiority. At least when they found out what she had been doing, it would be on her own terms. But not like this. Not a headline in the *Post-Gazette* that paints her as some temptress who may have deserved what she got. No way."

She was right. That's exactly how the press would have portrayed it. The headline would be too juicy to pass up: SEDUCING STUDENT FALLS VICTIM TO OWN GAME.

"And the older boyfriend? Was that part of her plan?"

V stood up and walked over to the stand that held photos of the girls and their families.

She answered, "No. That was something different. She tried to work her magic on him, but somehow he read into it. Lindsay told me that he completely turned the tables on her and she felt guilty for trying to reel him in. She ended up telling him what she was doing and he actually supported her. He told her that the university system needed a good purging and that she was doing society a favor. It wasn't long until they were involved. Can you believe that bullshit? I told her that she was being played, but she wouldn't listen. And since I was so adamant about her breaking it off with him, she never did tell me who it was."

She sat down on the beanbag chair and it molded itself around her tiny body. The tear factory started churning out products again.

"I should have tried harder. I told her that the project was going to get her in trouble. I told her that the guy was playing her. And then this psycho goes and kills her. He knew what she was up to, so why would he get mad at her? Why would this Steven guy promise to give her a future filled with romantic nights on the water and foreign vacations, and then kill her?"

I was standing by a window and looking out onto a quad filled with students.

"I don't think he did."

The speck in the middle of the bag stared at me in wonder. I realized I better quickly clarify what I said.

"He killed her. I don't doubt that. But he wasn't dating her."

"He wasn't?" was all she managed to squeak out.

"No. She must have been seeing another man. Like you said, an older man. Steven was a lot of things, but he was certainly not a charmer. I don't see how he could have turned her around like that and ended up in a relationship with her. He didn't have the charisma. And besides," I sorted through some appropriate words and chose some, "I don't think she was his . . . type."

The beanbag rustled. V asked, "Then why did he kill her?"

"I don't know."

I lost several seconds as I watched a young man set up an easel on the grass outside and begin painting something. He had probably just come from the art supply store where I parked my car earlier.

"Where are her notes and recordings, V?"

She didn't answer.

"I need to know. There might be something there that explains why she died."

The only sound was the fading chatter of students exiting another apartment. She wasn't denying that she knew where they were. There would have been an instantaneous denial if that were the case.

"Are you going to trash them?"

"I need to review her notes and listen to the recordings. I just want to know why this happened. Two people are dead and I'm not real comfortable with that. Are you?"

"After you see the stuff, then are you going to trash it?"

"Do you want me to?"

She looked over at the photos again. Then back to me.

"I don't know. I didn't agree with what she was doing, but it was important to her. I just don't know."

I thought about how damaging the information could be. Lives could be ruined. Marriages torn apart. If Lindsay was targeting full-time professors, not grad students, then careers could be ended. The scandal could destroy reputations regardless of whether sex was involved. Part of me felt sorry for the men who fell into her trap. On the other hand, those guys made their own beds and they wanted to hop into those beds with a girl who was probably young enough to be their daughter. I made a decision.

"How about this? I'll go over the information and then give it back to you in a few days. Then you can decide what to do with it. If you want, you can explain things to Lindsay's parents, and then send the info to the other girls working on the project. Or, if you prefer, you can burn everything. Your call."

She immediately liked this idea. The beanbag spit her out and she walked over to the mantle where the ashtray was. There were candles on either end of the mantle and next to the candle on the left was a small figure, standing in a pose. V pulled it down and tossed it to me. I examined the tiny replica of a recent U.S. President. V noticed my confusion and rolled her eyes at me. Walking over to me and taking it from my palm, she pulled the figure apart. It was a USB flash drive. Lindsay had saved all of the information in the storage device and all that was needed to access it was a computer. V handed it back to me.

She told me, "The police came here and searched the place after they found Lindsay's body. I guess they thought this was just a decoration."

"It's easy to miss," I remarked. Then, rejoining the halves of the politician back together, I faced the implement in V's direction and looked at her questioningly.

Explaining the odd coupling of the device with the likeness, V said, "Lindsay said it was appropriate. Both were divisive and full of all kinds of crap."

We both smiled and I put Mr. President into my coat pocket.

"You said the guy she was seeing knew about the project, even encouraged it. Did he know about the recordings?"

"No. She told me that I was the only one who knew. She said if word got out that she was wired, her work would never get out there." She gestured toward a wall that represented *out there*. We must have read the same geography textbook.

"In this state, you can't record people without their consent," V continued. "She was afraid she would get charged and everything on the flash drive would be taken as evidence."

Another question crept into my mind.

I asked her if she had looked at the information on the flash drive. She told me she hadn't. She had never wanted anything to do with Lindsay's plan.

Returning to what V had said earlier, I asked, "What did you mean earlier when you said that Steven, or whoever the boyfriend was, promised her romantic nights on the water?"

She rewound the conversation in her mind and remembered. "Lindsay said that when it got warmer out, they were going to go out on his boat. She said he had just bought a new one."

How nice.

I knew a business professor who had done the same exact thing.

Mile 12

The nightclubs become intermingled with more upscale retail stores further down East Carson Street. The runners are completely spread out now. No more accidental bumping of elbows followed by breathless apologies. This makes it easier to navigate the streets, but harder to blend in. If I get too close, he'll see me coming. He may not have any suspicions as to my intent, but I can't take that chance. I need to stay out of sight, tucked away behind him, until the very moment of his death. I knew my vision would be limited here by the morning sun, so I pull down the sunglasses I've had propped up on the top of my head. They have small vents at the tops of the lenses to prevent them from fogging up. I have to see clearly.

A man in an old white T-shirt and black pants hoses down a sidewalk in front of a jazz club. He waves at a pair of runners in front of me, a couple wearing shirts that read, FOR LINDA on the back. A tribute to a lost friend or family member. They don't look like brother and sister. More likely a married couple who are running in remembrance of a mother, or sister. We do things that remind us of our own mortality in order to remember the dead.

The hard left onto the Birmingham Bridge is when I feel the first signs of fatigue. Even at this slower pace, eleven miles is more than just a leisurely stroll. My legs feel solid, but of all things, my shoulder is starting to hurt. Despite it being a long way from my feet, the repeated pounding on the pavement still vibrates through my bruised bones. It's like Chinese water torture. Each step is a drip on my shoulder. After 20,000 steps or so, the drips become hard jabs. By the end of the race it will feel like Steven is still behind me, whaling away with that tire iron.

—◦◦◦—

Kaitlyn returned from a morning meeting with a patient and was working in her den. She and Sigmund heard me come in and they both came out of her hideaway. She was still in business attire and cradling a half-filled mug of tea with both hands. Noticing that my hands weren't holding any bags filled with carpet tape and drill bits, she asked me where I had been. I weighed the value of telling her about what I'd been doing and what I had learned against keeping her in the dark. Usually, I shared everything with her, but I really wasn't sure what I had yet. She was still shaken up about the attack; and while the cuts and bruises on my face were healing, they were still visible reminders of how close I had come to buying the farm. If I told her I was out there interviewing Lindsay's roommate and uncovering information that might be related to the murder, her fury would be something to behold. Our full disclosure rule would be put on hold. Later on she would surely understand that my secrecy was for her benefit. Right?

Not that I'm scared of her. I'm the man of the house. I just didn't see any need to concern her. I can do whatever I want. Really. I can get her permission anytime I want.

"I needed to go for a drive. Cabin fever," I lied.

"Oh, I've been meaning to ask you. Have you noticed any problems with the Wrangler?" she asked.

"Other than the engine convulsing, the bad windshield wiper, the rusted bumper, the possible oil leak, and the ripped seat cushion in the back? Nope, not a thing."

She ignored my sarcasm.

"When I drove it back from the university, it felt like it was shaking when it got over eighty. You never noticed that?"

She was completely serious. I had pleaded with her for years about her lead foot.

"I hadn't noticed. Of course, I don't try to drive it fast enough to go back in time."

She grinned, rolled her eyes, and headed toward the kitchen to warm up her tea.

Turning her head back over her shoulder, she suggested, "Well, you should get it checked out. The alignment may be off."

I didn't respond. I knew the car was on its last legs. I was just hoping it would make it through the summer, but that was looking less and less likely.

I raised my voice so she could hear me in the kitchen and said, "I'm going to be working at my computer for a while. I've got some ideas for research studies I need to sort through."

"Alright. Have fun."

My home office was really nothing more than a desk, a computer, and a couple of crammed bookshelves. Sigmund decided that the sunbeam coming through my window was more inviting than Kaitlyn's windowless lair, so he curled up in it and started snoring immediately. I closed the door and pulled the flash drive from my pocket. Pushing the mouse on my desk, I woke the computer up and pulled Mr. President apart. Plugging his feet into a USB port, I clicked on a couple of icons to see what I had.

The files were separated into two main folders—audio files and text files. I clicked on the folder with the audio files. Subfolders appeared on the monitor, each of them labeled with different names. Rippoli, Parisi, Pasquinelli, Bandi, Wolfe, Jaworski, Caferty, Kelly, Kasko, Wainwright, Norris, Walker, Robbins, Baird, Harper, Smith, Maynard, Chrusciel, Hamluck, Cassidy, DeJohn, Esposito . . . Keller. I knew all the names. All were my colleagues, and most had families. Individual conversations were organized by dates. How many had she been successful with?

I began opening the audio files, one by one. I started with mine. Four short conversations filled with increasing amounts of amorous advances and awkward deflections. The audio recordings didn't do justice to her attempts. The gentle touching on the arm and revealing displays of her upper body couldn't be captured this way. The final recording of me was her visit to my office. My statement abhorring such conduct sounded strong and convincing. Again, I shriveled up inside when I thought about the chain of events set into motion because of that visit.

The quality of the recordings was good. She must have worn a digital recorder with a microphone tucked under her shirt. Obviously, not the top portion of her shirt. These days, recorders were so small they could be nearly invisible. I sifted through the conversations. Some were short—offended educators who wanted nothing to do with her.

Most were longer—interested men, feeling out the situation. Prodding. Testing the waters. Those men were recorded on several occasions, each one becoming more daring. Eventually, most caved in and were willing to meet for private study sessions at their homes, or some motel. A couple of them were more blatant and described in fantastic detail what they wanted to do to her. It was disturbing. Discouraging.

I saved the files of the people I knew best for last. Only a couple of weeks had passed since I had looked on as Aaron Caferty was teased about how he would incur his wife's wrath for buying a bigger bass boat. As I waited for the audio to start playing, I thought about what V had said. *Romantic nights on the water.* A bass boat wasn't exactly a luxury yacht, but I could see Aaron trying to depict it as such. I tensed up as the audio started to play.

The first two conversations sounded as if Lindsay had approached Aaron after class. It was almost identical to the way she approached me. Small flirtations. Subtle innuendos. Nothing tangible. When Lindsay became more direct, Aaron didn't shy away. When she complimented him, he flattered her. He was loving it. Back in the locker room, when I told Aaron, Jacob, and Randy about Lindsay's murder, Aaron had said that he *thought* she was in one of his classes *last* semester. I checked the date of the recording. It was this semester. He knew exactly who she was and he hadn't even batted an eyelid when I mentioned her name.

The rest of the recordings with Aaron's voice made me sick. These conversations also sounded like they took place after class. He was doing his best Donald Trump imitation, talking big, referring to his waterfront property on Lake Erie and his extensive travels. Yes, he was married, he told her, but they had an *open* relationship.

I happened to know that Aaron owned a cheap condo in Erie, his extensive travels consisted of one weekend in Bermuda, and I had met Debbie—who I was quite certain hadn't been fully briefed on their open-marriage arrangement. Lindsay sounded as if she was dazzled by the business guru. She began to suggest that they meet off campus somewhere, when another voice became audible. Then more voices. I was able to guess that students were filing in for the next class that was to be held in that room. There was an awkward goodbye between the two main speakers on the recording and then nothing.

I clicked on a date that was about a week after the last as my mind was cycling through this new information. Was there really any connection between this and Lindsay's death? How did Steven fit in? How hard should I punch Aaron when I saw him?

My daydream of pounding Aaron into the ground was interrupted by the start of the next recording. It was Aaron speaking. He was proposing that he and Lindsay go away for the weekend. His house in Erie was being renovated, so they could just slip off to a hotel in Harrisburg. What a class act. The next part made my head ache with frustration. Lindsay turned him down. She told him she had thought about the two of them together, but she just couldn't go through with it. He was a married professor and had too much to lose. She thought it was best if they kept things platonic and went their separate ways at the end of the semester.

Aaron pleaded at first. He sounded so pathetic that I momentarily forgot that I wanted to pulverize him for being such a scumbag. When Lindsay refused to change her mind, his change in demeanor bled through the computer's speakers.

His voice boomed when he asked, "What is this, some kind of game to you? Do you like playing with my head?"

Lindsay started to speak but was cut off.

"You're trying to make a fool out of me!"

I heard a thumping noise that I assumed was Aaron pounding a desk or podium as he spoke.

"I'm not some college boy who will be made a fool of! What am I, some sort of bet with your slut friends? Some sort of running joke? Is that what's going on here?"

He sounded extremely—*troubled*.

"Are you laughing at me? Are all of your friends laughing at me? You and the rest of your slut friends can go straight to hell!"

The next set of sounds was a girl who realized that she had taken things too far. Some wires had accidentally gotten crossed and a devastating malfunction had occurred. She sounded scared. Like a child who wanted nothing more than to get away from the source of ugliness that stood before her.

Her words were unsure and rapid. She tried apologizing. She tried telling him she really did like him, but their being together just wasn't right. She wasn't laughing at him. Nobody was laughing at him. This was all a mistake and she never meant to cause trouble. She had to go now. Another class. Friends were waiting. Things to do. Someplace she needed to be. Somewhere else. Anywhere else.

The fast-paced clicking of heels remained at a constant volume, as a voice in the background faded away. The last words that could be deciphered from the distant voice were, *"You bitch! You're all bitches!"*

The recording stopped and I double-checked to make sure that it was the last one in that folder. No other dates. I didn't know if that was the last conversation Aaron and Lindsay had, but it was the last I had access to.

Aaron wasn't the boyfriend. That wasn't charisma. That was volcanic rage that had been pent up for a long, long while. Lindsay had triggered something in Aaron and she never saw what was coming. He had a boat—but she would never have set foot on it with him after this episode.

I stood up, and paced back and forth across the small room. Sigmund woke up, noticed the sunbeam had relocated without his permission, and readjusted his sleeping position accordingly. Steven killed Lindsay. I knew it. Without a doubt.

Maybe Aaron's tantrum was unrelated to Lindsay's murder. As far as I knew, Aaron didn't even know Steven. I didn't know why Steven had strangled Lindsay, but I knew why he *didn't* do it. I felt that the reason had to be here in these files.

Yes, some murders happen for no reason. A stray bullet enters a bedroom window and a wife becomes a widow. A nutcase enters an elementary school and starts shooting. It happens. Sad, but true. But this was no stray bullet. This was a man putting his hands around a woman's windpipe and squeezing until the life disappeared from her eyes. She had fought back. She tried to hang on to her life with her fingernails, but it slipped away. Steven must have looked into her eyes and watched the light go out. That takes a certain level of conviction. Not random. Not pointless.

Having re-convinced myself that I was headed in the right direction, I found the next name that was most familiar to me. I opened the folder for Randy Walker expecting to find incriminating recordings. Randy was a three-time divorcee who didn't have much respect for men, much less women. I once heard him refer to female police officers as glorified meter maids. Hearing his voice suggest a rendezvous with Lindsay would come as no surprise.

Boy, was I disappointed. There was one recorded conversation in the file. It was from the previous semester and it lasted less than two minutes. It was Lindsay making her initial approach, full of flirtatious energy and false adulation being directed at Randy. The stone wall she hit was immense. He would have none of it. He was arrogant, condescending, and sexist. He was as repulsive to her as he was to anybody else.

"What the hell are you doing? You're a child. Go find yourself a boy your own age and focus on making him happy and raising some kids!"

I had to give the guy credit—at least he was a consistent jerk. I could hear Lindsay go in full retreat.

The last thing I heard before the recording ended was her mumbling to herself, "Asshole."

Randy's repellent personality had finally paid off for him. He wouldn't hop into bed with a twenty-two-year-old. I made myself pledge to only loath the guy for the thousand other legitimate reasons. Nobody can say I'm not fair.

The last folder I opened was titled "Jacob Kasko." Jacob had said that he didn't know Lindsay. In fact, he said that he knew all of his students and he rarely forgot them. I looked at the date of the recording. December. The end of the previous semester. Maybe Jacob's memory wasn't as keen as he thought. Maybe it was.

I tried to imagine Lindsay approaching the eternally proper, prominent professor and trying to convince him to have a fling with her. She had guts—I had to give her that. He made me self-conscious about my tattoo and she was going to try to seduce him.

The first few short conversations mirrored the others. Some brief encounters after class, some compliments, a few subtle hints. Jacob was polite and dismissive, without offending. Lindsay turned on the heat. She pressed him to talk about his background and his experiences. What did he like most about being a professor? Where did he get his doctorate? What did he do on his days off? Maybe they could spend some time together outside of class and he could help her decide on what graduate school to attend?

I wondered if she knew that he had lost his wife recently. If she did, would she still have pushed so hard?

That's when Jacob said it. I stopped breathing when the words came through my speakers. I followed the image of sound waves bouncing across my monitor with every syllable.

He calmly entreated, "Lindsay, why don't you tell me what it is you're working on?"

Then, silence. I thought the recording had stopped, but it hadn't.

The male voice I knew well continued, "I'm not mad at you. I simply want to know from an academic standpoint. What's the endgame here?"

The girl's voice changed from tigress to kitten in a flash. She didn't even try to lie.

"It's a project, of sorts. You would call it a study in human behavior."

"Interesting. Tell me about it. You have complete confidentiality with me. Social scientists have to depend on confidentiality."

And she told him. She told him about everything except for the names of the men she had approached and the existence of the recordings. He didn't interrupt, and he asked follow-up questions about how she planned on presenting her findings. He told her that the venture had real potential, but that she shouldn't limit her work to the field of journalism. If she developed it as a true research project, and presented it as an academic pursuit, as well as a journalistic piece, she would be taken more seriously. She wouldn't be regarded simply as an aspiring young reporter who was starved for attention. She wanted to be more, right? Not just a flash in the pan.

He was smooth. Inviting, but professional. He sounded earnest and interested. I could see where this was going and I didn't like it.

He made a few suggestions about the way she could organize the data by categorizing her subjects by age, race, field of study, years in academia, and marital status. The possibilities were endless.

"You're an exceptionally bright girl," he told her. "You seem to have lots of potential. Good luck with your project. With a little refining, it may work out well for you."

It sounded like he was packing up a briefcase.

For a brief second I was hopeful. Then the second passed.

"Wait," the female voice was strong again. "Can you please help me? I mean just with the organizing and writing part. I really do want to be taken seriously."

There was a pause, and I could hear the softest of breaths being picked up by the microphone. The lines on the monitor were low ripples.

Then a nonchalant male voice said, "I suppose we could discuss this further."

I could practically see the heartwarming look on his face when he said, "I'm always available for a worthwhile project."

I didn't want to believe it, but I knew it was true. Jacob had told me before we set off running down the river trail, but I wasn't listening.

For most of the city, it's just some blonde girl who had her future snuffed out like the flame on a candle.

How did he know she was a blonde?

Jacob had said he didn't know who Lindsay was. Every television station and newspaper had shown her photo while telling the story. A photo of a young freshman who had dark hair interrupted by a red streak. I had seen Jacob Friday afternoon. He had been in Morgantown on Monday morning. It wasn't likely that he had a conversation with someone over the weekend who just *happened* to mention her hair color.

How did he know she was a blonde? I hadn't even asked myself that question at the time.

I'm kind of an idiot sometimes.

Mile 13

The unmemorable mile after coming off of the Birmingham Bridge creates a brief psychological strain. The vacant lots and graffiti-covered walls are a reminder that progress can be slow. Recovery takes time. Bent and rust-covered rebar sticks out of chipped concrete where a commercial building once stood. Windows on the front of a forgotten warehouse have served as objects of dissatisfaction for rock-throwing youths.

The road has been sewn together with tangled strings of tar. The pavement at the corner of Forbes and Craft resembles a Rorschach test. I try to occupy my mind by assigning a perception to the blackened shapes, but all I can come up with is an octopus. No crowds line the streets. The distance between me and the next runner is thirty feet. The married couple running "for Linda" have fallen back and vanished. It's weirdly quiet.

A medical center approaches on my right. The massive University of Pittsburgh Medical Center system has sprawled into this wasteland. I'm sure the property was cheap, and the main campus is just up the street. A few UPMC employees stand outside the newer buildings and smoke cigarettes. Why is it that nurses and firefighters smoke so much? If ever there were two professions you would think would avoid the flaming cancer sticks, those should be them.

The only good thing about this stretch is I can see ahead for nearly two miles.

This is the third place it could happen. This would be the worst place. It could all be for nothing if it went down here—and I wouldn't get a second chance. Not here.

Later.

For some reason, this area has an odd Lord of the Rings feel to it. The road turns from destruction to renewal and expansion. All the time we are moving closer to a huge tower that appears to be the end of the world. It's called the Cathedral of Learning. Seriously. Maybe it's more of a Brave New World feel. Are we chasing the ideal? Are we running toward a mythical concept that will never really get any closer?

I need some water, I'm not thinking clearly.

I need calories.

I chew some sugar and grab a paper cup from the water station. Looking ahead, I see nothing important. No sign of him anywhere. I better pick up my speed, just in case. I can't miss him. What if he's having one of those days when he's faster than normal? I can't miss him.

Not now.
Not after all he's done.

—⟨⟩—

I closed the folder that contained the audio files. I knew what I needed to know. Jacob was seeing her. I heard it in his voice. It was the same polished way of talking that Kaitlyn used when the psychologist in her came out. The difference was, when I heard it, I knew what was happening. Lindsay didn't.

He had spoken with a certain rhythm and level of compassion that could charm a cobra. For a man of his experience, a young girl was an easy mark. Part of me wanted to give him the benefit of the doubt and allow his wife's death to serve as an excuse. Part of me wanted to sympathize with him and I tried to imagine him supplying me with a reasonable rationale why he would have gotten involved with Lindsay. But the way he turned the conversation around—the way he played on her ambition, her desire to be somebody . . . something more. Any hopes I had for feeling exhilaration on learning the truth were gone. I wished I didn't know.

Staring at my screen, I allowed my eyes to focus on the other large icon that had originally popped up. It was a set of text files organized the same way as the audio files, by names and dates. I clicked on the image and several subfolders spread across the screen. There weren't as many of these files as there were audio files. I assumed that these were simply her written notes and they would summarize the recorded conversations. I was wrong.

When I opened the file labeled "Craig Bandi"—a colleague from the English department—what I found was much more than typed out notes. A lengthy list of document names filled the screen. I knew from the recordings he was one of those who had succumbed to Lindsay. There were different file types: PDF, Word documents, Excel spreadsheets. I started reading each file.

Lindsay had done a lot more than record unsuspecting professors. She had been data-mining information from the internet. She had paid online services to research the details of Bandi's life. For less than fifty bucks per request she had obtained information about his real estate purchases, property taxes, family members, utility bills, political affiliation, involvement in lawsuits, business ties of family members, phone numbers, records of his marriage and subsequent divorce along with terms of the settlement, and a plethora of other details. Since TRU received some funds from the state, she had even found his salary information for the past several years.

The last document in Bandi's file was a Word document where Lindsay had summarized her findings. He had been a professor at TRU for the past five years. He had been cleaned out in a messy divorce seven years before when he lived in Michigan. According to court documents, his wife filed for the divorce and cited repeated instances of physical abuse. He had no criminal record. Just prior to beginning his employment at TRU, Bandi rented a modest apartment in Robinson Township. His spending seemed to be in line with his diminished income. Lindsay's summary was well written and detailed. She would have been a good investigative reporter.

Even before getting any guidance from Jacob, Lindsay had been doing much more than posturing to get on television. She was really digging into peoples' pasts. She was looking for damaging information—apart from what she was able to elicit through her approaches—and hadn't limited herself to those men she had tried to lure. There were other names here. Names of male and female faculty members. My name.

My file consisted of the same type of information as Bandi's. There was information on my finances, marriage, etc. There was a small press clipping that detailed an arrest I had made in Baltimore and the citation I received from the department. That was it. The most damaging information about me was a speeding ticket I received in Kentucky.

I spent the next two hours reading every page Lindsay had accumulated. I assumed that there were fewer of these files than the sound recordings because she hadn't received all the results yet from the data-mining services she was using. Again, I looked closely at those I knew best.

Dr. Jacob Kasko's file contained a huge amount of data, as you would expect for anybody with a lengthy career in academia. In addition to the basic items, there were some press clippings about academic awards received, grant money obtained, and journals and books authored. The relatives section still listed Jacob's wife, Tabatha, as living. Lindsay hadn't known she was dead when she first approached Jacob.

Finding nothing of interest in that folder, I moved on to the folder bearing the name Aaron Caferty. His life filled my screen and I picked it apart. Again, there was nothing of real interest in most of the documents. The only item that drew my attention was a six-month gap in employment. I thought it could have been some sort of sabbatical, taken with the university's permission. I checked his financial records. Somehow a company had managed to obtain his credit card statements. This couldn't be legal, but I assumed that at fifty dollars per request they made enough money to hire some really talented lawyers.

I found one that matched up with the dates of his brief period of unemployment—a large charge to the Timberlake Retreat. Figuring that he put himself in debt to vacation at some plush resort, I did an online search for the establishment. The Timberlake Retreat was not a luxury beachfront hotel. They did not offer valet parking and rooms with balconies that had breathtaking views. What they did offer was high-quality inpatient psychiatric care and drug and alcohol rehabilitation services.

Lindsay's summary on Aaron had connected the two. V was right. Lindsay hadn't been some ditz who was going to get by on her looks. Lindsay had typed out two short paragraphs mentioning the probable visit to the funny farm and little more. In red text at the bottom of the page were the words *Follow up on this*.

The next file I checked was Randy's. The pages Lindsay had received were dated after she had tried to tempt Randy. My fellow Criminology professor had been so rude in his deflection of her that I could imagine her crossing her fingers and praying that she could find dirt on him. She did.

Good ol' Mr. Walker had made his reputation from a well-known study he had conducted over three decades ago. It was a brilliant analysis of how the construction and layout of a prison could affect inmate behavior. I had read it years ago, and I have to admit it was groundbreaking. He systematically broke down the way everything inside prison walls was set up, from the size of the mattresses to the color of the food trays. He compared four prisons, studied the prisoners and their behavior, controlled for all of the right variables, and wrote an exceptional article that detailed his findings. He singlehandedly changed the way prisons were built in this country.

After Randy's blast onto the academic scene . . . nothing. He ground out a spattering of weak articles that couldn't even be categorized as research. His writings became nothing more than slanted editorials under the guise of social science. That was the case until fifteen years ago.

Then the name Randy Walker reappeared in the most respected academic journals. He had conducted research on juvenile crime and the negative effect that could be seen when both parents in a family worked. It was an increasingly common scenario as the American middle-class disappeared. He studied families with parents that worked full-time, part-time, the same shift, and different shifts. He followed the activities of their children for nearly two years and watched how their lives were affected. He wrote up the results and became semi-respectable again. I had seen that study too, and while not great, it was decent. Regardless of how people felt about the results, the methodology behind it seemed to be solid. Randy didn't publish much of substance after that, but he put himself back on the map and he was granted tenure at TRU just after the study had been made public.

Good for him. Even a stopped clock gets it right twice a day.

Better for Lindsay, who didn't need an online information service to do any work for her on this one. There have been some amazing technological advances in the last ten years. A lot more information is readily available now than there used to be. I didn't know what possessed her to do it, but she ran Randy's study from fifteen years ago through a new database that compares writing samples. The program searches for key words, lines of text, and finds duplication or similarities. Colleges use it to make sure their students turn in original work. Older studies are constantly uploaded to the system in order to make it more complete.

The smile on Lindsay's face must have been a mile wide when she saw the results. The study I was looking at had been scanned from a hard copy. The typeset was blocked off and some letters looked like small nibbles had been taken out of them. It had been written on a typewriter, not a computer. The content was exactly what I remembered it to be: An analysis of how juvenile crime may be affected by the increase in two working-parent families. The only problem was the author wasn't named Randy Walker. It was Marie Miller from Carson-Newman College in Tennessee. And the study had been conducted eight years prior to Walker's plagiarized version.

A quick internet search told me that Miller had died of cancer just after she authored the article. The name of the journal that she was published in was unfamiliar to me, so I looked it up too. It was an obscure journal that ceased publication not long after Miller's death. It was a forgotten article, in a forgotten publication, by a forgotten researcher.

I conducted another search and pulled up the article under Randy's name. It was nearly identical in every way. The only difference was that Miller followed families in Knoxville and Randy claimed to have conducted his work in Pittsburgh. Randy must have been desperate to get tenure, knowing that his star had long faded.

Somehow he found this article and realized the author and journal were both obscure and no longer functioning. He changed a few details, put his name on it, and reclaimed a little credibility. TRU had never questioned him and nobody had done any fact checking. In the academic world, any level of plagiarism was an intolerable offense. If discovered, his career would be over and he would go down in history as a fraud. Any work he ever did would be assumed to be fraudulent, including his landmark study on prisons. I closed Randy's folder and reminded myself to get a better running group.

I was down to the last three folders, when I noticed one of them wasn't actually titled with a person's name. It was just labeled with initials "D.A.A." I hadn't remembered seeing any names on the audio files that had those initials, so I was curious. What I found made me a lot more than curious.

The information in the file was similar to the others. Money, land, associates, driving record, the works. What was different was the story that it told. Accusations of embezzlement at a university in California five years ago. An overly aggressive admissions department and campus police department. A lawsuit filed by the accused, and directed at the school and the cops for slander, unlawful arrest, harassment, and unlawful termination. A small financial settlement. An expunged record. Legally binding agreements to not discuss the case. Everything swept under the rug. Somehow one of the investigative services Lindsay employed had found all this information, and had passed it along to her in a series of neatly formatted electronic documents.

They had also uncovered the sordid details of the initial accusation. An imaginative manipulation of numbers had resulted in nearly $350,000 disappearing from the school's annual budget. A forensic accountant had followed a questionable trail back to one person. The accountant then bypassed the police and leaked the story to the press. The police then felt compelled to make a premature arrest, rather than look incompetent. The fact they didn't have any real evidence, along with the small matter that the forensic accountant was really just providing an educated guess, produced a lawsuit, gag orders, and expunging of the record. No further investigating took place out of fear of being sued.

But Lindsay had some information that the people in California didn't have at the time. In a totally unrelated set of documents in the file, information about relatives and their business ties sat innocuously in neat paragraphs. I studied it carefully.

The accused man's sister owned a struggling transportation service in Arizona which owned a handful of buses catering to groups of senior citizens who wanted to visit the Grand Canyon or Las Vegas. Around the same time the money disappeared from the university, the transportation company bought out a competitor, purchased some new buses, and underwent a major expansion. The company became very profitable and all of its partners began to collect some nice annual profits. In fact, over the next few years several people involved with the company became very wealthy. A fortuitous turn of events, indeed.

Of course, the data-mining company hadn't connected the dots. To them it was just a compilation of random facts and it was their job to simply supply the information, not interpret it. Lindsay did the rest. She saw the names, numbers, and dates, recognized exactly what happened, and wrote a summary linking everything together. She also noted that the defrauded university was a public institution which utilized state money. She had copied a portion of a state law that informed the reader that in

California there was no statute of limitations when embezzlement involved public funds. The case could still be prosecuted.

I scrolled back through the documents until I found a list of the transportation company's partners. I had missed it the first time in the cascade of data. The fourth name on the list was the same one that was on all the other documents. The initials D.A.A. on the folder's icon weren't the initials of somebody's name. The initials stood for a title. It was a title I was very familiar with. I wondered how long the Dean of Academic Affairs would keep me waiting in the lobby the next time I paid him a visit.

Mile 14

I always pin my bib number onto the leg of my shorts before races. Most people pin it on the front of their shirts, but I prefer not to in case I want to lift my shirt up and wipe the sweat from my face. I broke tradition today and centered the number on my chest. I'm number 1863. I just happened to get that number assigned to me when I registered. Any single or double-digit bib numbers are reserved for the elites.

As we move through the campuses of Pitt and Carnegie Mellon, fatigue is intruding on my mind and my legs. I occupy my mind by trying to find some significance in the number 1863.

Civil War era.
Battle of Gettysburg.
Little Round Top.
Joshua Chamberlain leads a heroic bayonet charge.
Probably won the entire war in that moment.
He was around my age then.
He was a professor. Rhetoric, I think.
What else?
Vicksburg. Grant.
He would have been a good runner.
Wait your opponent out if you must—plow through and destroy when the opportunity is there.
He liked cigars. Maybe not a runner.
Probably not.

Museums and classroom buildings stand in the shadow of the tower. Lots of fast food and music stores here. Dozens of shops for students advertise candles and Bob Marley tapestries. Barricades and police cars are at every intersection. Even on Sunday morning, there can be a lot of traffic on 5th Avenue. There's always something going on. I see some well-dressed people walking to one of the local churches. Pittsburgh has a lot of churches. Maybe I should start going. I would have to be a Unitarian Universalist. They don't discriminate.

I wonder what he's thinking right now. Is he thinking about churches? About the Civil War? Is he thinking he got away with it? Did he think I wouldn't figure it out, or if I did, that I would just let it go? Three of them are up there somewhere, but only one has to die.

———

After I had gone through the entire contents of the thumb drive, I sat there in my office and tried to figure out my next move. I knew I should have taken what I had to Shand and Hartz, but that course of action came with its own set of problems. First, I still didn't know if this had anything to do with Lindsay's death. Steven's name was nowhere in the files and, as far as I could tell, he didn't have any connection to the people who could be harmed by the information. Second, these were career academics, and the minute a cop showed up knocking on the door, they would be on the phone with their lawyers. Third, I made a promise. My promise to V was that I would let her make the call. Promises should be kept.

No. No cops. Not yet.

Lindsay had plans to use this information to make a name for herself, and I didn't want to doubt that fact. Unfortunately, I had to account for another possibility. She could have been blackmailing any of a number of people. She could have tried it on the wrong person. But she wasn't blackmailing the man who killed her. Steven's name wasn't in the files.

I concluded that if I kept taking the facts at face value and didn't start thinking outside the box, I wasn't going to get anywhere. I decided to let my intuition run wild and see where it took me. I just hoped I still had some good instincts.

I talked it out and Sigmund twitched an ear.

Lindsay was not dating Steven, but from the way they looked at each other in my office, it was clear they knew each other. Lindsay had recorded numerous embarrassing conversations with faculty members. Did she die because of a recording?

Stop.
Was an embarrassing conversation worth killing for? Probably not. Men can lie. They can make up excuses. They can claim that it wasn't their voice. They can beg their wives for forgiveness and say they never would have actually gone through with it. They can seek redemption. And besides, nobody but Lindsay and V knew about the recordings.

Okay. Scratch that theory. Move on.

I decided that I was going to assume that Steven killing Lindsay wasn't a coincidence. He didn't kill her while she just happened to be discovering destructive information on university employees.

Would Steven kill for somebody else?
Sorry, Cyprus. Can't take the chance.
Sorry? You don't say you're sorry if you are mad enough to kill. But you might say it if you are killing *for* someone else.

Who would he kill for?
  Cui bono? Who benefits?
  Several people.

Lindsay had found out that Aaron was off his rocker and had enraged him in the process. But did Aaron even know Steven?

Okay. Maybe. Hold onto that.

Next.

At a minimum, Silo could be facing a criminal investigation and possibly a prison sentence if his fraudulent dealings became known. Out of all the people in Lindsay's files, he may have had the most to lose.

Stop. How would he have known that Lindsay had the information?

Throw that one out.

No. Wait. Not yet.

Jacob was seeing her. He's the most prominent professor at the school. He values his reputation more than anything. His wife is gone. His name is all he's got. He knew Lindsay the best. He seduced her. He promised her a future.

He didn't have a link to Steven. Did he?
No, he didn't. Steven didn't seem to have a link to anybody. Who is Jacob linked to?

He's linked to Aaron. To Randy. To me.

To Silo.

Lindsay could have confided in Jacob. She could have told him about Silo's crime. Jacob could have told Silo. They're friends.

Weak, but possible. Hold that one.

Lindsay knew that Randy was a plagiarist and a sexist jerk. She could have ruined his career and his life's work.

Stop. Assume he didn't know about the recording.

But, Randy teaches in the Criminology department. Steven studied Criminology. They could have crossed paths. Randy knew Lindsay and may have known Steven. Randy doesn't like me, but would he go as far as sending Steven after me? If so, how would he benefit?

Hold on to that.

Look for connections.

If Lindsay was hiding Jacob from V, then she had no reason to hide Steven from V.
Right?
So, Steven wasn't a large part of Lindsay's life, but they knew each other somehow.
Right?
They *were* connected in some way by *someone* who had something to lose.

Right.

If I was going to move ahead by operating on wild assumptions, then there was one big fact I was going to have to accept. Steven killed Lindsay because he thought he was protecting someone else. When he said, *Sorry, Cyprus. Can't take the chance,* he meant he couldn't risk that Lindsay *did* come back to talk to me later like she said she would. That she *did* tell me something. He wouldn't have known that she wanted to get a recording of me stating a university rule in order to help some off-the-books journalism project.

He would have thought that either she was going to pursue a relationship with me . . . or . . .

Connection.

Or, he would have thought she was going to tell me about another relationship. One she was involved in.

The relationship with Jacob.

Steven *did* know Jacob.
Jacob knew Steven.
They both knew Lindsay.
It's the only connection that makes sense.

There were three flimsy lines of reasoning to follow and one slightly more solid.

Randy could have known both Lindsay and Steven. But, did he know that she knew about his plagiarism? Doubtful.

Or

Silo discovered that Lindsay knew about his past crime and somehow used Steven. Again, a stretch.

Or

Aaron cracked, knew Steven and somehow got him to do his dirty work for him. Also requires massive speculation.

Or

Steven was protecting Jacob.
Logical.
Maybe.

All of this was conjecture and not particularly insightful. However, it needed to be investigated properly.

Now I knew what I had to do next.

Mile 15

The change of scenery gives me a boost. Transitioning from the realm of student housing and rat-race retail to the established businesses and residences in Shadyside gives me the feeling of permanence again. The walls of trees on each side of Walnut Street aren't fully in bloom yet, but after the vacant lots and shells of transience I saw over the last two miles, I feel an unusually strong desire for stability. How could that have only been one mile from the heart of a bustling area full of young energy? The beautiful, well-kept houses here make this street look like the background in a Norman Rockwell painting. All that are missing are the flags and the 4th of July parade.

Just one mile. That's 5,280 feet. I estimate my stride length to be about two feet. So, that's only 1,140 steps. In just 570 steps I'll be halfway to the next mile. I inhale every three steps and exhale at the same rate. So, that's twelve feet covered with each full breath. That equates to 440 breaths per mile, or 220 breaths per half mile. I could actually count 220 breaths in my head. Counting steps is too cumbersome, but I can count breaths. I'm wondering if I should start counting on the inhale or the exhale. When I get a drink of water at the upcoming water station, will that throw me off? Should I give myself a margin of error of plus or minus three? Maybe four.

I have to stay distracted to endure the race. I have to stay focused for other reasons. *Distractedly focused*. That will be my new power phrase. *Chasing the ideal* no longer works for me. *Distractedly focused* seems more applicable these days. Distract myself with numbers and facts, but be on target when the time is right. By the time I've done the math and figured out the feet, strides, and breaths, another mile has passed. One more tumbler falls into place.

⟞⟐⟐⟝

Time to back off. I knew who had killed Lindsay and I had some crazy theories as to why. I didn't have the whole picture yet, but I didn't need to. I had gone above and beyond what I should have done, and I reminded myself that I wasn't a cop anymore. My mind was made up.

I decided I would give the flash drive back to V, persuade her to talk to Lindsay's parents to explain what their daughter had been doing, and then give the information to the police. Once they analyzed the information, they could run down the leads.

It was time for me to take a bow, exit stage left and get back to my normal life. I considered making a copy of the files on the flash drive, but I didn't for a few reasons. First, I didn't see any real benefit. I knew the information and hopefully the police would too soon enough. Second, Steven had been the man who murdered Lindsay and none of this changed that fact. The rest of this was scandalous and sad, but circumstantial and mostly unrelated. Third, I was afraid that I would be tempted someday to use the information for my own benefit. I couldn't imagine myself doing that, but why take the chance.

Before heading out to return the flash drive, I needed to tell Kaitlyn what I had been doing and let her know that it was over. Full disclosure could only be delayed for so long. I knew she wouldn't be particularly happy about my going off and playing detective, but the woman had advanced training in conflict resolution and crisis management, so I was sure she would handle it like a champ.

"You're a damn idiot!"
Well, she didn't handle it quite that well.
"I know."

Sigmund had followed me to her den, but made a hasty retreat. *Coward.*

"Who told you that the girl had an agenda?"

"You did."

"And then you went and actually interviewed her roommate?"

"I talked to her. Just a conversation. I wouldn't call it an interview, per se."

In the way a parent scolds a four-year-old, she asked, "Oh, well then, let me ask you this about your *conversation*, Dr. Keller. Did you lean in when the questions got tougher? Did you change the inflection of your voice when addressing certain topics? Did you monitor her body language and look for signs of deception? Did you perhaps, catch her in a lie, hold it back, and then throw it in her face? Did she happen to be crying when she gave everything up?"

Where the hell was Sigmund? I needed backup. He needed to come back in here and do the cute head-tilt thingy.

"I may have interviewed her."

"No kidding. I'm shocked!"

She wasn't.

"I'm furious at you."

She was.

"What if the cops find out that you were spending your days on suspension running down leads and interviewing people?"

"I'll say I'm with the neighborhood watch?"

"Oakland is not your damn neighborhood!"

After some more advanced conflict resolution, Kaitlyn descended to a safe altitude and the conversation became much more productive.

"Do you think you can get the roommate to talk to the police?"

"I think so. V is pretty worried about Lindsay's reputation, but I'll explain the importance of it." I thought about the potential fallout again. "A lot of people may get hurt by this, depending on whether the police release the information."

"V? The roommate's name is V?"

"Her real name is Virginia Richmond."

"What's wrong with some parents? They can try to be too clever."

"I agree."

I got back on the road and headed back into the city to return the memory stick and convince V to turn it over to the police. On the way, my cell phone rang. Brent Lancaster was calling to let me know that he wanted me to come down to TRU the day after next, and give my official statement regarding my outburst. He had been appointed by the panel to get a short summary of what happened and a promise from me to be on my best behavior in the future. He assured me it was just a formality and he would simply take my statement, write it up, and submit it to the Criminology department panel members.

A smile crossed my face when he said it was likely that I would be reinstated by the end of the week. He let me know where he would be teaching class that morning and asked if I could meet him there at nine forty-five. He said the class should be finishing up at that time and he could get my statement right there. I agreed, and felt a sense of relief. All of this was wrapping up.

After arriving at V's apartment, my conversation with her went even better than I expected. As promised, I returned the flash drive and assured her that it was her choice about what to do with the information. Some rags in her hand told me that she had been cleaning. Quite a neat little doper. I never knew wacky weed could make you OCD.

While trying to ignore the odors of lemon cleaner and burnt marijuana in the air, I told her, "Some of these files will really hurt some people, but any evidence of misconduct should probably go to the police. In fact, I think you should turn the entire thing over to them. There's some interesting stuff on there."

I knew the police wouldn't concern themselves with all the dirty little details of the professors' lives, but they would certainly be interested in Silo's financial dealings and possibly Jacob's relationship with Lindsay. Even though most of the incriminating information on the stick wasn't criminal in nature, I could see the cops turning over the information to the university or letting it get leaked to the press.

V told me she would think about things for a few days, but I got the impression she was leaning toward giving everything to the cops. I was about to mention that there was no real reason to bring my name into the conversation, but she beat me to the punch and said that she had never seen me before.

I thanked her, we shook hands, and I was on my way. En route to the Jeep, I passed through the quad outside of the building and noticed the same guy with the easel and paints set up facing away from the apartments. He looked to be working furiously to beat the setting sun and the accompanying colder temperatures. As I passed behind him, my eyes traced a path over his work and I could see what he was painting. Less than a quarter of a mile away, the Cathedral of Learning projected itself into the dimming sky, while a miniature version of the same tower stood twelve inches from the artist's face. I told myself that I would have to remember to use that building as a landmark in a few weeks.

Mile 16

Victorian houses and one hundred-year-old trees change into brick apartment buildings when we turn onto Highland Avenue. These apartments are much different than those around the colleges. These look to be more upscale. Maybe some students can afford these, but they are more likely filled by recent graduates who hop on a bus to exciting new jobs downtown or over in Squirrel Hill. Some of them probably ride bikes to nearby companies in Shadyside when the weather is nice.

Eventually, I'll have to get a bike. Cycling is supposed to be easier on your joints. If my knees start failing me after a few thousand miles, I'll be one of those guys you see in the fancy shirts that zip up in the front. They wear spandex shorts and fly down narrow roads, just daring a truck to pancake them. The thrill of the speed must be irresistible. I can see myself weaving in and out of other cyclists as the road flies by beneath me. Or, I'll learn to play golf.

It's probably similar.

I once read that Lance Armstrong had a resting heart rate of something like thirty-five beats per minute whereas a normal person's is seventy or seventy-five. I measured mine once and I was thrilled when I calculated it to be fifty-eight. A low heart rate means less strain on the body. You take fewer breaths, expend less energy, and you operate more efficiently.

To run efficiently you have to maintain proper form by not leaning over too far, but not leaning too far back. You keep your stride length comfortable, run heel to toe, swing your arms, and let inertia help you along. A body in motion tends to stay in motion. That's the rule. There are always going to be times when you find yourself being brought to a violent halt. You just have to get started again, even after you bounce off a wall or two.

———◦◦◦———

That night, I slept better than I had since the day I'd found out about the murder. My shoulder seemed to feel better, Kaitlyn was relaxed, and even Sigmund snored a touch louder. The best thing about carrying around a burden is the feeling you have when it gets unloaded.

Yes, a student of mine was dead. Yes, my graduate assistant had been the murdering wacko who killed her. Yes, my running group had been a collection of morally corrupt and mentally unstable hypocrites. Yes, the Dean of Academic Affairs was an embezzler. But hey . . . welcome to Three Rivers University. Let me show you some brochures.

I woke up the next morning refreshed and ready to tackle the day. Of course, I still had nothing to tackle and I think the Home Depot had me listed as a stalker, so I went for a run. It was cool and overcast with temperatures in the high forties. An hour into my run a light drizzle floated in and the tiny dabs of water felt great on my skin. I cranked out fifteen miles and felt good while doing it. There were just four weeks until the race and, other than my shoulder, I was doing fine. I told myself that I would work my way up to running twenty miles, and then taper off the final two weeks so my legs would be ready for action. Confidence: regained.

Kaitlyn had gotten up before dawn and had gone to Philadelphia for a three-day conference and to visit a college friend through the weekend, so Sigmund and I had the place to ourselves for a few days. When I returned from my run, Sigmund greeted me like I had been gone for a week. That's one of the great things about dogs. Whether it's five minutes or five weeks, they are always happy to see you when you come home.

After a long stretching session, I got in the shower and planned the rest of my day. I decided that I would have one last lazy day before rededicating myself to work. I was going to meet with Brent the next morning. Being reinstated was a foregone conclusion after he submitted my statement. This day was going to be completely about watching some movies I had on DVD, but never had time to watch, and finishing that book about the Unabomber. No stress.

Determined to take this mini-rebellion all the way, I threw on some sweat pants and a fleece shirt after getting out of the shower. I was going to stay in total bum-gear all day long and nobody could do a thing about it. I went to the kitchen, poured myself a cup of coffee and turned on the TV. Walking to the stack of unwatched DVDs next to the TV, I picked out a feel-good movie about some kid who went from poverty to making millions in pro football. I was about to change the TV from its normal setting to the DVD mode, when the local news interrupted some game show with a breaking story. I heard only the first few bits and pieces as I struggled to unwrap the plastic that was keeping me from opening the case that contained my movie.

Tragedy . . . Oakland . . . students shocked . . . dead . . . KDKA Newsforce on the scene . . . getting reaction of owner . . . nearby business . . . Ernie's Art Supplies . . .

I dropped the movie and grabbed the remote. I turned up the volume and hoped for a recap. The desk reporter didn't disappoint me. She pasted on a look as if her own child was in danger and used her best dramatic voice. She described how the details were sketchy, but a young female had been found dead in the early morning hours. The police were not releasing any further information, but students who lived in the building said the occupant of apartment 301 was a sweet girl who never bothered anybody.

A neighbor who knew her had noticed her door standing open around six in the morning and decided to check up on her. She said there was no way that the victim would have left the door open since her roommate had been murdered just a couple of weeks before. The neighbor found the body next to a blood covered fireplace poker.

The neighbor, a girl who looked to be about eighteen years old, said she was in total shock because she had never seen so much blood. She described all sorts of bruises on the face and neck. She hadn't heard anything during the night, but some guys had a loud party in 307. They always threw parties that were *off the hook*. She said they were great guys. She mentioned again that she was totally in shock. Of course, that didn't stop her from excitedly describing the scene while looking into the camera.

The press was salivating over the story's potential. Two room-mates murdered. Was there a connection? Did the police miss something? Was this a terrible coincidence? The Newsforce team would be following the story all day. They promised.

The police weren't releasing the name of the victim, pending notification of the family. To my amazement, the news crew re-fused to release the name as well. Probably out of fear of getting shutout by the police. They wouldn't say the name, but I knew the name.

The police *had* missed something. They had missed what I had held in my hand yesterday afternoon. They had missed what I had failed to give them. Somebody knew what V had and they decided to kill her for it. I had to assume the flash drive was gone. The bruises on her face told that story. V had some fight in her, but she was basically a kid. If somebody decided to beat the information out of her with a fireplace poker, they got what they wanted.

I turned off the television and looked out a window into the woods. The light drizzle had turned into a steady rain. I gripped the window frame and closed my eyes. My head pounded.

I wasn't fully responsible for Lindsay's death. I couldn't bear that cross. I wasn't fully responsible for Steven's death. He came at me. I *wouldn't* bear that cross. But I *was* responsible for *this*.

I could have gone to the police. I *should* have gone to the police. I could have told V that I was taking the files to the police—to hell with Lindsay's reputation. Lindsay's minister father and saint of a mother would have just had to deal with it. That's what I should have done.

I didn't do any of that. And now a death was squarely on my shoulders. That was unacceptable. Killing V was unacceptable. She was a bystander by circumstance; and somebody had attacked that petite little girl, who barely created a dent in a beanbag chair, and had beaten her to death.

No. Unacceptable.

Chase the ideal? I wanted to chase the ideal? This was not the ideal.

I opened my eyes again. At that moment, watching the raindrops cry down the window, that's when I decided that detectives Shand and Hartz were *not* going to hear from me. I was *not* going to call the police. I was *not* going to trust the system. I was *not* going to rely on statutes and procedures. I was *not* going to let one goddamn lawyer get near any of this. I was *not* going to chase the ideal. I was going to chase something else. Someone else.

I was going to find the man who killed that tiny girl with the purple hair, who missed her best friend more than anything. I was going to deliver an imperative reckoning. I was going to watch that man die. I was going to become a murderer and it didn't bother me in the least.

Now that drastic measures were going to be taken, I had to stop functioning on assumptions. Taking a man's life should never be based on any level of uncertainty. My first move had to be to confirm that the flash drive was taken when V was killed and that meant going into her apartment. Walking into a recent crime scene is a risky proposition, but I had to know if that data was still there. Even if the police found the small presidential figure and recognized it for what it was, which was unlikely, they probably wouldn't have taken it. They had no reason. Students always have flash drives lying around and rarely do they contain anything more than schoolwork.

Sometimes people think that crime scenes stay guarded twenty-four hours a day. They don't. Generally, urban police departments don't have the manpower to post a guy at the door for very long. Besides, once the photos have been taken, the forensic teams have processed the scene, and the body has been removed, the room ceases to be of real evidentiary value. There isn't any reason to guard it anymore. The cops put a piece of crime scene tape across the door and hope for the best. That's it.

Since a murder had been committed in a building full of college kids and parents would be frantic, I could easily see the Pittsburgh PD or one of the nearby universities maintaining a heavy presence in the neighborhood. If the city cops decided to handle it, they would make sure to drive by the building as often as possible and maintain high visibility. That's what I was hoping for. If some university cops caught the assignment, then a couple of other problems presented themselves.

First, the university cops had a smaller area to patrol, and I was afraid they might post an officer in a stationary car outside of the building. That officer would stay there until another call came over the radio. I thought the campus cops might even offer to pay overtime to one of their off-duty officers, who would therefore have no patrol responsibilities, and keep him posted there all night long. The other problem with the university cops would be vigilance. City cops are used to dealing with bloodshed and high-profile homicides while the campus cops aren't. A city cop might be more complacent about watching a useless crime scene, where a university officer might think that the assignment is his fifteen minutes of fame. I wanted complacence.

Timing was important too. I needed to wait until the crime scene had been cleared and sealed up. That would take several hours, probably into the night. I would have to wait a while. A rookie mistake would be for me to head down there at four o'clock in the morning and try to get into the building. It would be just as bad if I made the attempt at eight o'clock. If I tried to sneak in when the streets were completely empty and everyone was asleep, I would stick out like a sore thumb. If I went too early, like at eight in the evening, the area would be busy and attentive eyes would be roaming the streets. But if I made the attempt around midnight, I might be able to blend in with the last of the day's foot traffic and still avoid watchful crowds of people.

My appearance was another factor to consider. Even at my age, I could possibly pass for a graduate student, but a trained officer might raise an eyebrow and decide to ask questions. Creating some sort of disguise wasn't an option either. If I went and bought some coveralls to transform into a maintenance man or janitor, or if I dirtied myself up like a homeless man, I would only be asking for trouble. A student had just been killed, and some of the first people the police focus on would be people who work in the building or members of the local transient population.

I thought about my limited options and decided to go in a totally different direction—hiding in plain sight. It would be risky, but I felt certain I could pull it off. As I continued to hash out the plan, my confidence grew with every passing moment. The best part was, I had everything I needed right there in my own home.

When I left the department in Baltimore, some friends of mine had given me a Baltimore PD badge encased in Lucite. It was supposed to be great for displaying the badge on a desk or shelf and evoking fond memories of locking up bad guys. I found the badge in a box in the garage marked MEMORABILIA and dug out the badge. It didn't take me long to figure out why Lucite was used instead of glass. Even with the use of a hammer, it took me several minutes of chipping away at the shatterproof plastic compound before I could free the badge.

I headed upstairs to the master bedroom, walked into the connecting bathroom, reached into a cabinet beneath the sink, and started untangling a cord. Sigmund stood at the bathroom door with judgmental curiosity. The buzzing sound made his head tilt and the growing pile of debris on the floor was a major point of fascination with him. I hadn't used the set of clippers in a long time, but the vibrating teeth seemed to remember the shape of my head. In minutes, I was able to look up and see a man that part of me had missed. Most of me did not.

Next, I stood in my bedroom closet and picked out a pair of slacks and a jacket that seemed appropriate to the mission. The Goldilocks rule. Not too nice, not too rough. Just right. Shoes were important. I found a black pair that had scuff marks and worn soles and threw them next to the bed where I had laid out the rest of the outfit. Then I grabbed a belt that had some broken stitching showing, as if it had previously carried more than just the occasional cell phone.

I undressed and redressed in my new outfit. The last thing missing was the one thing I absolutely didn't want to carry. I went to my nightstand and grabbed the item from the back of the drawer. It was in its holster and I knew it was loaded and ready to go, but I checked it anyway. Taking it out of the holster, I extracted the magazine and racked the slide back, ejecting a round from the chamber. The .357 round traveled end over end and made a dull thud on the carpet. I thought of Steven's semi-conscious body rotating toward its fate.

I picked up the cold, shiny bullet from the floor and looked at the bronze-colored end. The hollow-point would expand rapidly upon entering a body and commence to do the maximum amount of damage possible. If the shot landed *center mass*, pieces of hot shrapnel would scatter throughout a person's chest cavity and cause considerable internal bleeding. If one shot was placed right, death was possible. If more shots followed, death was probable.

I stared at this tiny instrument of destruction and marveled at the amount of energy we put into developing more effective ways of killing people. I remembered back to a class I took at the University of Maryland. A student was arguing with a professor about how modern times were no worse than the mafia-infested decades of the 1920s and 1930s. The student proudly sat up and stated that the similar homicide rates proved his point. The professor of the course did well to not show any satisfaction in disappointing the undergrad when he pointed out that if you got shot in the arm in 1930, you were much more likely to die than in modern times. Medical advances had tried to keep up with the development of killing devices. Tried.

I put the magazine back into the Sig Sauer P229 handgun and racked a round into the chamber. I de-cocked the weapon, took the magazine back out, and pushed the previously ejected round into the top of the magazine. Then I reinserted the magazine with a telling click. Thirteen rounds. A jury of twelve in the magazine, one alternate in the chamber. The weapon didn't have a safety. You just point and shoot. The first trigger pull would take about twelve pounds of pressure. Every pull after that would take only four. When all the bullets were expended, the slide would lock back and the open mouth of the gun would smoke and beg to be reloaded. Hungry for more brass.

Carrying the weapon would be necessary. Using the weapon would be tantamount to suicide. With forensic technology, a bullet from my gun could be matched in no time. Gun powder residue, gun oil, fingerprints, epithelial DNA—they all could send me to prison with minimal effort. Cops and former cops don't do well in prison. So I couldn't use the gun, but I needed it for show. I thought about carrying it unloaded, but the voice of my old training officer kept ringing in my head. *Better to be tried by twelve than carried by six.* I put the gun in the holster and clipped it on my right hip. I took my recently freed badge and clipped it on the left side, slightly toward the front. The small metal clip on the back of the badge wasn't really meant to hold it on a belt, but it would have to do.

The badge could be a problem. It was different from a Pittsburgh detective's badge. My badge was silver, with some traces of color in the middle. And while Pittsburgh detectives' badges were silver, they could be distinguished by a small bronze plate reading DETECTIVE across the front. My old badge would have to do. I would just have to hope that in the dark, behind a flapping sport coat, nobody would notice.

I walked over to a long mirror hanging on the bedroom wall and looked myself over. Dr. Keller wasn't there. Cyprus wasn't there. A detective was there. The outfit was right. The equipment was close enough. The hair was perfect. My demeanor would be the determining factor. I had to believe. I had to *know* who I was. I knew if I looked like I belonged—if I sold it right—then I could pull this off. I glanced at the clock and realized it was time for the hardest part. The ticking announced each second as if the previous was a forgotten nuisance. I waited for night to fall.

Mile 17

A rock band is set up in front of Mellon Park on 5th Avenue as we march into Homewood. A man in an old concert shirt is singing Bryan Adams' song "Run to You." When he arches his back to bellow out the chorus, I can see his belly flash some December skin under the black shirt. His three band members gyrate behind him and the bassist looks like he has to be the lead singer's brother. The drummer is a woman who must have idolized Joan Jett in the 80s. I can't see the guy on the guitar clearly because he's behind a large amplifier.

It doesn't take much to figure out what other songs they have been playing for the last hour or two. "Born to Run" by Springsteen. "Runaway" by Bon Jovi. "Runnin' Down a Dream" by Tom Petty. It's the same at any race that has bands comprised of middle-aged men and women. Occasionally, some jokers will sing "Heat Wave" by Martha and the Vandellas or "God's Gonna Cut You Down"—recently revived by a Johnny Cash rendition. Those songs aren't very inspiring.

The bend from 5th Avenue onto Penn Avenue introduces us to houses that were probably considered mansions several decades ago. Most of the dwellings are in good condition, but overgrown shrubs and dislodged bricks on walkways serve as a precursor to trouble. It's called the Broken Windows theory. Once neighborhoods become disorganized and worn down, the criminal element starts to move into the area and a chain reaction occurs. Dilapidation begets dilapidation. Transgressions beget transgressions. In most cities this is a foregone conclusion and Pittsburgh is really no different. It's a city of recovery, but usually things have to be worn down to the skeleton first.

I've sped up because it's that time.

This is the fourth place it could happen.

My adrenaline level is up again, but not like before. The fact that it didn't happen at the previous three points tells me that everything is on schedule. The plan was far from infallible. Variables are always present when it comes to killing.

Knives are rudimentary and require you to be close enough to feel your enemy's breath. Handguns are noisy and can be traced. Explosives cause collateral damage and have to be timed perfectly. Even a sniper with a rifle has to account for wind direction, visibility, elevation, and distance, and must remain concealed. Always variables.

All you can do is control them as best you can and play the percentages. If my plan fails, then I can still deny and escape. My opponent will know it was me, but it won't matter. My biggest problem will be getting another opportunity to kill him because he'll know it's coming. His personal window will have been broken and he'll see the enemy closing in on his neighborhood. His clock will be ticking and he may decide it's time to move on to a safer neighborhood. I can't let that happen.

———∞∞∞———

I circled the block twice and mentally recorded what I saw. Once wasn't enough, three would be suspicious. Things were as I had hoped. The news crews were packing up from their eleven o'clock broadcasts. They would show back up in a few hours to rehash the story before the morning rush hour. A few students walked down the narrow sidewalks and illegally crossed darkened streets. A heavy bass sound thudded from a distant car. Everything was as it should have been with one exception.

The university cop in the well-marked patrol car sat directly in front of the building's entrance. Other than an illuminated dashboard, the inside of the car was dark when I first drove down the block. It was on my second pass that I caught a glimpse of the officer. She had turned on a dome light in order to read some papers on a clipboard she held in front of her. The white light bounced off the papers and brightened her face. Somebody should have told her to change out the bulb in the car to a dim red color, or to put some dark tissue paper inside the plastic cover. Once she turned on that bright light, her night vision was out of commission for at least twenty minutes. That would help me.

I pulled the Jeep into a space one block south of V's building and started walking toward the entrance. With every step, I worked on boosting my confidence and simply looking like I belonged. When you look like you belong, people rarely ask questions.

I slowed my pace and watched a student crossing the street in front of the building. He had a backpack slung over one shoulder and was twirling a set of keys in one of his hands. He was heading toward the entrance and I wanted to time my approach with his. I needed someone to open the door for me, and students who see a badge usually don't question authority.

Walking past the patrol car, I made sure to make eye contact with, and give a little nod to the officer behind the wheel. She turned off the dome light and I just happened to move my right arm so she caught sight of the badge. Just for a second. There was no way she could read BALTIMORE, MARYLAND at a distance of ten feet in the dark. She gave me a non-smiling wave, turned the light back on and continued reading off of her clipboard.

I slowed down to a near stop in front of the building's entrance, and watched the approaching student out of the corner of my eye. He was coming at me from the right side and the building was on my left. The police officer was parked on my side of the street and I had walked only a few steps past the front bumper of the car. It was going to be alright. I had it all planned out. The kid would open the door and before it closed behind him, I would catch the metal frame with my arm and hold it open, being careful not to touch the door with my hand. No fingerprints. If the kid turned around, I would simply flash the badge, say thanks and walk right past him. No explanation. None needed.

I was the police and if there were questions to be asked, *I* would be the one asking them.

I belonged here.

I belonged wherever *I* was and *I* had the badge.

That had to be the attitude.

Live the part. No doubt. Rock solid. Tougher than Lucite.

The student with the backpack was almost to my side of the street and heading right for the entrance when he did something I didn't expect. He turned left and passed by me in the opposite direction. He pushed a button on a keychain and a loud beep came from a car three spaces behind the police car. My friend with the backpack slid into his car and drove away. I found myself standing all by my lonesome, in the cold, outside of a crime scene, with an old badge and a loaded weapon.

I rolled my eyes at my own predicament and thought about what would be more noticeable to the officer, who by now had to have refocused on me. Walking away was suspicious. Standing there purposely didn't seem like a good idea. The keypad next to the glass door was begging me for an entry code that I didn't have. My mind was suddenly flooded with some discouraging thoughts.

I wasn't really with the police and *I* didn't want to answer questions!

I didn't belong here!

I didn't belong *anywhere* near here and *my* badge was as valid as a three-headed alien Elvis baby!

A good twenty seconds had passed and I decided to move on and hope the cop wouldn't follow me. Time to go.

As I took a step, a hand on my shoulder jolted me into the stratosphere.

"They didn't give you a code?"

It was the police officer from the car. The lighting in front of the entrance was terrible, but I could make out some of her features. She was a decent-looking lady in her late twenties. Her black hair was pinned back in a short ponytail. She looked the type to be either the most helpful officer you ever met, or the type to quickly douse you with pepper spray—depending on how you treated her. Time to go with the flow.

With a cynical smirk, I replied, "Nah, sure didn't. Apparently, I'm supposed to be psychic or somethin'."

"Yeah, they had the door propped open all day, but once the crime techs left, they shut the whole thing down. You with the city?"

When she asked me, her eyes had sunken down toward my obscured badge. It was almost imperceptible, but it was there.

Not wanting to take a chance that she would realize the badge didn't have a bronze plate across it, I took a big leap.

"Nah, state Attorney General's Office. You know, state university, state money, state interest. The governor is going to take all kinds of shit about this. Girls getting killed on his watch . . ." I shook my head as if trying to imagine the fallout. "He's gonna get killed in the press. Soft on crime and all that. You know how it is."

I hoped she didn't, because I sure didn't. I had no idea what the state Attorney General's Office did or what their badges looked like. I was banking on the fact that she was as ignorant as me.

I said, "Law enforcement and politics just don't mix. I should have worked a beat, like you. You get to do real police work and you don't have to deal with all the political B.S. At least *you* know why you're here."

My partner in conversation was getting hooked, so I kept going.

"So they tell me to get my butt down here to take a look at things and report back." I threw my hands up in disbelief, "But what the hell am I gonna tell 'em? The girl's dead. Cops are on it. It sucks, but it happens. But they say, 'get down there pronto and find out what you can,' so I do."

I saw a question brewing with my new buddy and I knew what it was.

I quickly added, "But I'm not gonna rush down here in the middle of a damn press event. I figure, she's just as dead in the middle of the night, so I'll glide on in here once the newsies are packed up and that way nobody is sayin' the governor is worried about this. Can't have the man lookin' worried. No way. It's bad *perception management*." I let the last two words drip off my tongue with utter distaste.

I leaned in to share a secret with OFFICER M. NOKES—that's what her nameplate read.

I whispered, "Of course, he *is* worried. He's pissin' his pants over this. But I'm not gonna be the one who takes the hit if that's what the reporters start sayin'. Ya know?"

I hoped she did, because I sure didn't.

"Aw, that sucks. Who was supposed to give you the code?"

Good question. For all I knew, this lady knew every detective in the city. For all I knew, she knew every patrol officer in the city. Not a single bright idea crossed my mind.

"Detective Shand. I tried to get up with him, but apparently he's been up forty-eight straight and he's not returning his messages. I was hoping to still catch somebody down here."

"Naw, they're all gone for the night, but I can help yinz out. Gave me the code since there's a bathroom in the lobby. Here ya go."

Officer Nokes reached over and punched the keypad four times. A latch clicked and she pulled the door open for me.

"I don't know if they ever got that door locked back up, but if they did, you're out of luck. I don't have a key for that," she said helpfully.

"Thanks. I'll go see. If it's locked up, I'll just get with one of the city guys tomorrow and get the grand tour."

She walked happily back to her car, having helped a fellow officer of the law. I moved quickly toward the stairs, having tested my bladder to its fullest.

The hallway looked exactly like it had on my previous visit. The only distinction was the splash of yellow at the end of the tunnel. Crime scene tape was strung across the doorway and formed an X. It took me only a second to understand what Officer Nokes meant about the door being locked. Even from a distance, I could see that the entire area between the doorknob and the frame was broken into splinters. Somebody had kicked in the door on his way to attack V. Music thumped from one of the apartments and camouflaged my steps. My anger grew as I moved closer.

After sliding my hands into a pair of leather gloves, I pulled down the crime scene tape and inspected the splintered area. The cops must have had the maintenance guy from the rental agency come by and put a temporary lock on the door. It wasn't a deadbolt, just a simple rod that slid into a loop. It was secured with a small padlock. A deterrent, not a countermeasure.

I thought about the girl with pigtails, who I had made cry, and I kicked the door with all my might. It flung open easily and revealed a dark interior. Pulling a tiny flashlight out of my pocket, I started scanning the area. Some of the windows were visible from the street out front, and I didn't want to turn on the lights in case any passing city cops got curious about why someone was in their crime scene.

The first thing my beam caught was discoloration on the floor. Blood was soaked into the carpet about four feet from the door. It had pooled heavily in one particular spot, and there was some splatter all around. Somebody had really worked her over before delivering the killing blow. I took care to walk around the morbid puddles and streaks.

Remembering how V had pulled the flash drive down from the mantle, I headed in that direction. The unlit candles stood at both ends, but there was no sign of the flash drive. Not wanting to spend any more time in the apartment than absolutely necessary, I began searching the place. Lindsay and V had separate bedrooms and it was easy to distinguish between the two. Lindsay's walls were bare, with the exception of some framed movie posters. They were from recent dramas that I hadn't watched, but I remembered seeing the commercials. I looked in every conceivable hiding place. The flash drive was nowhere to be found.

V's room had walls that were covered from top to bottom with Salvador Dali prints, signs from environmental rallies, and a wrinkled print of the painting *The Lady of Shalott*, inspired by the Tennyson poem. A copy of *Zen and the Art of Motorcycle Maintenance* waited for her on a nightstand. Not one picture of a half-naked guy, or an issue of a magazine inviting her to throw-up after eating, found its way into the flashlight beam. Sadly, the memory stick wasn't in view either. A wave of guilt hit me when I held the flashlight in my mouth and searched through her dresser and desk, but only a few marijuana leaves on the bottom of her underwear drawer gave me pause. She must have stored a small stash in the dresser. Most likely, the cops had searched the place and taken the drugs with them for disposal.

I stood up, turned off the flashlight, and let my eyes readjust to the dark. Rotating my sore shoulder to loosen it up, I readied myself to search the living room and kitchen. Reigniting the beam, I followed the lit circle on the floor out of V's room. The circle flickered and I smacked the side of the flashlight to bring it back into line. I decided to start with the furniture and then move on to the fireplace before giving the kitchen a quick look.

When it's dark, your other senses awaken to compensate for what you have lost. Therefore, my hearing should have warned me that someone else had entered the apartment while I was in V's room. What would have been even more helpful would have been if my ears had alerted me to the fact that I was about to feel a freight train burrow into my skull.

The pain was more shocking than excruciating. I had once been in a small room when a flash bang went off. When in close proximity, the reason that police occasionally throw the non-lethal stun grenades into a particularly dangerous room before entering becomes very evident. The concussive force of the mechanism creates several seconds of disorientation and blindness. If you are within fifteen feet of the short controlled blast, you'll feel like every cell in your body has front-row tickets to a Metallica concert. That's similar to what I felt when the impact hit me above the left ear.

Somewhere between unconsciousness and consciousness, I knew a light was being shined into my face. Mentally, I started doing a diagnostic check, much like a mechanic looking at a car.

Body—
    Feeling in hands: Check.
    Movement of toes: Check.
    Vision: Minimal.
    Hearing: Breathing and footsteps—not mine. Check.
    Position: Floor. Check.
    Pain level: Awful. Fail.
Equipment—
    Flashlight—I felt the area on the floor around my left hand. Check.
    Gun—Don't reach to see if it's still holstered. Not unless you absolutely have to. Unknown.

My overall status read more like a magic eight ball.

Outlook: Not so good.

Standing over me was a ball of fire being held by a thick hand wearing a glove. The voice behind the light was one I recognized.

My attacker demanded, "Where is it?"

Another glove came into focus. A gun was being leveled at me by the same man. The smack of the gun barrel had been what brought me to the floor. This was turning out to be a terrible semester. First, I was attacked by my own graduate assistant with something that looked like a lead pipe and now by a man holding a gun. What the hell was this, a game of Clue? If Ms. Scarlet had come at me with a rope in the conservatory the very next day, I wouldn't have been surprised in the least.

"Where is it?" he repeated impatiently.

"Where is what?"

"Don't screw with me! I'm not letting you take me down. Not *you*. I've worked too hard. And I certainly won't be blackmailed!"

My eyes started to focus past the light and I oriented myself in the apartment. I was on the edge of the living room. The door stood a lifetime away. A sliver of flickering fluorescence trickled in under the exit. So far away.

The kick to my side was unexpected. He moved quickly for a big man. I fought to regain my breath.

"I don't have it," I sputtered as I searched for oxygen. "The police must have it. There's nothing you can do."

"Bullshit!"

This time I protected my ribs with my arm. My arm did not thank me after the foot left its second impression.

"I got your message and now you're going to get mine." He put the gun a little closer to my head, but still out of reach. "I don't care what you think you know, but you're going to give me that flash drive. I followed you from your house, so I know you came straight here. There's no reason for you to be here unless the information is still in this apartment."

Trying to sit up, I managed, "Look around dammit! It's not here. And I didn't leave you any message! What the hell are you talking about?"

The light dropped down to my chest and I could see a perplexed expression. The expression rapidly changed to unbelieving.

"Don't even try it, kid. You think you're so smart. I watched you badge your way in here. Ever hear of a back door, moron? Smokers prop things in the latch and forget to lock them all the time. I walked right in and walked the floors until I found the crime scene."

Huh. Score one for the opposition.

"You had to *find* the crime scene?" I asked.

He stood silent. Empty breaths filled the room.

I followed up with, "So, you didn't kill V? And what message are you talking about?"

The light dropped a little further down my chest. He was really confused now. I was a little confused myself.

The voice replied, "If you didn't put that letter under my office door threatening to . . . threatening me with what's on some flash drive, then why would you be here?"

"It's a long story. Let's just say that we are looking for the same thing for different reasons. Maybe we can help each other."

I started to stand and my chest was greeted by a size 11 in the sternum.

"Where do you think you're going?" he menaced. "If you're looking for the flash drive, then what did she have on you?"

"Nothing. I think this all ties into Steven Thacker and Lindsay Behram. I think . . ."

The light was back in my eyes and another kick was delivered to my side.

"You know what's on that thing! You *do* want to blackmail me! You almost had me, you bastard! Now, where the hell is it?"

Through gritted teeth, I explained, "I honestly don't know. We both know you aren't going to kill me, so let's just talk about this."

There was a canyon of silence while he thought this over. I had presented him with a logical option that made sense. Surely, he would see the light.

"Here's the way I see it. Regardless of whether or not you know *where* the information is, you must know *what* it is."

Uh oh.

"And here you are, impersonating a police officer in order to gain access to a sealed-off crime scene."

He wasn't seeing the light.

"And even if you do have the information stashed somewhere, you can't really use that information if you're dead, now, can you?"

He continued the lecture with, "And after I shoot you, I'll search your body for the flash drive, leave this unregistered handgun behind, slip out the back door, and disappear into the night before anybody is the wiser."

He smiled as another thought came to him.

"Who knows? A gunshot wound to the head in this apartment . . . sounds like remorseful suicide to me. When I realized where you were going, I assumed you killed the girl. I bet the cops will think the exact same thing. Cops love open and shut cases, don't they? Yes. I think this would—"

The voice came through the apartment door before the person.

"Awwww, what the hell? I told you that if the door was locked then you were out—"

The silhouette of Officer Nokes filled the doorway, but only for a moment. The man standing over me turned in a panic and fired in her direction.

It's called muscle memory. If you practice something enough times, then your body reacts to certain situations or stimuli in a particular way. You don't mean to do anything, your reflexes just take over and you move from point A to point Z without even remembering passing through any other points. It just happens; and even after years of not practicing, you would be amazed at how the synapses in the brain tell the tendons, ligaments, and muscles to act under extreme circumstances.

I don't remember thinking about reaching for the holster. I don't remember smoothly unsnapping the holster and drawing the pistol in one fluid motion. I don't remember lining up the sight at the end of the gun's slide in between the two rear sights. I don't remember pulling the trigger. But I did.

It's simple cause and effect. The finger pulls the trigger. The hammer gets pulled back and releases forward. A firing pin slams into the primer of the bullet, causing a minute explosion. The bullet is propelled forward at over 1,200 feet per second and twists as it hits the grooves in the barrel. The slide of the weapon moves back and forth causing a sensation called recoil. The casing of the bullet ejects from the chamber and free-falls to the ground, having served its only purpose. The bullet spirals away from the gun and leaves all judgments, opinions, and traces of a conscience back in the shooter's hand.

In this particular case, the hollow-point bullet struck Dr. Randy Walker in the side of his head. The entry point was small. The exit point was not. His corpse folded to the floor a beat after Officer Nokes fell victim to Randy's shot. My training had taught me to shoot for the middle of the chest, but he had been turned toward Nokes and the light from the hallway had illuminated his head. I had automatically aimed at the best available target on his body.

I stood up and surveyed the dimly lit room.

Blood.

The smell of burned gun oil.

I checked the officer for signs of life.

Gone.

No need to check Randy.

His plagiarizing mind was on a wall.

Even with the music blaring from a neighboring apartment, the noise was surely going to attract attention. I had to make a decision. Stay and explain why I was in a crime scene with a Baltimore badge, a gun, and two dead bodies, or leave and continue my search for V's killer. I used my flashlight and checked where I had been lying to see if there was any blood from my head on the floor. None. It was time to go. I searched for, and found, the shell casing that had ejected from my gun. I pocketed the warm brass and took one more look at those who had been living just seconds before. If I played this right, nobody would ever know that I was here. As I fled the apartment, I remembered some words often attributed to Ben Franklin: *Three may keep a secret if two of them are dead*. Seemed about right.

Mile 18

Most cities hide their defeats. They don't hold parades through crime-soaked gutters or hold community picnics in postage stamp patches of grass that have seen too much. And most places certainly don't send thousands of athletes through beaten streets—lined with beaten buildings— that are filled with the echoes of beaten people. This city isn't most cities. This part of Homewood isn't where dreams go to die—they were never dreamt. This town isn't hiding its slow motion Hiroshima. It says: *Here it is. This is us too. We know . . . we're trying.*

Like many parts of America, this neighborhood has transformed into a gangland where the vibrations of the honest are drowned out by an earthquake of violence. Bars on windows are useless to the innocents whose affliction comes from their own broken circle of trust. Illegitimate businesses operate on broken glass, in alleys behind abandoned storefronts. It's real. It's here. It's no lie.

Exhaustion is blinding for most of us at this juncture, but we all see this. The race fires right into the heart of this disparity— a column of positive light being projected through the damaged streets. Police block the intersections, but there is little else to do here on a Sunday morning. Any wounds inflicted were done in the darker hours and only scar tissue remains. No water station here. No volunteers placed on the streets here. Not this place. The silence on these blocks isn't peaceful, it's a tiresome exhale.

This is how it should be. Not that this disrepair and neglect should be accepted, but it shouldn't be hidden. To show off statues, stadiums, and successes and hide those who have missed out, is nothing more than a hypocritical shell game. Allowing the runners to see this area is a way of saying that we still have farther to go. We haven't finished moving forward. This is truth. No recovery here. Not yet.

———

I burst out the back door that Randy had used and came to a halt to compose myself. A square piece of cardboard was lying near my feet. At some point, the square was some smoker's ticket back through the door. A cold rain was falling as the metal door slammed behind me. I realized I was still holding my gun, so I quickly de-cocked the killing machine and put it back in my holster. I started moving away from the building, not a run, but not a walk. Pulling the collar of the jacket up, I kept my face shielded from both the rain and anybody whom I might pass, as I made a wide circle around the block. Approaching my Jeep from behind, I slid into the driver's seat and pulled away. In all my years in law enforcement I had never killed a man. Now I was setting a new standard of two a semester. I thanked God TRU wasn't on the quarter system.

Ballistics: The science of the flight of and effects caused by flying projectiles. In this case, I was in possession of a handgun registered in my name that also happened to be a murder weapon. The chances were good that the hollow-point round that ended Randy's life had fractured into tiny pieces, but the forensic techs would possibly be able to determine the caliber of the round. If the bullet stayed relatively intact, the striations from the grooves in the barrel could be matched to my gun. Taking the shell casing may have only served to make sure my fingerprints weren't left in that room. Nobody wears gloves when loading a gun.

Checking the spot above my ear where Randy's gun had struck me, I found no blood. That was good. Trace evidence can be enough to convict and certainly enough to arrest. I wasn't too worried about fibers. People watch too much television and they think that crime scene technicians can find every little fiber and solve a murder in an hour. That's not the case. Besides, there were countermeasures for that.

I pulled the Jeep into my garage, got out, and stripped off my clothes. When I entered the house, Sigmund took a run at me, observed my state of nakedness, hit the breaks, cocked his head, and decided not to lunge at me. Thank God for small favors.

From a cabinet, I grabbed a large garbage bag and put everything in it except my gun and wallet. After throwing on a pair of sweat pants, sweatshirt, and tennis shoes, I vacuumed the Jeep. I would have to shampoo the carpets and clean the upholstery the next day on my way to take care of my gun problem. In the meantime, I emptied a can of aerosol disinfectant into the car in order to add as many contaminants as possible.

Pulling the car back out into the driveway, I rolled down all of the windows, and let the rain in to soak the seats and carpeting. Temporary, but effective. Back in the house, Sigmund looked at me disapprovingly and walked out the doggie door into the backyard, rain be damned. I looked at the clock and realized I had only a few hours until I had to meet Brent Lancaster and give him my statement.

By the time the police found the bodies, processed the scene, identified Randy, and started looking for a suspect, it would be well into the afternoon. The people at TRU wouldn't even hear about it until then, since any family members would have to be notified first. By the time anybody thought to connect the dots, take a close look at me—and check to see if I had a gun registered in my name—I would have taken care of everything.

Throwing the gun away wasn't a good option. Having some lame story about it being stolen wasn't going to help my cause. I had a better idea. For the time being I decided to hide the weapon, just in case. I put the gun into a waterproof bag and took a shovel from the garage. Sigmund watched me through the small openings between the fence boards as his idiot owner dug a hole in the mud out in the dark woods. In case I had any inquisitive visitors, having a bad story about a gun being stolen would still be better than being caught with conclusive evidence. I just had to make it until the afternoon. Then I would be able to regain some control over the situation.

Taking off my muddy shoes, I walked back through the house and grabbed my third pair of shoes for the day. I walked back through the garage, picked up the garbage bag, and took the hangman's evidence out to the Jeep. A short drive later, I tossed the bag and my muddy shoes into a dumpster behind a strip mall. My clothes and the seats of the car were soaking wet and chilled my bones. Coming up on a traffic signal, I pressed down on the brake pedal, looked in the rearview mirror, and saw nothing but red-tinted rain behind me.

The shower at home was steaming and the hour of dampness had pruned my fingers. The steam filled the bathroom and clouded the mirrors. Water washing over water. No real cleansing, just immersion. Facts floating around in the steam, unable to find each other. Unable to connect. The rush of escape was fading and my entire body raged with pain.

Randy had searched the building for the exact apartment in order to find me.

He didn't know where it was, because he hadn't been there. He didn't kill V.

My message? He received a message with my name on it threatening to blackmail him? Somebody knew that I knew. V had told her killer everything. The flash drive was history. The killer had it. But I knew what was on it.

I was the threat, and the killer had unleashed an angry desperate man on me. What did Randy think that I knew? Merely about the plagiarism, or did he think I had more? It didn't matter. I couldn't ask him. Somebody had pulled his strings and counted on one or both of us dying.

This was hand-to-hand combat. Somebody was using my strength against me. They knew the source of my power—I would keep pushing. I would always keep coming. Pursuing. And he just kept pulling. Using my force as a weapon. Letting my momentum pull me right past him, into one obstacle after another.

No more mistakes. Cut the strings. Randy didn't do it. One more kill, but one less suspect.

It's always good to look at the bright side.

Mile 19

Descending through Homewood West the houses stand a little taller. Torn sofas in the front yard are gradually replaced by shrubs. A local business appears on one block, two on the next. A gulp of water from a volunteer's hand washes down a tasteless piece of my pastry. Continuing hurts, but stopping would hurt worse. This is when the body just keeps moving because it doesn't know any better. The autopilot is turned on, but can't be fully trusted. The sun has pushed my shadow in front of me and the dim silhouette is pulling my chest toward the ground. I have to run tall. Maintain form. Don't even let your shadow see your pain.

Frankstown Avenue is the start of the runway to the finish. The sun on my back means the city is to my front. A few more hills will taunt me, but most of the course will slouch into submission if I can just keep moving.

Ignore the shoulder.
Ignore the legs.
Remember the mission.

Liberty Avenue is up ahead. The beginning of the civilization we choose to accept. Not rich, not poor, the last of the middle-class warriors. Finding the right pace is becoming more difficult than I thought. I have to move slowly enough to stay behind him and fast enough to outrun my doubts. For the first time, I feel them gaining on me—honing in on my location and trying to lock on. I thought I could outrun them, but now I'm not so sure. Can I pull this off? Have I left out any details? Did I miss something crucial? Something damning? It has to be perfect. The worst questions of all creep into my thoughts.

Am I right?
Should I be doing this?
Am I any better than him?

This can't be the ideal. This is something much more savage. If Dostoyevsky were writing my story, he would have my conscience compel me to fall to my knees and answer for my sins. Confess all and the human spirit will overcome. He would have me lower my head in defeat to the detectives and unload all of my burdens. The ideal is right in front of me. I can still touch it. Questions hit every time my soles compress against the warming road. Stop this madness before it gets any worse. How many hearts have to stop beating to make this right?

I think about Lindsay. The fear that must have been in her eyes when she realized she was overpowered. Her panicked lungs begging for air. Her desperate clawing, knowing it was all coming to an end.

I think about V. Pigtails dipped in blood after what must have been a torturous few minutes with a sadist wielding a fireplace poker. The fear. The pleading. Any remaining innocence extinguished. She gave up everything and it still wasn't enough for him. Only death was payment enough.

I think about Steven. The blackness in his eyes. The premeditated attack from nowhere. His arrogance. I think about that day in my office when he held up that paper with the misspelled Latin phrase. He pointed to those words with condescending disbelief. He couldn't believe anybody would misspell that phrase. I mentally focus on those words. I can still read his correction, written in big red letters.

Lex Talionis.

The law of retribution.
An eye for an eye.
Exact reciprocity.

Doubt will have to wait. I have only a few more hills to go, and the wind is at my back.

———❦———

I found Brent lecturing in the auditorium of Voorhees Building. The screens behind his head held images of explosions, damaged buildings, bloody sidewalks, and weeping faces. Block letters, spelling out names of locations, identified each tragedy. Lebanon, Cairo, Madrid, Paris, London, Mumbai, New York, Tel Aviv, Munich, Washington, D.C. The screens transitioned and images changed along with the names. New nightmares in new settings.

I stood in the back and looked down the filled rows of the academic arena. Not one student was texting, emailing, or chatting with a neighbor. All eyes were focused on the man in the suit guiding them through this class on terrorism. The day's topic of assassination was right up the former Secret Service man's alley.

Walking back and forth on the stage, the lecturer effortlessly discussed the subject without the assistance of notes. He tried to keep the listeners involved by eliciting their opinions.

"Now, let's look at these scenes. Some of these targets were assassinated and some survived the attempt. Ford even survived two attempts." Lancaster directed a thumb toward the screens. Names like Caesar, Ford, Reagan, Sadat, Rabin, Truman and others situated themselves into precise positions on top of the images. "What do all these attempts have in common?"

A male student in the second row answered first in a serious, yet questioning tone.

"The attackers were all crazy?"

A few snickers rose up throughout the auditorium.

Brent silenced the light laughs with a raised hand and a smile.

"No, no . . . don't laugh. Many successful or would-be assassins have been mentally ill. It could certainly be argued that the attacks on Ford were perpetrated by insane individuals even though the courts disagreed. Any other guesses?"

A moment of stumped quietness passed before Brent relented.

"All these attacks took place when the target was stationary. What I mean is, the person attacked was either on foot at a particular site or seated at a designated location when the attacker or attackers struck. Most attempts occur at a point where the target is either coming from or going to, and not between those points."

"What about JFK?" yelled a rumpled-looking young man near the back row. When he leaned up I could see a shirt with the logo of a mixed martial arts company that had become popular.

"Oh, don't get me wrong. There have been several attempts made on targets in moving vehicles, but they aren't quite as common. There are a couple of reasons why. Would anybody like to venture a guess as to what those reasons are?"

"It's harder to hit a moving target." came one response from the middle of the sea.

"That's one," agreed the professor.

Thoughtful faces stared at the screens.

Brent paused for a few seconds and then said, "The second one is easy. *Predictability.* Most of the time an assassin knows where the target will be coming *from* or going *to*. Whether it's Caesar sitting in the Senate or Reagan exiting the same Hilton hotel he had been to a hundred times, it is predictability that becomes our adversary."

With a slight touch of a button the screens changed to a map of Washington, D.C. Two buildings were circled.

"So let's say that the target lives here." Brent used a laser pointer to identify a street in Washington's Northwest quadrant. "And an assassin knows that the target is going to be here." The green dot moved to a block in Southeast. "Do you think the attacker would rather try to anticipate which of these fifty different routes the target might take," the dot bounced all over the nation's capital. "Or, do you think he would prefer to set up at one of these fixed locations."

Nobody answered. Nobody needed to.

"*Predictability* is what gets people killed. Now does that mean that threats should be ignored along the routes? Of course not. People in the security business have a tendency to drop their guard when they are in between the departure point and destination. That should never happen. Those of you who go on to work in law enforcement or security would be well served to remember that."

Following a brief look at his watch, the speaker dismissed the class with a reminder about a reading assignment. As the students filtered out, he looked up at me and nodded hello.

On the stage, we shook hands.

"Hello, Brent. It's good to see you."

"Same here. Your face seems to have healed up nicely."

When he said it, I saw his eyes move to the fresh bruise above my left ear which my short haircut did nothing to conceal. He seemed to be in a good mood, and there was no indication that word had gotten to him about Randy's death. If I was right, I still had a few hours.

I liked Brent. There wasn't anything phony about him and he didn't put up with anybody who tried to snow him. Since I started at TRU we had gotten together on a few occasions when the weather kept me from running, and I let him mop up the racquetball court with me. We weren't close friends, but we were certainly friendly. Last year, I had tried unsuccessfully to get him to join my running group. Boy, was I glad now that it didn't work out.

He gestured to a desk at the corner of the stage and said, "Well, I brought the paperwork with me, and there isn't another class in here for a couple of hours. Want to knock it out right here?"

I agreed, and let him have the "control side" of the desk. Nothing to fear. Just a formality.

Brent asked me to give a recounting of my initial comments to the police about Steven and his subsequent attack on me. Despite having gotten no sleep the previous night, I told the story perfectly, leaving out all the right details. I was afraid that Brent would slip back into law enforcement mode and start asking more pointed questions, but he didn't. A half an hour passed before I'd finished the story and Brent had written out my statement. He asked me to read it, and if I agreed with the content, to sign the document at the bottom. I did, and I did. Packing up the papers, Brent stood and I mirrored him.

"I'll type this up later and get you to sign the final version. Do you have a fax at home?"

I told him I did and gave him the number.

"It must suck being on that side of the table."

"It does," I said.

"Every time I had to take a polygraph or get re-interviewed for my security clearance, I walked out of there feeling guilty for breathing."

"I just hold my breath."

We shared a tension-breaking laugh.

Smiling and putting a hand on my back, he said, "Come on. You look tired. Let's go grab a cup of coffee. If you promise not to whack any grad students on the way, I'll even pay."

"I can't make any promises. I'm a little irritable until I have two cups."

We walked out of the building into sunlight that was drying out the night's rain. We were surrounded by a return to normalcy that I knew was about to be disrupted by more news of death. When the news about Randy made its rounds, the school would be in a frenzy. Three TRU people—dead in a matter of weeks. Another girl at a nearby university—found bludgeoned. Parents would flood the university switchboards demanding action. Police patrols would double if not triple. Reporters would write heartless headlines and teleprompter jockeys would paint themselves with sorrowful looks as they spoke through a camera to a rattled populace.

Brent looked up at the struggling sun as we stood on concrete steps that unfolded down to an active pedestrian-filled street.

After a long inhalation, Brent spoke. "I think spring is almost upon us. It's about time. Winters in Atlanta were sure a lot easier. Hell, even D.C. was a little better."

He looked down the street at some approaching runners.

"Isn't that your running group?"

I tried to focus my eyes on the passing runners. They were making a turn around the corner.

Three of them.

Three.

I could see Jacob and Aaron paired together, talking and smiling. It looked like Jacob turned his head just enough to address the runner trailing them.

Speechless, I stood and stared as the new addition appeared behind Jacob and Aaron, and then vanished around a brick building.

"Well, what do you know?" asked Brent. "You never told me that ol' Silo was a runner."

Still looking at the corner as if it was going to reveal something new, I could only answer, "I didn't know he was."

Mile 20

This is the wall. When you enter the community of runners, you always hear them talk about hitting the wall. The twentieth mile is that wall. Even for the most experienced runners, something happens at this point where the tank runs empty and the sleek sports car you were cruising along in becomes an antiquated contraption. Some people are limping; others are flat on the side of the road. The medical crews were wisely placed in the middle of this mile so they could attend to the delirious and unconscious. A lady in a pink tank top is bent over crying. Her hands are on her knees and tears are splashing between her laces. Tomorrow, she'll be embarrassed for crying and she will wonder what caused her to react that way. She'll eventually realize that it wasn't from pain or frustration, it was her mind and physical being saying—*enough.*

The refuse of misfortune is scattered throughout the rest of the East Liberty and Highland Park neighborhoods. The pleasant two-story houses, behind fifty-year-old trees, look on sympathetically. Wrought-iron fences that have no gates are for aesthetic purposes only. These streets have seen the bad times and bounced back to solemn respectability. No need for gates. The battle-tested faces of those who sit on their porches and watch us pass by are protection enough.

Medics are working on a torn man splayed out by the seminary. His head is turned toward the contemplative brick structures and he mouths something. He gets no response. On the opposite side of the street sits a football field surrounded by empty bleachers. God on one side of the street, gridiron on the other. I wonder which side hears more prayers.

Some more race photographers are on a scaffold up ahead. I prop my sunglasses up on my head and let the breeze evaporate some sweat on my face as I pass by. That's another eighty-dollar picture I won't purchase, but it will be invaluable to me.

I'm not going to hit the wall. This is too close to the end for me to stop. Again, I try to distract myself with scattered thoughts of measurements.

Only about 6 miles to go. And don't forget the .2. A 5K is 3.1 miles. I've run dozens of those with no problem. This is two 5Ks. I can run two 5Ks. At this pace I can be finished with this in less than an hour. I can do anything for an hour, right?

Just 6.2 miles to go.
Only 7 more turns.
5 more water stations.
And 1 murder to commit.

It's almost time.

———

The ground behind my home was still moist enough for me to easily retrieve the gun from the accomplice soil, and take it out of the waterproof bag. Having previously discarded the holster with all the other potential evidence, I had to tuck the firearm into the back of my waistband and cover it with my shirt. I drove to the local library and used one of their computers to do some quick research. It took me the better part of an hour, but I found what I was looking for. I filled the Wrangler's tank with gas and took off for a small town in Ohio. The round trip took me only four hours. The Jeep smelled clean from the thorough shampoo treatment it had received on the way back.

Back at home, I once again took a walk into the trees. This time I walked nearly a mile into a deserted area. One of the benefits of living in hunter-filled western Pennsylvania was nobody thinks twice about two quick gunshots in the woods.

I walked back into the house, pressed a button on the remote control, and the television blurted out the story I didn't really want to hear. I reloaded two rounds into the gun's magazine as I watched. The names were released, an academy photo of Officer Nokes was plastered on the screen, and then the mention of the TRU professor found dead in the same room. The reporters recapped the entire history of Lindsay's death, the murder of her roommate, and now this. This time the newscast didn't break away to cover anything else. This was big time.

I checked a national news site on the computer and sure enough, there it was. A photo of the apartment building was front and center with a beckoning link sitting below. It took them no time at all to put a name on it: *The Bloody 'Burgh.*

The story detailed everything up to the most recent deaths. My stomach contracted when I saw my name mentioned as the professor who killed Steven Thacker in self-defense. The police were still investigating the deaths of Virginia Richmond, Randy Walker, and Officer Monica Nokes. They had no information to release as of yet. The police refused to comment on whether Dr. Walker was a victim or a suspect. They refused to speculate as to why he would have been at the apartment. They said it would have been irresponsible for them to speculate about who shot who. One thing they did confirm was that Officer Nokes' weapon was still in her holster. They were looking for a third party.

I needed to call Kaitlyn. She was certainly going to hear about this, and I needed to give her a heads-up. It occurred to me that I hadn't seen my cell phone in a couple of days, and it took me several minutes until I found it on the dining room table. When I opened it up, blackness stared back at me. Dead. I wondered how long it had been out of commission. I found the charger and plugged it in. Picking up the landline in the kitchen, I dialed Kaitlyn's cell phone. It went straight to voice mail and I left an overly calm message asking her to call me when she got a chance.

The couch swallowed me up, and I pressed a button on the remote control sending the reporters into the media abyss. Within seconds, my eyes were closed and I left the world I knew for one where my hands were clean of blood, and ghosts of dead students and colleagues fell into submissiveness and rattled their chains no more.

I jumped up in the room that had become dark. Instinctively, I grabbed the gun that was still tucked in the back of my waistband and tried to scan the room for the threat. I saw nothing but heard everything. If an air horn could catch a cold, that's what a beagle's bark sounds like when it wakes you up. Sigmund was up near the front window and his bellowing was sincere and alert. Walking down the hallway toward the front door, I found my canine alarm clock with his front paws on the windowsill, and his attention fixed in the direction of the street.

At the door, I peered out of a small pane of glass and caught sight of the cars blocking my driveway. Three men were approaching, and the light from a post in my yard showed me their faces. Detectives Shand and Hartz were scanning the windows as they headed toward the front door and they didn't look happy. In tow was a local uniformed officer, there as a courtesy to two detectives who were a few miles out of their jurisdiction.

I knew that whatever they wanted to talk about, they would want to discuss it inside the house. I didn't have time for this, and I needed to get rid of them. Once I let them in, they would be hard to get rid of. Playing the part of the unfairly persecuted was probably the quickest way to send them on their way and leave them guessing.

Quickly, I retreated back to the living room and put the gun behind a pillow on the couch. I only had to wait a few seconds before the doorbell rang. Waiting for a second ring, I opened the door and said hello to my guests.

"Dr. Keller, we were hoping to talk to you," announced Shand, wearing a brown leather coat that partially covered a blue polo shirt.

Shaking my head and allowing myself a slight sigh, I said, "I heard about Randy. I can't believe it."

Detective Hartz asked, "Would you mind if we came in?"

"Don't take this the wrong way guys, but actually, I would. It's been a rough couple of weeks and now this news about Randy. I really don't know how I can help you. Do you have any leads on who killed him?"

Shand ignored my question and countered, "Well, we were thinking you might be more help to us than you may realize. Maybe we can just come inside and talk for a while."

"Sorry, guys, it's really not a good idea. The place is a mess and my dog can be pretty tough around strangers."

Detective Hartz leaned slowly to his right and looked at the front window.

With one eyebrow raised, he asked, "Would that be the little pooch there in the window with the tongue hanging out, tail wagging?"

"He's different once you're inside. Quite vicious. Trust me."

"Dr. Keller, you know how these investigations work, right? Different detectives work the investigations in whatever areas they are assigned. If cases seem to have similarities in them, no matter how small, the detectives get to talking. They start comparing notes and throwing theories around."

I waited.

"And here's the thing. We've got Lindsay Behram, Steven Thacker, and now this Walker guy all dead. And we sit down and comb through these cases and, sure enough, guess what three of them have in common?"

"Three Rivers University."

"That's right. And the Richmond girl, she was roommates with Lindsay, so I think we can safely say there's another connection as well."

I kept my mouth shut.

"But the thing is . . . they don't all just have Three Rivers in common. They have you in common too, don't they?" Shand accused.

"Was the Richmond girl a TRU student? I thought the newspaper said she went to Pitt."

"She went to Pitt, but did you know her?"

"Why would I know her?"

"Maybe you would like to come with us down to—"

On the off chance that they would find one of my fingerprints in V's apartment from my first visit, I decided it was best not to answer the question about knowing V; and I certainly wasn't going to let myself be put in an interrogation—an *interviewing* room. Time to be indignant.

"Are you kidding me? Because of you guys, my school thinks I'm a homophobe. Aside from that, I can't take two steps on campus without people whispering, *Hey, that's the professor who killed his grad assistant!* Now one of my coworkers is dead! And let's not forget the fact that a student in one of my classes got herself killed—and that's what set this whole thing in motion! Now you think *I* might know something about Randy and that officer getting killed? This is like a sick joke! What more do you want from me?"

The uniformed officer was standing in my yard, just off the porch. When I started yelling, I saw his hand move closer to an expandable baton on his belt.

Hartz and Shand were in no mood for this. They probably hadn't had much more sleep than me. Hartz seemed to take particular exception to my attitude.

The giant detective leaned down six inches to look me in the eye.

In a deep, deliberate tone, he said, "You didn't let us finish."

He straightened up and left his pupils indented on my forehead.

"Maybe if you would come down to our place, you could help us exclude you as a suspect. You can tell us where you were last night. Maybe . . . maybe you could even let us take a look at the Sig Sauer P229 that is registered to you."

"My gun! Now you want to see my gun!" I incredulously threw my hands to the sky. The uniform took a step closer. "Oh, you two are really something. Do you have a warrant?"

I felt cowardly even saying it.

Shand stepped in. "You have connections to at least three dead bodies and you own a gun that happens to fire .357 rounds. The same type of round that killed your professor friend. If you were in our shoes, what would you think?"

I knew what I would think. I knew what they were thinking.

"I didn't kill him."

"Then help us out. Give us the gun."

"No. I've had enough of this. I want things to go back to normal."

"What's normal?"

"Not this."

Shand reached into his jacket and pulled out a hand clutching a neatly folded set of papers.

"I was hoping you would just consent to this, but here you go."

He handed me the warrant. Some judge in this area had a very loose definition of *probable cause*. They were going to take my gun. I stood reading, wasting time.

Hartz spoke from above. "Save us some time. Where is it?"

I opened the front door and led the three men into the living room, turning the lights on as we walked. Sigmund greeted each one with a wet nose and attention-wanting whimper. His tail shot back and forth in sheer delight at having visitors.

Quite vicious.

I pointed to the pillow on the couch. Hartz donned a pair of latex gloves and retrieved two evidence bags from his pocket.

"Got the box?" he asked.

"No."

"Is it loaded?"

"Yes."

Moving the pillow and carefully holding the murder weapon, he asked, "Expecting trouble?"

"If you expect it, it never comes."

He unloaded the weapon, including the round in the chamber. He separately bagged the gun and the ammunition, barely taking notice of the bullets as they poured into the bag.

"Normally I would never say this to someone, but you know how this works. You may be able to work out a deal. Get a lawyer and come in. The prosecutors around here are pretty levelheaded. If you give us some good reasons, you never know. Former cop . . . college professor . . . if you were painted into a corner or had no other way out . . ."

"I told you, I didn't do it."

"And all of this is just bad luck? People around you dying?"

"The worst."

"Let me ask you this—why do you think anyone would want Randy Walker dead?"

"I wouldn't know."

"What do you think should happen to the person who killed him?"

Basic question. Guilty people downplay the punishment. A subconscious desire to be vindicated.

"Them." I said.

"What?"

"Them. I assume that the same person killed the police officer too, right?"

"Okay. Them."

"The scumbag that killed Randy deserves something other than prison. And you shouldn't even have to ask me how I feel about cop killers. Whoever killed that officer deserves the same fate in return. No question."

"I don't suppose you would just want to tell us where you—"

"It's time for you to leave. Your cars are blocking my driveway. Good night."

Sigmund watched the taillights get smaller, and I sat back on the couch and counted my borrowed time. The clock was ticking and no amount of willpower could stop it. My hands were starting to tremble. It was all catching up to me. Everything comes back to you. It always comes back.

I got up and poured myself a scotch to steady my nerves. I took a long pull from the glass and plopped down on the couch, placing my drink on an end table. Of all the things to worry about, I realized I hadn't used a coaster. Kaitlyn hates water rings on the tables. Draping my arm over the armrest of the couch, I felt my way around the end table and found a magazine to put my drink on. Without looking, I expertly relocated my glass and slid the periodical closer to my comfortable reach.

Silo. Jacob. Aaron. The other names of the condemned in Lindsay's clandestine files. The message to Randy. V. Poor V. My gun on its way to some lab. Steven. The parking garage. Me on my way to the car. The blood-filled apartment. Where was Lindsay killed? Nobody knows. Probably ambushed like me. Like V? Stationary targets. *Predictable.*

Like Brent said in his lecture. Like Brent said. He must have noticed the fresh bruise on my head, but he didn't say anything. Why?

Sitting up, I cupped my head in my hands. The clock— ticking. Feeling for my glass, I couldn't quite reach it from that position. I turned and leaned toward it, afraid of spilling the warm massage. The wet ring left by my glass wrinkled the cover of the magazine.

Not a magazine. The bubbled-up words on the page started the reaction. I closed my eyes tight. My mind pulled the trigger back slowly, the hammer yawned toward me and my thoughts began to focus. I lined the sights up. Focusing on the front sight, the back sights began to blur. Everything else began to blur. I could almost see it. Then the hammer dropped and the percussion of fire jetted me into recognition.

Got it.

The last tumbler fell into place.

I had to talk to a person who I had all but forgotten, but regardless of what he said, I knew.
I knew.

Mile 21

The road transforms from semi-continuous pavement to giant squares of chipped concrete on Bryant Street. From high above, it must look like oversized bricks were placed down, and if one became damaged, it could be lifted out and replaced. The old Buicks that were parked on each side of the street have transformed into affordable foreign cars with names that are made easy to pronounce for xenophobic American buyers.

The pain is more than I anticipated. The sleep-deprived days prior to the race have piled on top of my battered head and chest, and it's all catching up to me now. I have to speed up. The gap has to narrow and I have to make a move now. Each of my hands has been balled into a fist and the tension in my forearms tells me that I haven't run in the relaxed way I should have. Too late to worry about that now.

Catch up to him.
Close in.
Kill the architect of this house of mirrors and try to set things right. Feel the remorse later.
If you can.

—⟡—

It's not paranoia if someone is really after you. At least, that's what I kept telling myself every time I checked the mirrors. It had become a habit after Randy had followed me to V's apartment. At night, detecting vehicular surveillance becomes more difficult when headlights on city streets are as common as fireflies in a meadow. I probably wouldn't have noticed the tail if I hadn't blown through a red light on Western Avenue. It was three cars behind me, and all I could discern was that it was a sedan. I couldn't afford to let my adversary see where I was headed and who I was trying to find. It was too soon for him to know.

In the movies, the *pursued* always screeches away and attempts to lose the *pursuer*. There is usually some elaborate chase where pedestrians have to jump out of the way and horns blare with hostility. This wasn't a movie and I had had enough of the games.

Slamming on the brakes, I caused all of the cars behind me to do the same. I opened my door and sprinted down the center line toward the sedan. I had expected the driver to attempt an escape by suddenly throwing the car in reverse and executing a three-point turn in the middle of the road. I was hoping either to reach the sedan and confront the driver, or at least be able to see past the headlights and confirm his identity before the car inevitably sped away. None of those things happened.

My move was countered by the sound of acceleration, and the pursuing car's headlights swiftly became larger and more daunting. The car sped forward, causing me to come to a stand-still beside one of the cars I had forced to stop, and rethink my brilliant strategy. Leaping onto the hood of a yellow Mustang, I felt the toe of my right shoe catch the front the sedan. The force spun me awkwardly and I rolled off the hood of the car, and into the street, as the fender of the Mustang crunched from a collision.

A stream of profanity came from the driver of the Mustang and horns began to sound all around me. I stood up to see where the aggressor sedan had gone. With the headlights now shining in the other direction, I was able to get the make of the car, but I couldn't read the plate or see the driver. I didn't need to. Just as the car had reached me, I was able to see the hands on the steering wheel. Hands I hadn't expected to see. Tiny hands with white knuckles that stuck out of an oversized coat.

Ignoring the irate driver, I dusted myself off, got into the Wrangler and sped off. I still had to see someone. I would deal with the man who'd tried to turn me into road kill later.

Mile 22

eavy breaths come at me from behind, and even at my accelerated pace, several people pass me. The last relay station is now behind me, and those fresh-legged competitors on this final leg of the relay are trying their best not to disappoint their teams. Worry creeps in as people continue to pass me, but then I catch up to a pack of four running the full marathon and I easily pass them.

This straight stretch on North Neagley Avenue is the ideal place for me to make my move. Not slowing down at a water station, I snatch a cup of water from a young teen wearing a shirt that reads VIRGIL'S CHILDREN'S CAMP. Throwing the water into my face causes goose bumps to populate my sweat-covered arms. My strides lengthen and my breathing becomes deeper. For some reason I glance at the long scar on my forearm. Pain has a way of either making you focus or making you lose focus. This is the most focused I have ever felt.

Pulling back into the driveway, I hit the button to open the garage door. When I saw the Ford parked there sloppily, I did a double-take and brought the Jeep to a quick stop. Lightly pressing the accelerator, I parked against one side of the garage as I worried about why Kaitlyn was home early. She wasn't due back for a couple of days, but there was her car. I reached down on my belt to check my cell phone for messages and remembered that I had left the dead phone charging in the house.

After the police left, I took a trip downtown to find the man who could fill in the last few blanks. He did, and now I had all the right cards. Nothing I knew would ever stand up in court, but it didn't have to. It was good enough for me.

I had missed my wife over the last few days, and turning the doorknob to go into the house, I imagined briefly what our reunion would be like. Surely, I would open the door and be met with my soul mate wearing a tight white blouse and dark blue jeans. Her hair would be disheveled in the most beautiful way I had ever seen. Her lipstick would be perfect and she would smell like vanilla. Before I could get both feet into the house, she would plant a passionate kiss on my lips and say, "No need for words. Take me upstairs and make love to me. I've missed you so much. I couldn't stay away." I would do so, and we would explore each other until late the next morning. She would tell me that she was lucky to have a man like me and I would agree wholeheartedly.

I held on to that fantasy up until the moment I actually started turning the doorknob. What I was greeted with when she yanked the door open—nearly taking my hand off with the knob—was slightly less than I had hoped for.

"Where the hell have you been? I've been calling you for hours! I saw the news! That's the girl, right? Virginia Richmond? And Randy? Why was Randy there? They said he was shot! What happened? Are you alright? Do you know how worried I was? Why the hell didn't you answer your phone? I caught a glimpse of it on the TV and I started driving home! Why didn't you answer your phone? Why did someone kill that girl? Is it because of that flash drive? Did Randy have something to do with it? What happened to your hair? Are you bleeding? Is that a new bruise?"

At least she was wearing a tight blouse.

The deluge of questions dwindled to a stream and finally a trickle. I told her I was fine and took her by the hand into the living room. She sat on the couch with one arm pressed against the pillow that Detective Hartz had lifted a short while before. I paced through the living room and stayed silent. She could tell that if her usually articulate husband was struggling to assemble his thoughts into words, then something was definitely off.

Sigmund took up a position at Kaitlyn's feet and listened to inclemency settle around us. One of the most overused phrases in the English language has to be *love of my life*. But in this case it was absolutely true. From the moment I met her, Kaitlyn had been the most important thing in my life. She was my protection from having the empty pit of regret that so many people have when they take their last breath. I counted myself lucky to have wasted less than three decades before I found the greatest treasure I could ever have sought. To lie to her on this day would have been to lie to her forever. I couldn't do that.

I told her everything.

I told her what I had done.

I told her who was behind it all.

Regret, hesitation, ambivalence—those were feelings I had repressed until then. When I saw her start to cry, that's when the totality of everything hit me. I could tell she was half-crying out of concern for me and half-crying out of anger at the entire situation. I started getting choked up myself as I watched her accept the bitter realities one by one. What I had acclimated to over the course of a few weeks, I was now asking her to absorb in one sitting.

She wiped her eyes and without looking at me, she asked, "You can't come clean with the police, can you?"

"No. I don't have the level of evidence they need. Besides . . . too much blood on me."

"So, he's just going to get away with it? All of this?"

I tried to look out a window, but caught only my own reflection.

"No," I said quietly to her. Or to me.

When no other sounds came from the couch, I turned and looked straight at her. She looked up at me with eyes that were wet stones, drying out in the desert sun. Our eyes latched onto each other for an immortal moment.

She disrupted the visual exchange long enough to pick up the scotch I had left on the end table, and finish it off with an impressive swig. When they projected back in my direction, her blue-gray eyes were hardened steel.

With the sincerity of a wrecking ball, she said, "You have to do it smart. You can't get caught."

Taking a seat beside her, I told her my plan.

Mile 23

My shoulder throbs and my lungs burn as I summon all the energy I've tried to conserve by running at a slower than normal pace. Weaving around two runners who look to be on the brink, I take care to do it gradually enough not to attract attention. I don't know these runners.

I passed two of the men who were involved in this mess long ago. Neither is innocent, but neither of them is the one who set the wheels in motion. Slipping by people unnoticed isn't difficult when the streets are wide and eyes are filled with sweat. I won't be slipping by the next one.

Far ahead in the distance, skating near the center line—there he is.

He's on the route.

His guard is down.

He shouldn't have let his guard down.

Around the time he comes fully into focus, I pass a sign announcing the irony of the situation. The uncomplicated marker tells me we're passing through FRIENDSHIP.

—◦◦◦—

When the phone rang on Monday, I had been cooling down from a painful eighteen-mile run. The marathon was less than a week away, and although I hadn't been able to train the way I would have liked, I felt I was ready. The voice on the phone was that of Beatrice Holbrook. With all of her usual pleasantness, she informed me I was reinstated and expected back at work the following day. Her words were more of a demand than an invitation, and I could tell she had really been hoping to speak to an answering machine.

Not being one who wants to end calls on a negative note, in the most congenial voice I could muster I said, "Why, thank you so much *Mrs*. Holbrook. It is always wonderful to speak with you. And might I add, you *look* lovely today."

She cackled back, "What in the world are you talking about, Keller? You haven't seen me today. And it's *Ms*. Holbrook."

"Oh, it wouldn't be if I would have met you years ago, you sly minx."

She hung up. Rhetoric is a lost art.

There had been no word about my gun. For a nationally publicized homicide, the lab must have rolled out the red carpet for its arrival, but I still hadn't heard from the boys in blue. If I were them, I would let me sweat a while too.

On Tuesday, I decided to skip stopping by my office, instead reporting directly to a classroom full of uneasiness. The messages I had left with the graduate student who had been teaching my classes had gone unanswered, so I asked the students in my first class where they left off. After a long, nervous delay, I finally got an answer and picked up the lessons from that point. The tautness in the class was unbearable. Several seats were empty and I had received email notices that a few students had dropped the course. The combination of the killings and my newfound reputation as Dr. Death was creating a less-than-optimal learning environment. Regardless, the semester would be over in a few days and perhaps everybody could step back and reset. From the thorny expressions I observed in the classroom, I concluded that it would probably be a good idea for me to get a fresh start somewhere else.

After class, I went to my office and the sun beamed through my window as I tried to decipher some notes left behind by my timid substitute. The ink had smeared across the pages the way that happens when left-handed people write. It took me an hour and two cups of hazelnut coffee before I felt like I was up to speed. The next few minutes consisted of me deleting phone messages from reporters who wanted to get a comment from me. I had screened my phone calls at home since the story broke nationally, and persistent journalists had taken to calling my work number as well. I was only a minor part of the story, and not demonized in the least, but it was still an aggravation I didn't need.

While deleting the twelfth message, there was a knock on my door. Fearing that a reporter had decided to pay me a personal visit, I stayed seated and hoped for the best. Along with the second knock came a question.

"Cyprus? You in there?"

Without getting up, I told Aaron to come in.

My two cups of coffee paled in comparison to whatever Aaron had in his system. His eyes darted around the room like they were following an angry fly, and he tapped his right forefinger and thumb together rapidly like he was transmitting Morse code.

"Hey . . . Cyprus. I wanted . . . I just wanted to come by and see how you were doin'. A lot of crazy stuff around . . . We've missed you on the runs. Not the same without you . . . and now Randy. The papers say that he may have fired the gun that killed that police officer. Doesn't make sense, does it? You think you know somebody and . . . WHAM! Out of left field, there it is."

I waited to speak, in the hope that his eyes would settle on me. For a brief moment they did, and I could see his pupils. They were dark saucers that were taking in too much for the mind to handle. If I had to guess, I would have said that at least one of Aaron's reasons for obtaining psychiatric treatment was for manic-depressive disorder. Mr. Manic was the one speaking to me now in staccato sentences and fidgeting madly.

"How have you been, Aaron? Have you been holding up okay?"

"Yeah . . . you know, you do what you can. Ever since that Lindsay got killed . . . ever since then, it's just been one thing after another. She goes and gets killed and all hell breaks . . . well, we've got jobs to do, you know? How do they expect us to do that when people are getting smoked? Randy . . . you know, he wasn't a bad guy. Sure, he was kind of a prick sometimes, but not all the time. I just don't know what . . ."

I politely pushed my way into the conversation with, "The semester's almost over. If you aren't working the summer session, maybe you and Debbie can get away from here for a while. Take a vacation. Maybe take that new boat out. Come back in the fall with a fresh perspective."

"Oh, that would be a real treat!" Aaron's hinges came off. "Sit in a car with her pecking away at me the entire time! And she won't get on the damn boat! Seasick! For twenty years she never got seasick, and now she says she gets seasick when we're out on a small lake! Doesn't make sense, does it? I don't think . . . I know she's not sick. She sits at her damn book club, sipping tea, bragging about how her big dope of a husband thinks she can't go out on the boat because she gets *seasick*!"

I let my right hand find a desk drawer where I kept a pair of scissors. Silently, I wrapped my fingers around their wide base.

"That's what they do! They talk and ridicule . . . soooo superior. Soooo condescending. And if you don't agree with them one hundred percent, then there's something wrong with you! *You* need to adjust. *You* need to see your . . . *You* have to give in to their demands! When you've been married as long as I have, you'll see. You'll see . . ."

The last sentence trailed off as he drew in a breath. With the influx of air, came a change in disposition.

"You're still going to run the race, right?" he said. "It should be a good one. The weather is supposed to be great!"

Aaron's switch had again flipped, and it was as if we had been discussing what type of sealant was best for a wooden deck. He was halfway out the door before I could answer him.

Releasing the hidden scissors, I assured him, "I'll be looking out for you."

Mile 24

Pulling my sunglasses back down from the top of my head, I leave Friendship and charge into Bloomfield on Liberty Avenue. Houses vanish as some of the last independent drugstores hang on to real estate pressed between car dealerships and bakeries. Bloomfield could be a snapshot from 1975. Even the Starbucks is embedded in a building that used to serve as a movie theater. Pubs on each corner pledge freedom while a magistrate's office promises consequences.

Just as I had hoped, he's right where I need him to be. His stride is powerful and purposeful, but I have pent-up fury at my back. Just like clockwork, he's done exactly what I expected him to do. Making the exact movements I had envisioned so many times over the past few days, he carries on unsuspectingly. From behind the tint of my shades, I take him in and observe the man run down the hill, past deserted sidewalks on a street where most of the thinned-out runners are spread out in gaping intervals.

The course map had spelled it all out. This was the perfect place. There is a wide spacing between medical stations and few spectators who would notice or be ready to assist him. Any serious spectators have already gravitated to the finish line. Really—who cares about the twenty-fourth mile? It's the finish that people live for.

My heart skips a beat when he slows down. First to a jog, then to a walk. Even from a comfortable distance behind him, I can feel his entire being radiate *distress*. He walks past a few locals who are too busy waving at their neighbors from across the street to notice the man pass them. Out of habit, and traditional runners' courtesy, he moves to the right side of the road to give any pursuing runners a wide berth. I slow down even more, but not so anyone would notice.

One stumble forward, one to the side. He's in limbo between the street and the sidewalk—the purgatory of dry grass seems to slow him even more. Next, he's on one knee with one hand clutching at his throat and another waving above his head. Pure hope that someone will notice him. *I* notice him.

Finally, he puts himself on his back and continues to raise an arm. He turns his head toward a little African-American girl in a church dress. She's holding her mother's hand and seems anxious to leave. Her mother is oblivious and converses with a heavyset woman in blue nurse's scrubs. He raises his hand, pleading. The tiny girl waves back and giggles.

Before I reach him, an elderly Korean man bends down beside him. The Korean man is trying to ask him if he's alright, but the sick runner can't seem to respond. Words won't come. The Good Samaritan says something to the woman in scrubs and she runs over to her new patient. I can tell from the way her lips are moving, and the exaggerated head bobs, that she's trying to get answers from him and she's not having any luck. The nurse turns toward the little girl's mother and I see the woman dig in her purse for a cell phone. She finds it and dials. Then the nurse speaks to the Korean man, who starts running toward the next medical station. It's too far away. I know. It's on the map. I've done my homework.

I drift to the right side of the street and drop my speed down one more gear.

Turn.
Look at me, you bastard!
This direction! She can't help you! Look in this direction!

As if he could hear me, his red, puffy, weakened neck surrenders and his hive-covered face is unveiled to the street. He looks blankly toward the loose gravel around a storm drain and then up at me. Without breaking stride, I raise my glasses and silently confess. Before the race, I told myself I would smile at him, adding insult to mortal injury, but I don't. I can't. I'm ending his life and he knows it. There is no further insult needed.

Just as I pull past him, his jaw falls open and awareness leaves his body. His respiratory system has failed him. His throat is closed. The arm he had placed across his chest slides down and off of its lifeless table. As concerned citizens start to form a circle around him, I can still see his arm dangling off the curb.

Feeling a little lighter, and a lot heavier, I pull the sunglasses down again, and continue at the same pace. No rush now. It is a beautiful day for a run.

—◦◦◦—

It was the Friday before the race and a spring rain had blown in from the west. It would be a few weeks until the cold rain would be replaced by turbulent thunderstorms. The structure hosting the school's athletic facilities and the surrounding fields were nearly empty as most students and professors focused on final exams and made plans for adventurous summer trips.

From the laughable shelter of a half-bare tree, I watched the front of the recreation building and waited for him to arrive. Right on schedule, he ran to the front steps and checked the device on his wrist. He surmounted the steps leading up to the entrance with easy bounds.

Aaron was nowhere to be seen. It turned out that in the morning some thug had walked into the parking garage and committed some terrible acts of vandalism on his car. What a shame. He was going to be very busy talking to campus security and his insurance company for quite some time. That garage was becoming a very dangerous place.

When the right amount of time had passed, I flashed my university ID to a student employee who never looked up, and entered the locker room. I turned to my left and waited near my usual spot.

Jacob had a white towel around him when he appeared at the lockers. A drop of water from the shower was still clinging to his earlobe when he saw me sitting in front of my locker. The false display of perfectly white teeth was a nanosecond too late.

"Cyprus! Where have you been hiding? I've left you several messages! I thought you would be at Randy's funeral, but I didn't see you there."

"I've been busy."

The coldness of my voice caused his mouth to straighten out, and he retracted a hand he had expected me to shake.

"It's understandable not wanting to go to a funeral, but it does help us deal with our grief on some level. We need closure more than we realize," he said matter-of-factly.

"True."

I started to stand and then stepped forward and delivered a strong punch to his stomach, taking care to miss any ribs. A gust of wind escaped him and he stumbled back onto another bench. He tried to speak, but nothing was forthcoming.

"I wonder what your next move was going to be," I said. "Were you going to manipulate Aaron into coming after me? Drop him a message? Convince him that I was out to get him? You must have picked up on the fact that he's unstable, so taking advantage of his mental state had to have been one of your better options."

A cough from the bench told me that air was starting to flow back into him.

"I'll admit it. You had me running in circles for a while. You had everybody running in circles. It stops now."

Gasping, Jacob pleaded, "Cyprus. I didn't . . . I don't know what you're talking about."

"Don't! Don't even think about trying to spin this. Steven would have done anything for you. He killed Lindsay for you! He tried to kill *me* for you!"

"You . . . you're confused. I didn't even know Steven. Why would he—"

I lowered my voice and said, "You knew him very well. You've known him for years. I did some snooping around. It had never occurred to me that his first two years of undergraduate work weren't in Criminology . . . he was a Psych major right here at TRU. In fact, he took several of your classes."

Jacob tightened the towel around his waist and held a hand over his stomach.

"I wonder, how long were you seeing Lindsay before you introduced her to Steven? And don't waste my time denying that you were sleeping with Lindsay. She was in one of your classes. You called her a blonde when every photo of her used by the media showed her with dark hair. Your lies are your admission."

I balled my right hand up a little tighter and prepared to hit him again at the first indication of a denial. To my surprise, I didn't get one.

"You can't blame Steven. He was only trying to protect me. To protect my reputation. He was a brilliant student and I took him under my wing. He was dedicated to me. I mentored him and he looked up to me like a father. Did you know that his father died when he was just a boy? A drunk driver hit him head on. Steven never got over it. I served as a surrogate for his father. I didn't see how his loyalty to me had gotten to the point that he was irrational until it was too late."

His eyes filled with tears.

"It's my fault. I had come to realize what a bastard I had been and I told Lindsay that I was breaking off the relationship. Since Tabatha's death, I had become a lonely man. I let the loneliness get the best of me with Lindsay. At first, she came on to me, but I wasn't naïve enough to think a beautiful girl that age would naturally be attracted to one of her professors. Despite what you may think, I'm not a complete narcissist."

Yeah . . . really, a guy would have to be pretty full of himself to . . .

"I asked her what she was up to—why she was acting like she was attracted to me. After a while, she told me about a project she was working on. She planned on exposing the degenerates and hypocrites who are taking over academia while getting famous in the process. I won't bore you with the details, but I was fascinated with her boldness. I didn't discourage her in the least. In fact, I told her it would be better received as an academic piece rather than some internet sensation. She asked me to help her with her work and I agreed.

"Needless to say," Jacob dropped his head, "over time, I became what I was hoping to help root out. Words aren't enough to express my shame."

Dripping from the showers in the next room filled a few seconds. Jacob snapped back from a moment of introspection.

"When Steven heard Lindsay's conversation with you, he showed up at my home and told me about it. He was convinced she was going to expose my relationship with her. He told me my career would be over and my name would be tarnished forever. I told him to let it go. I told him I would try to reason with her. He told me that he was going to try to scare her. We fought about it, and in the end he stormed out of the house and sped off."

Jacob held his head in his hands and sobbed openly.

"He showed up again later that night and his arm was bleeding. He told me what had happened. Steven had looked up Lindsay's address and gone down there. He went to her apartment to talk to her. Lindsay was determined to ruin me and she told him so. Things got out of control, and Steven said the next thing he knew she was dead on the floor and his hands were around her neck. He used a duffle bag he found in her apartment to carry her body to his car. Then he dumped her body in the Hill District, figuring she would be written off as the victim of some drug dealer."

I unclenched my hands and took a step back.

"And you didn't think to call the police?"

"How could I? He was like a son to me. Much like I feel about you sometimes."

I leaned down and said, "The last time I saw him, he didn't seem to be in a brotherly mood."

"I don't know what he was thinking. His protective instincts had turned into the most dangerous kind of obsession. Steven said that we couldn't chance that Lindsay had talked to you after he left your office. He said that there was a chance that she could have told you everything. I told him I wouldn't turn him in for killing Lindsay. I knew I was the real reason she was dead, and Steven going to prison wouldn't bring her back. It was a terrible mistake, but I selfishly thought we could get past it if we sat back and did nothing. I told Steven that if he harmed you, I would have no choice but to go to the police and tell them everything. He calmed down, and by the time he left my house he had convinced me that he had regained his senses."

"So you were obviously mortified when you found out that Steven had tried to kill me."

"More than I can ever say. My sorrow was twofold: Steven was dead, and he died while attacking my good friend. But at that point, my going to the authorities wouldn't have done anybody any good. Steven had sinned, and unfortunately, you had to be the one to deliver the inevitable retribution."

Calmly, I said, "And if I would have faced criminal charges for killing Steven, you would have come forward, right?"

"Of course! I couldn't let you be punished for my mistakes."

Walking a slow circle around Jacob, I asked, "And what about Randy?"

Jacob turned around and followed me with a confused look.

"I don't know exactly what he was up to. The only thing I can figure is that Randy had succumbed to Lindsay's advances while she worked on her project. Randy must have thought that either Lindsay left some of her work in the apartment—or perhaps her roommate came across something and threatened to expose Randy. I think we have to assume that Randy killed the roommate."

"Her name was Virginia."

"Virginia," he said as if he were uttering the opening syllables of a eulogy.

He withdrew his focus from the name and said, "As to who killed Randy, I have no idea."

"That's an easy one. I did."

Jacob's neck twisted unnaturally and revealed a look of horror as he slung it around to watch me walk behind him.

"Wha . . . why?"

"I really didn't have much choice. He was about to give me a pretty serious case of suicide."

"I don't understand why you were even there, but I'm not going to judge you, Cyprus. You've always shown strong moral character. More than I have, I'm afraid. I'm sure you did what you had to do. As far as I'm concerned, your secret never has to leave this room. If you feel you need to tell the world about my relationship with Lindsay, then I'll understand. No matter what, I'll never tell a soul about what you have just revealed to me."

My series of circles came to an end right in front of the weeping genius. His eyes were puffy and he was the picture of emotional atrophy.

"My God, Jacob."

"I know. I'm so—"

"You—are—a—complete—fucking—sociopath."

The puffy eyes sought clarification. I stared down and provided it.

"Let me give you another version of events. We'll put this one on the *nonfiction* shelf."

My orbit resumed, but in the opposite direction.

"You were having an affair with Lindsay. You got that part right. After that, your facts are a little shaky. And I don't doubt that you were very close to Steven. In fact, I'm sure of it. The guy who told me about Steven being a Psych major was very helpful in that respect. He told me that during his freshman year, Steven talked constantly about the brilliant mind and extraordinary talents of one of his professors. This guy told me that it didn't take him long to figure out that Steven was head-over-heels in love with this professor. At first this was very upsetting to this fellow, since he and Steven were lovers. But over the years the man learned he was going to have to share Steven, if he wanted to have any kind of relationship with him. My new friend says that he's always been a big believer in practicing monogamy, but he became very tolerant of Steven's divided attentions because he wanted him to be happy.

"Up until your sicko-protégé's death, this guy got together with Steven only occasionally, but he always cared about him. Now, I've only seen this guy twice, but he sure seems like the honest type. The first time I saw him he was kissing Steven at the front door of his townhouse. The second time was when I recently found the house again and he opened the door and tried to punch me. It turns out that he's pretty mad about Steven being dead. So much so, that once I calmed him down and told him a story about a sneaky, manipulative man who turned Steven into a coldblooded killer, he came around nicely. Chris . . . that's his name, Chris Monroe, and Steven talked openly about you when it was just the two of them. Chris didn't like discussing you, but he really loved Steven, so he put up with it."

"Cyprus," Jacob said as he craned his neck, "Steven was like the child I never had. You can't possibly think I was romantically involved with him, whatever some *associate* of Steven has told you."

"Because you wouldn't lie to me?"

"I know I've been less than honest with you up until now, but I was hoping we could put it all behind us." Jacob wiped an eye that didn't need the attention.

Briefly pausing in my steps, I said gravely, "I'm not done."

My sole audience member resumed listening.

"I went looking for Chris only because I wanted to make sure I hadn't missed anything. Up until that point, I had missed way too much, but I finally got it. It was the lecture that sealed it for me."

Jacob waited. He stopped tracking me and was simply looking straight ahead.

"You were the only person who I told about the time of death. I told you what the cops told me—nine thirty. I told you I

-- 218 --

had a solid alibi because I was at the lecture. The lecture dealing with cognitive ability in apes. The lecture that I still have a program for—it's at home next to the couch. The small print on the bottom of the cover says it all: SPONSORED BY THE TRU DEPARTMENT OF PSYCHOLOGY. For events like that, the sponsoring organization maintains all of the attendance records. Records that would go straight to the head of the department. Records that would have gone to you. I didn't think much of it when my name wasn't on that list, but I'm sure thinking about it now. You took my name off that list and eliminated my alibi.

"Maybe Steven had given you enough details that you thought that the cops had gotten the T.O.D. wrong—maybe he didn't. Either way, you had no qualms about leaving me out there as a suspect for Lindsay's murder. It was just bad luck for you that I was covered for the real T.O.D., which was two and a half hours earlier than I had told you."

I was behind Jacob when I finished this point, talking to the back of his head. As I rotated back into his view, a maniacal grin was stretched across his face. The fake tears were gone. My feet froze when he looked at me.

"Very good. Very, very good."

Mile 25

Two EMTs carrying backpacks run past me in the opposite direction. They are speaking loudly into the radio, trying to identify the problem. They'll need a Ouija board if they want to hear anything from the casualty behind me. This time the water station gets my full attention. I wash down my usual triangle of sugar and carbohydrates, and take care to thank the volunteer this go-round. Several police officers are blocking the usually busy intersections, insuring my safe passage. Unknowingly, lining the streets for a murderer. From a third-story window, a shirtless man peers out and is holding a loud conversation with a man passing in front of his building. The man in the window starts to tell a joke, but now I'm too far away to hear the punch line.

——❧——

Jacob stood and walked over to his locker. Pulling out several articles of clothing, he began getting dressed.

He asked, "Anything else?"

"V." I answered.

"What?"

"Virginia."

"I think we can safely assume that Randy killed that poor girl. We could ask him, but you seemed to have made that impossible."

"I did ask him."

"And?"

"And you killed her."

"He told you that? I don't think so."

"It's the only logical conclusion. Let's put aside the fact that Randy was so disgusted by his own sweaty clothes, and anything else dirty, he most likely wouldn't have been able to go swimming in blood the way you did."

I fought back vomit as I said the words.

"The files on the memory stick were a well-kept secret. V knew about them and she told me. When I gave the flash drive back to her, she was still debating what to do with it. Anger got the better of her and she opened up the files. She must have read the documents and listened to the recordings."

Jacob said nothing and continued to dress. If he acknowledged that he knew about the files, he was confessing to murder.

"I asked myself, what would have been the most upsetting thing that she would have seen in those files? Her best friend was gone forever. Lindsay had been involved with an older man and V didn't approve. Steven was already dead and she wanted somebody to pay. She didn't care about academic fraud, professors going to treatment centers, or even about your pal Silo and his checkered past. The recording of you and Lindsay was the one thing that would have made her do something rash. She picked up the phone and called you. I don't think she was the extorting type, so what did she say?"

Jacob walked over to the mirror and, with the confidence of a king, straightened a sky blue tie. I looked on from the background.

His reversed image told me, "Young girls are so wonderfully innocent. She told me she hated me for taking advantage of Lindsay. She said that she didn't know if I had anything to do with Steven killing Lindsay, but part of her wanted to see me burn for taking advantage of my position. She told me about the flash drive, the recordings—everything. She said her first instinct was to release the information, right then and there."

"And you talked her out of it," I saw myself say.

"I didn't even have to. I said she told me that *part* of her wanted to see me burn. The other part seems to have been quite the pacifist. She told me she would give me an opportunity to resign from the university before she sent the files to Lindsay's blogger friends who run the scandal sites that Lindsay wanted to be a part of. I used my best humbled-and-humiliated voice and begged her to give me twenty-four hours. And like I said . . . young girls can be so wonderfully innocent."

"You could have just stolen it." I growled. "You tortured and killed her."

I felt something inside me coming apart.

"Proof or no proof, you know she would have shouted my private affairs out from the rooftops. I couldn't let that happen. People would have asked too many questions; and the next thing you know, they're digging around and probably find out about Steven and me."

He turned from the mirror and returned to the locker to pick up his belongings.

He said, "You still haven't got it all figured out, have you?"

"If you mean, how the relationship worked among all three of you, and why Steven thought Lindsay was going to expose you—I have a theory."

"Do tell," was all he said.

"Lindsay was outgoing and flirty, but she was essentially traditional in her beliefs. I don't think she knew about you and Steven in the beginning."

"Go on," Jacob prompted.

"According to the police, Steven was into some pretty unorthodox behavior. One of the things the cops mentioned finding at Steven's apartment were photos of group sex. Chris Monroe confirmed that Steven was always trying to get him on board with having others join them. I figure you're probably twice as arrogant as Steven ever was, so trying to pull Lindsay into that world would seem like a simple task to you."

Continuing the thought, I said, "The way Lindsay and Steven looked at each other in my office that day, it was a nauseating awkwardness that hit her, not frustration with me. She was so uncomfortable at the sight of Steven that she bolted out of the room the first chance she got. Since you obviously enjoy having men and women, I think you introduced Lindsay to Steven and tried to work out a nice little threesome. You must have been pretty steamed when she told you to go to hell."

With a chuckle, Jacob said, "I have to admit, she didn't handle it well. People think that today's young people are ultra-liberal sex addicts, but I think in many ways they are more reserved."

"And Tabatha? I suppose your marriage went to hell because she knew you were a freak. How did you manage to get her to stay with you all these years?"

"Tabatha was actually very tolerant of my occasional . . . indiscretions with men. She understood I had needs that she couldn't possibly meet. It was when she started suspecting that I was sneaking off to see other women—that's when things went downhill."

"Did she really die of an aneurysm, or did you take her out too?"

"That was a bit of good fortune, I suppose. I was tiring of her company and she was becoming less understanding of my needs. Fate intervened and I didn't have to lift a finger."

Smugly, Jacob looked at his watch and said, "You seem to have pretty much nailed down everything. I really have to be getting to class. Is there anything you're still fuzzy on?"

"Just two things," I said while stepping closer to him. "Did you send Steven after Lindsay and me, or did he do it on his own?"

"I simply told Steven that if I was publicly raked over the coals, then I would have to leave this town and our relationship would be over. Steven . . ." Jacob searched for the right words, "chose what he thought was the best course of action."

I edged closer to him.

"You said there were two things," Jacob reminded me.

"Obviously, you talked to Silo before I had my meeting with him. How involved is he?"

"Silo is a good friend," was all he would say.

I grabbed the lapels of Jacob's suit and slammed him against the lockers.

"You're getting sloppy, Jacob. I could be wearing a wire. I could have all of this on tape."

Shoving me back with surprising strength, he said, "You have already told me you were the one who shot Randy. The police may buy that you killed one man in self-defense, but two . . . ? No, I don't think you can afford to gamble on that."

He was right. They would crucify me.

"I suppose the flash drive is long gone. What did you do, drop it off the side of your new boat?"

"So, Lindsay mentioned that to somebody, did she? You try and try to tell a girl that secrets are everything, but in the end, who can you really trust? I tend not to flaunt things like our friend Aaron does, but it is a beautiful boat. As for the flash drive, no reason for me to hold on to it," he said. "What would I do with it? Blackmail my colleagues?" With a cocky flash of teeth, he added, "I'm not a monster."

He slipped into a raincoat and drew it around him.

"Now, if I were you, I would try to put all of this behind me. No reason for this to drag on. And you should have a talk with Monroe. Tell him you were wrong. I would hate to have to stop by his place to have a fireside chat."

I had already told Monroe to get out of town for a few days, but Jacob couldn't have known that.

Throwing all of his gear into a gym bag and walking toward the door, Jacob left me with one last piece of advice.

"You seem stressed, my boy. You should keep your options open. This job isn't for everybody."

The locker room door swung closed and sealed in too many secrets. Making my own exit, I reached into my jacket pocket and withdrew the contents. After making sure to wipe off any fingerprints, I tossed the contents into a trash can. The rustle of discarded paper towels cushioned my crime.

Mile 26

There is a half block between me and any other runner. A few pockets of people are grouped on the corners. They are holding their four-dollar coffees and chew on day-old pastries. A few people throw me some applause when I pass them. If they only knew.

I find myself wondering how many of the people here, given the same circumstances, would have done what I have done. If the truth was placed in front of them, how many would understand the necessity of my actions? This is a hardened city where statues of miners, steelworkers, firefighters, soldiers, and police officers tarnish but never disappear. It's a city that can be short on compassion, but understands justice. The people here cheer for the virtuous and damn the wicked. How would they view me?

The Strip District looks much different now than it did when I passed through so long ago. Discarded paper cups and pools of water line sparsely populated streets that, much like the legs running on them, are no longer fresh. The echoes of the sign-holding crowds no longer reverberate off the antiquated store-fronts. It's a post-parade street waiting for the cleaning crews to arrive. The war is over. We won. Now we slog through the confetti and live with what we have done.

Lonely pockets of people are on each side of the road, hobbling toward me. Couples and families pat the backs of loved ones with drained faces who left everything they had at the finish line. They slowly make their journeys to parked cars where dry clothes and ibuprofen await. A husband admires his wife's finisher's medal that she couldn't care less about right now, but will proudly hang up later. It doesn't matter whether it was the full-marathon, the half, or the relay. Covering the distance is everything.

A father and son sit on the front steps of a nightclub that was once a church. The man squints down Penn Avenue hoping to spot some loved one. The boy is too small to see in a crowd, so they are avoiding the smothering finish line area. They'll wait here in the quiet. For the first time in an eternity, I hear my own footsteps underneath my breathing. Steps and breaths. That's what I've been reduced to. Once you sort through the detritus and tune out all the static, that's all that's left. Steps and breaths.

Like a drowning sailor being hoisted up to a helicopter by a rope, I can feel the crowd pulling me in. The incoherent collection of noise from the convention center becomes louder and louder with every few strides. A cocoon of full grandstands and rocking bicycle racks are imploring me to find a way—*any* way to let them embrace me. It makes no difference to anybody there that the winner of the marathon finished long before me. For these few moments, I may as well be running into a stadium to claim my Olympic gold.

All of these people have become fans. They aren't my personal fans. They clap and yell for anybody who passes by and once that person moves on, they drop them from memory and turn their adulation to the next unknown. It should feel shallow, but it doesn't. The applause is genuine. The excitement is real. Most of them will walk away not knowing why they are still hemorrhaging exhilaration, and most of these people will never get to know the feeling I'm experiencing now. Less than one percent of people ever run a marathon. Perhaps less than one percent of people have ever really lived.

—————

I said that I was going to kill someone during the race. It probably would have been more accurate for me to say that I killed someone the Friday before. While I was waiting for Jacob to finish his shower, I busied myself by inspecting his running belt that was always stored in the locker we shared. As he had done countless times before, Jacob had finished his run and loaded his gel packs for his next run—in this case, Sunday's marathon. Until then, the belt would sit untouched, somewhere in Jacob's house or car, since Saturday is always a rest day. The five packs were neatly arranged in their assigned slots until Jacob pulled them out one at a time at designated points in the event. The fifth pack would be the last one of his life.

How many times had he harped on me to properly refuel during a long run? He had it all figured out. He would go straight down his line of gel packs, from right to left, like a home inspector working his way down a checklist. Mile 5. Mile 9. Mile 13. Mile 17. Mile 24. The only thing I had worried about was him grabbing the wrong pack at the wrong time, perhaps in front of the UPMC medical center, or switching out the packs before the race; but true to his habitual nature, Jacob would be deadly accurate.

Walking through the rain, I thought about all I had done and what it all meant. I thought about my job and where my life was going. I thought about Kaitlyn. I thought about the lovely psychologist who volunteers her time at the children's hospital. I thought about her trusted celebrity status there, and how she basically had free reign while she went from room to room counseling families. I thought about how she somehow had been able to pick up an unattended vial of liquid penicillin and a syringe. In a children's hospital, those items are as commonplace as pop-up books. If a vial of the usually innocuous antibiotic was found to be missing, the hospital certainly wouldn't investigate too carefully.

Then I thought about how Jacob would consume his tainted gel when his heart would be racing, his blood would be pumping wildly, and his physical abilities would be strained to the max. I could practically see him squeezing the liquid into his mouth and mindlessly tossing the pack onto the side of the road with the thousands of other packs and cups that would be swept away hours later. I thought about how he would make it only a few yards before he realized that something was wrong. I contemplated how I expected him to die immediately. The entire process should normally take several minutes, but in Jacob's exhausted state, death would come quickly. Finally, I wondered what was wrong with me.

I was fine.

.2

Nobody can really explain it. You are completely tapped out of energy and every fiber of your being is telling you that you aren't going to make it. Even visions of crawling to the finish line and reaching out for it like it's an oasis in the desert seem unrealistic. Then, with no fathomable explanation, you find a barbaric source of power usually reserved for cornered animals.

With the end in sight, my legs are churning relentlessly, although I don't remember asking them to take on this terrible task. My arms are pumping harder and I stand a little straighter. The ground scrolls beneath me. I'm not in control now. It's something else.

Not once have I been one of those people who break down at the end of a race, and the lump in my throat is unnerving to me. I have tried my best to balance the scales, but the loss feels so much greater than the gain. The deafening ovations from those around me aren't loud enough to soften the screams of the dead. Fighting back tears, I find myself engaged in a final sprint against an invisible competitor. The line is moving toward me— faster and faster. Unwittingly, I let out a guttural cry of pain, frustration, and finality. Leaning forward, I'm crashing through an imaginary barrier and arms reach out to slow me down.

Somebody wraps a crinkly blanket around me and my hand suddenly holds a sports drink. A faceless woman who is shorter than I am is trying to put a medal around my neck. She keeps repeating something I can't understand, but when I lean over and the medal slides into place, she is pacified. Getting my bearings, I follow a line of people through a corral where cookies and watermelon slices are ravaged as if this is a food drop at a refugee camp. Beyond the commotion is a small plaza shielded by the overhang of the convention center. People are walking in every direction, finding family members or looking for a place to sit. One face is still. She sees me and we are walking to meet each other. I'm telling her that it's over. She's saying that she loves me.

This is my favorite part of the entire journey.

EPILOGUE

The majority of the students vanished along with the semester. The school barely had time to mourn its latest loss before the dorm rooms emptied and the classrooms became empty shells. The unexplained death of Dr. Jacob Kasko was a final slap in the face to a university that had endured too much. Tear-jerking words were spoken, cards were sent, and another funeral I wouldn't attend was held. The media gave little attention to Jacob's death, and any time they did mention him in *The Bloody 'Burgh* stories, it was only as an aside. Another tragedy for a small school, but not really newsworthy. People die during marathons. It just happens.

Wearing old jeans and a brown leather jacket, I walked into the Whitlock Building where the most senior university employees were packing up their desks for the summer while the newer staff members looked on with intense jealousy. I headed right for a sign that read DEAN CLYDE SILO—ACADEMIC AFFAIRS.

I passed through the first door and into the dim waiting area. Beatrice Holbrook was coiled behind a stack of files on her desk. She elevated to a state of high alert when she saw me enter the empty waiting area. Without acknowledging her, I took a direct path toward the entrance that she so carefully protected. Her chair screeched angrily as she rose up and attempted to block me from the door. As always, she wore a crooked scowl, but her usual air of superiority was somehow lacking.

"He's not available. You need to make an appointment like everybody else," she said as she backed up against the door, made her arms parallel to the floor, blocking my path.

"Beatrice," I said coolly, with an underlying maliciousness, "get out of my way before I rip your arms off and use them to knock out what's left of those decayed fangs that you call teeth."

The arms lowered, the little bit of blood in her face drained away, and she obediently slinked back behind her desk. Apparently, killing a graduate assistant with my bare hands was having a positive effect on my ability to communicate with people.

Pushing the door open, I found Silo using his index fingers to perform wrathful acupuncture on a masochistic keyboard. He turned a shade of green when I walked up to his desk.

"What do you want? I'm busy. Make an appointment."

"Six-month paid sabbatical. No, you aren't. And my appointment is right now."

His face was turning from green to red. I suddenly felt Christmassy.

"Have you lost your mind? You're lucky you still have a job! If it were up to—"

"It's not. I'll also need a glowing letter of recommendation. You can leave the date blank; I'll fill it in later if I need it. Consider it your last official act before you resign."

Silo stood up and raised his head to look up at me. He moved back from his desk to minimize the effect.

"I'm not giving you anything! Get out of here now or I'll have you arrested!"

I leaned over and picked up his phone.

"The number is 9-1-1. Want me to dial?"

"My God, you really have gone mad. If you don't get out of here, I swear I'll—"

"Maybe we should dial 4-1-1 instead. They can probably give me the number for the Dry Creek Charter Service in Arizona."

He lowered the finger that he had been pointing at me and swallowed hard.

"I don't know—"

"Yes, you do. Missing money from a school in California. A sister who owned a small transportation company. A sudden influx of cash. Blah, blah, blah."

"You don't—"

"No, I don't have any proof, but I'm pretty sure that if the cops in California and the feds get together, it won't take long for them to indict you. If someone were to point them in the right direction, that is. Did I mention that there is no statute of limitations on what you did? They can put you away, Silo. They can put you away for a long, long time."

He thought about all of this and I could see him trying to come up with any possible way he could escape this. The sag in his shoulders stipulated some measure of concession.

"White collar cases are tricky. I could get a good lawyer. I could beat it. Hell, I could probably cut a deal and get off with probation and restitution."

He was right. Years had passed. Evidence could have been lost. Witnesses could have moved on or died. Any decent prosecutor would agree that any hopes for a conviction would be slim.

"They don't give probation on felony murder charges."

"I didn't kill anyone! What are you talking about?"

"You unleashed Steven on me. You saw an opportunity to take care of two problems at once. You saw a way to protect your big-money professor and friend, and get rid of me in the process. You sent Steven after me."

"I did no such—"

"How did you schedule your meeting with him, Silo? The day he died, you had an appointment already scheduled with him. I had tried to call him at home that day and got his machine. I even went by his apartment and he was nowhere to be found. Even the cops, with all their resources, couldn't find him, Silo. How was it that you were the only person in the world who seemed to be able to talk to Steven?"

With a shaky hand, Silo picked up a cup of coffee from his desk and took a long sip. He put the mug back down, having delayed long enough to formulate a thought.

"I called his cell phone. People carry cell phones, you know."

"Where did you get the number? It's not listed in the school directory. The police obviously didn't have it either. But somehow, the Dean of Academic Affairs happened to have his cell phone number."

Silo looked everywhere but my direction. He adjusted a suit that covered him like a tarp blankets a car.

"That doesn't mean anything. It doesn't matter how I ended up talking to him. It still doesn't have anything to do with murder."

"Oh, but it does. You see, when you sent Steven to kill me, it was a felony. And here's the best part—when I killed him, *you* became guilty of murder. *You* are responsible for the death that occurred during the commission of a felony. Not me. I was simply defending myself. Sweet deal, huh?"

"You don't have any proof that I told him to do anything! You're bluffing!"

I was exaggerating, but not completely bluffing.

"You see, it doesn't matter. Once the cops start combing through your phone records and ripping your life apart, they are going to come to one of two conclusions. Either you sent Steven to kill me or, at the least, you knew about Jacob's relationship with Steven. The way I see it, that's the only way you could have reached Steven—through Jacob. And if you knew Jacob and Steven had some sort of relationship and you hid that fact even after Steven died—" I made a whooshing sound and shook my head, "then your life will become a living hell. Cops don't like people who keep secrets from them, and I'm pretty sure that they would have talked to you after I killed Steven. Your unwillingness to come clean back then will be foremost on their minds.

"They will say that if you knew about Jacob and Steven, then you probably knew about Jacob and Lindsay. The criminal charges will probably be nothing compared to the lawsuits you will face from Lindsay's parents. Her father is a big-time, cut-throat civil attorney, and I'm sure he'll see to it that you die penniless in a state home for senior citizens. I don't know exactly how it will all play out for you, but on top of an indictment for embezzlement, I'm guessing it won't be good."

The cutthroat attorney thing was total improvisation. I was really feeling it.

"And don't think for a second that I've gotten over the fact that you tried to run me over. I'm still more than a little upset about that, and it's taking all of my strength to restrain myself from beating you senseless right here. But you know what? At this point, I don't even care if it was your idea or Jacob's. Both of you had a vested interest in keeping tabs on me and making sure I didn't learn the truth. So here we are. What's it going to be? Me, out of your hair and you riding off into retirement, or cops, courtrooms, and cameras. I have a pen right here. You can handwrite the letters if typing is too difficult for you."

I couldn't believe it. He actually acted as if he was thinking about it. He turned his back to me and looked out onto the ghost town. His ego just wouldn't allow him to completely surrender to me. I knew he was going to fall into line and so did he. He just had one last petty move to make.

"I need some time to think it over."

"Sure thing. You have until close of business today. Don't take too long; people around here are dropping like flies." In an ominous tone, I added, "Look what happened to Jacob. I wouldn't want anything to happen to you before you write those letters."

Silo turned in time to see me exiting the office for the very last time. Looking over my shoulder, I caught him curiously examining his coffee mug that was not precisely where he had put it down. For some reason, he looked concerned as he stared into the swirling whirlpool of caffeine.

If Beatrice had thought I had lost my mind before I entered Silo's office, the laugh I let out as I walked through the waiting room cemented it for her.

The Silesian Deli provided me with the best lunch I could remember in months. Lemmy had outdone himself. Or Lincoln. The deli guy. When I had finished, I dumped the contents of my tray, including the pen I had used to harmlessly stir Silo's coffee, into the trash. Pens are never the same after they get wet.

Three letters waited for me in my office. I was being granted a six-month paid sabbatical for unspecified research purposes. The letter of recommendation was sufficient, although I would have probably said more about my young Robert Redford good looks. The third letter wasn't an original. It was a copy of Silo's letter of resignation. The poor guy was retiring for health reasons. Good for him.

Did Silo actually send Steven after me or was it purely a malicious act perpetrated by Jacob or his overprotective lover? I never found out. Even if Silo admitted to knowing about Jacob's secret affair with Steven, or his manipulation of Lindsay, it wouldn't have mattered. Proving his culpability would have been nearly impossible and I was all killed-out for the year.

Several months after I last saw Silo, I did hear some terrible news about the former Dean of Academic Affairs. It turned out that his retirement wasn't all he was hoping for. Apparently, the university in California he had ripped-off received an interesting packet of information in the mail regarding an old embezzlement case. Somebody had hired an internet research company and uncovered some information regarding the nearly forgotten investigation. The FBI was called in, along with the California Attorney General's Office, and Silo was shortly thereafter relocated to one of the Golden State's less desirable retirement communities.

Anonymous packages . . . what can you do? At least I learned what an Attorney General's Office does.

—◦◦◦—

The cardboard boxes were splitting at the corners. One of them tore apart as I forced it into the back of the Jeep. It had been just two days since my conversation with Silo, but I wanted to get off campus as soon as possible. The loading zone near my office impatiently waited for me to let it start its vacation. Standing back from the rear of the vehicle, I wiped my forehead with my sleeve, surveyed my packing job, and noticed one of the signals wasn't flashing with the rest of the hazard lights. Just one more thing.

Aaron waved meekly at me from across the street and approached.

"Taking off for the summer?" he droned as he scanned the boxes. He was on the depressive side of bipolar today.

I told him I was. An uncomfortable silence put a wedge between us.

"I am too. I've been thinking that I may go away for a while. Go somewhere peaceful and get away from all this craziness."

"That's probably a good idea, Aaron. It's been a stressful couple of months. Everybody needs a break sometimes so they can step back and regain their perspective, right?"

He didn't immediately respond. He watched two squirrels dance around a tree.

"I've got some problems, Cyprus. I may not come back for a while. I've got some things to sort through. There's a place I go sometimes, it helps me . . . like you said, regain my perspective."

Aaron needlessly smoothed out his thin mustache.

"I just wanted to tell you in case I don't see you next fall. I'm on my way to see if Silo will let me take a semester off."

"That sounds like a nice plan," I said. "I'm not coming back until the spring either." I added, "I think we all need some time to recover if we expect ourselves to carry on."

"What are you going to do?"

"Kaitlyn and I want to spend some time traveling. Then I think she wants to get another dog—something called a Eurasier. So I guess we'll be busy training a new puppy."

Aaron smiled. A real smile.

"Man's best friend, huh?"

I shook my head.

"Kaitlyn's my best friend. But dogs are good company."

Aaron nodded his assent and scratched his neck. A full minute of nothingness passed before he started making small talk about the race. He told me he was sorry we didn't get to talk while we were there, and I said the same. He asked me how I did, and I told him it went about how I expected. We shook hands and made promises about staying in touch over the summer which we both knew we wouldn't keep.

He was nearly across the street when he turned back in my direction and said, "Do you think Silo will let me take the time off?"

Seating myself behind the wheel of my dust-caked machine, I responded, "Just tell him you want the same deal as me. I think you'll find him pretty agreeable."

The Wrangler had barely reached its second record-scratch gear change before the grill lights appeared in the rearview mirror. The unmarked car pulled close behind me, and behind the wheel sat a grim mountain wearing black Oakleys. My side mirror was swallowed by an eclipse as he approached the driver's side door.

"Detective Hartz."

"Dr. Keller."

He was wearing black dress pants and a forest green sport coat over a chalky white polo shirt. He was holding a small cardboard box similar in color to the ones behind me. His partner was nowhere to be found.

"I was on my way to your office when I saw you pass by."

His head pivoted as he took an inventory of the car.

"No summer classes?"

"No. Research sabbatical."

My reflection in his glasses moved up and down as he acknowledged his understanding.

"I was coming by to return this to you." He handed me the box that I knew contained my gun.

"Normally, we would have had you come down to get it, but I thought I would return this personally."

The way he said *personally* made my vertebrae tingle.

"You can sign this."

He handed me a pen and a receipt. Putting the box on the passenger seat, I used my dashboard as a table and signed the receipt without bothering to confirm what was in the package.

"You didn't have to do that."

"I know."

We listened to the Jeep's idling engine beg for euthanasia.

Becoming very disconcerted about this one-on-one meeting, I asked, "Where's Detective Shand?"

"He decided to take a few days off."

Hartz took the receipt and pen from me, tore off the thin yellow sheet on the back, and handed me back the illegible fifth copy.

"You see, he's a little newer at this than me, so he takes it personally when he fails to close a case."

I started to say something, but stopped myself.

"I try to look at things more objectively. The evidence is either there, or it's not. You do your job to the best of your ability and if the dealer still hits on eighteen and gets twenty-one, then you walk away knowing it was just his day."

The engine fell silent as I turned the key. He had something to say and he wanted me to hear it.

"Take the killings in Oakland, for instance. Walker's fingerprints were all over the unregistered gun at the scene. He had GSR on him, so it looks like he shot the officer. Of course, the scene could have been staged, but I don't think it was. As to why he was there in the first place . . . I have no idea."

Hartz looked up the street and then back past his car. An internal timer had activated an ingrained habit of assessing his surroundings.

"Then we have the question about who shot Walker. We thought we caught a lucky break when the bullet that passed through his head was intact enough for us to get a read on it. My partner is a smart guy. He suggested that we run every name we've come across in the TRU and Oakland investigations and see who might own a .357, and bingo! The computer spits out your name and the dots start to connect. We can't fill in all the blanks, but you're starting to look dirty as hell."

Looking through the dirty windshield, I reminded myself to breathe.

"I'm usually not sloppy, but when we were at your house and I bagged your gun and ammo, I didn't notice it." He smiled, but not really. "Let me tell you, I was pretty embarrassed when I took those things to the lab and saw that the bullets were .40 calibers.

"Now, I'm not a gun nut like some cops, so I was at a loss before the lab guys filled me in. Did you know that your gun can either be a .357 or a .40? Yes, sir. We carry Glocks, so I didn't know that. With your gun, it turns out that all you have to do is swap out the barrel, get yourself some new ammo, and then you have a weapon with a completely different signature. And the best part is, you can buy a barrel without having to fill out any paperwork. If someone were to pay cash for that baby, it would be damn near impossible to track that kind of purchase."

A stick of gum materialized in front of Hartz and disappeared into his mouth.

"Like I said, I'm not sloppy, so I had the boys check your gun anyway. Of course, it didn't match, but you probably guessed that. I even thought to ask them if they could tell if the gun had ever been fired. They told me that a lot of the parts looked well-used, but the barrel had *minimal signs of usage*. Strange, but nothing damning."

I really needed a sabbatical.

"Needless to say, I was pretty upset. I was about to follow my partner's example and take some R&R, when I remembered something you said at your house. Shand asked you what you thought should happen to the person who killed Walker and Nokes. It was a bush league question and he never should have asked it. You *had* to know that all you needed to say was, *Whoever did this deserves to get gang raped in prison until the end of time*, but you didn't. You just couldn't resist, could you? You said that whoever killed Walker deserved something *other* than prison. Then you said that we shouldn't even question what you think about cop killers. So here is what I think happened. For whatever reason, I think Walker shot Officer Nokes. Out of either anger or pure instinct, you shot Walker with that gun right there."

He pointed at the box on the seat, while I internally cursed my ego for playing word games with the investigators.

"Then," he preached on, "you bought a new barrel for your gun and made the switch."

He paused and scanned the street again.

"You could have simply replaced it with a new .357 barrel, but why not change it completely? I suppose I could spend the next six months going to every gun store in a 100 mile radius and hope I find some sales clerk who remembers a guy paying cash for that barrel, but even if I did, what would that prove. I'm sure the original barrel is down some storm drain by now."

A river outside Youngstown, actually.

"And judging by the immaculate carpets in that hunk of junk you're driving, I don't think searching for any trace evidence would get me anywhere."

For the first time in several minutes, I looked directly at him. Even with the sunglasses shielding his eyes, I could tell that there was no real malice there.

"What now?" I asked. I didn't know what else to say. No need to fake being offended and insult his obviously formidable intelligence.

"What now? I guess that's the question, isn't it? The way I see it, Steven Thacker killed the Behram girl. You killed Thacker . . . legally. Randy Walker killed a police officer and *somebody* took care of Walker. Maybe Walker killed Virginia Richmond and he doubly deserved a bullet in the head. So, what now? Now, I wait for the call that tells me to pin the Richmond homicide on Walker, whether he deserves it or not. Then I wait for some crackhead to smoke somebody over ownership of a street corner and I start working that case. That's what's now."

A woman in her late fifties passed by on a thirty-year-old bicycle. She smiled at the detective who was making an ordinary traffic stop. He smiled back.

He started returning to his car, but then stopped and said, "By the way, my condolences on the death of that other professor. What was his name? Kanto?"

"Kasko. Jacob Kasko."

"Yeah. Too bad. When I saw his picture in the obituaries, I thought I recognized him. He was running with you the first day we met, wasn't he?"

Seriously, I was going to throw up if this didn't stop soon.

"Just to make sure everything was kosher—because I'm not sloppy—I checked on that race he was running. I found out that you were registered to run in it too."

"I did run in it."

"I know. I'm learning all sorts of things these days. I've never done much long distance running. The most I ever had to run was ten-yard bursts so I could try to separate some running back's teeth from his gums. So I was very interested to learn about those clocking things they put down on the streets. What do you call them?"

"Timing mats," I answered a little too quickly.

"You can go back and check any runner's time when they cross those things. Out of curiosity, because I love getting an education, I checked your times against Kasko's. Do you know what I found?"

I let the rhetorical question hang in the air.

"According to those fancy computers, you were a long way from Kasko the whole time. Almost a full mile the second time you crossed a mat."

"He was a good athlete."

"Apparently he was. Especially for a man much older than you. Well, this got me thinking that only two timing mats don't tell me much and besides, you can't always trust computers. So I talked to one of the race organizers and he mentioned that if I was interested in seeing a particular person, there were official race photographers at a couple of spots along the course. Each photo is digital, so you can see the time that it was taken too. Amazing. Anyway, I told him that I would just love to see some photos of you since we're becoming so close, and he typed your name into a computer, matched you with a bib number and in a flash—there you were!"

"There I was," I said while trying not to look shaken.

"They had a couple of real good photos of you. I had no trouble picking out the number on your chest and making out your face. It didn't hurt that you had those sunglasses up on your head and not covering your face." He tapped a baseball bat finger on the frame of his shades. "In one of the shots, it even seemed like you were looking right into the camera."

"Did it?"

"Like I said, I don't know much about marathons, so I asked the race people if the times on those photos were consistent with the times when you crossed the mats. You know . . . if you were running at a pretty constant pace. They said you were. I then went through the same process to check Kasko's times. It looks like he was well ahead of you up until he collapsed."

Placing his giant mitts on the door beside me, he said, "There is one thing I wanted to ask you about. You must have passed right by your friend after he went down. Did you stop to check on him?"

"A lot of people had to pull off the course. I must have missed him."

The investigator looked at the ground and shook his head back and forth.

"Mmmm, mmmm, mmmm. That's a shame. You have to be thinking that maybe if you'd seen him and stopped, you could have helped him in some way. Or not. Anaphylactic shock is a real bear. It can take only a matter of minutes for a person to die. The medics who worked on him told me that he must have had an allergy to something he came into contact with during the race. Maybe even something he ate. You guys do that, right? Eat things during the race?"

I told him we did and why.

"You would think he'd have known better. He had a bracelet that said he was allergic to penicillin, but there was no reason he would be taking that at the end of a race."

I shifted in my seat and put my hands on the wheel. He changed gears.

"Being a detail-oriented guy, I pulled Kasko's phone records to see if there was any unusual activity before he died. Things like him receiving threatening calls or anything like that. Boy, was I surprised when I saw the same number keep popping up on his system. It was the number of a prepaid cell phone. Dozens of calls were on that list to and from that number, and the records I requested went just two months back. The number was for a cell we found in Steven Thacker's car after he died. Hell, nearly *every* call made from that phone was to Kasko or some office on the TRU campus. Did you know that Kasko and Thacker knew each other that well?"

"No. Neither of them ever mentioned it."

"Sure would have liked to talk to Kasko about those calls. Too late now."

Hartz rolled his neck and took a thoughtful inhale. He continued, "You know, it just so happens that Kasko received a few calls from Lindsay Behram prior to her death. On top of that, Virginia Richmond also called Kasko just before she was murdered. It's funny how people tied to Kasko kept ending up dead. Especially since Virginia Richmond only called him one time and the next thing you know, she's on ice."

The lady on the bicycle passed by in the other direction, and seemed to wonder why this guy wouldn't just give me the ticket and move on.

As if he was coming out of a daydream, Hartz shook his head and explained something I already knew.

"When a guy Kasko's age dies during a marathon, they don't normally do an autopsy. I was going to have him dug up and see what the M.E. could find, but at this point it might be impossible to detect anything in his system."

Several beats passed before the detective seemed to reach a final conclusion.

While coaxing his tree trunk legs to walk away from my car, he said, "Well, Karma's a funny thing. Maybe he had something coming to him. You can't mock the gods of fate and then stand outside in a thunderstorm."

With that, the detective covered the ground between our cars in six thunderous steps and drove back into a city that would never appreciate him enough.

———◦/◦/◦———

Six weeks passed before I found myself back on campus. Of all the stupid reasons to revisit TRU, I ended up back there because of $125. That was the cost of the extra pair of running shoes I had left in my locker. Earlier that morning, I had come to realize the running shoes I had been wearing had seen their last miles. That's when I remembered I had a relatively new pair sitting inside my locker at TRU. My locker—and the shared locker— still contained some of my personal items. The spare socks and Pop-Tart boxes didn't concern me, but the expensive running shoes demanded that I not leave them there to rot. As I drove south on I-79, I cursed my thriftiness and vowed to get on and off campus as surreptitiously as possible.

Less than two minutes after entering the recreation building, I was walking out of there with the pair of shoes tied together by the laces. Brent was standing beside my double-parked Jeep, admiring the fine machine. So much for my covert operation.

He wore jeans and a plain green T-shirt. The gym bag on his shoulder told me he was on his way to a racquetball game.

"I saw the oil burner sitting out here and figured you'd be right out. I haven't seen you around. Off for the summer, huh?"

"Gone for a while longer. I'm calling it a research sabbatical, but truth be told Kaitlyn and I will be traveling and researching the finest cafes of Krakow and Prague. "

"Uh huh," he replied after some hesitation.

Dragging a finger across the dust on the hood of the car, he said, "I guess you probably heard—the official word came down that Silo is hanging them up. Some health thing."

I shrugged and managed, "Well, I can't say I'll miss him."

Brent smiled without smiling.

He said, "Is it true that your buddy Aaron quit?"

Aaron had sent me a rambling letter from his treatment center in which he told me that his wife had filed for divorce, and that he'd made the decision to retire. He wished me well and made no mention of ever seeing me again.

"I heard something about that," I said.

Brent manufactured a lighthearted tone and said, "I need to stretch my legs before I go in there and clean Rixey's clock. You would think a Kinesiology professor would be able to win a few games. Walk with me?"

Without waiting for an answer, he started walking toward the center of campus. Not wanting to offend the last TRU employee who could stand me, I caught up to him. He let several minutes pass wordlessly before he broke the silence.

"Did I ever tell you what I did for most of my time with the Secret Service?"

I had always assumed that he had done things like protect the President, work some fraud cases, and arrest counterfeiters, and I told him so.

"Sure. I did all that, but most of my years were on the intel side of things. I kind of became an expert on what we called protective intelligence. Basically, I identified and evaluated people who were deemed to be a possible threat to anybody who we were responsible for protecting."

I really wanted to get out of there. Normally, I wouldn't have minded a nice round of war stories, but this wasn't *normally*.

"Brent," I interrupted, "Kaitlyn and I have to meet with the travel agent. Do you think I could call you—"

"I started off in Atlanta, did my time in D.C. and then back to where I started. I worked all kinds of threats: the nut jobs, lone gunman types, serial bombers . . ."

The way we were strolling leisurely through the open patches of the campus, you would have thought we were out bird-watching. My running shoes bumped against my knee as I dangled them by the laces. I silently scolded myself for not throwing them in my car when I had the chance.

"But my real specialty was working the groups. Militias, biker gangs, drug organizations . . . the groups like those were the interesting ones. Usually, they kept to themselves, but every once in a while they would get it in their heads to knock off one of our people—the politicians, I mean—and that's where I came in. I teamed up with some DEA and ATF guys and we kind of started our own little task force. Between drugs, guns, and threats, we pretty much had everything covered. Mostly we just watched the groups and prepared to jump in if a threat started to look credible."

We were almost to the yard in the center of the campus by this point. The skyline of the city peered over the tops of the university bell tower.

"So every once in a while some gang leader or wannabe-military commando would start firing an AK-47 in the air and start talking about taking out the old government and building a new one, or some similar craziness. And do you know what happened after that?"

"You arrested them."

"Wrong. Nothing happened. That's the thing, Cyprus, ninety-nine times out of a hundred, nothing happened. Studying the group dynamics of these whack jobs was fascinating. As soon as some loudmouthed leader started spouting off reckless threats, four or five strong personalities in the group would start to push back. They didn't want all the heat that some grandiose plan would bring down on them. They went into self-preservation mode. They positioned themselves to wrest control from the leader who was becoming the threat; the infighting would start and before you knew it—Boom! All-out war would rip through the organization."

Brent came to a halt and turned to me when we reached the statue of Gadson, overlooking the fruits of his labor.

"The most interesting aspect of all was that whenever the smoke would clear from their civil war, and all the main players had duked it out, there was always just one of them left standing."

He paused for effect and squared up to face me.

"It wasn't always the loudest. It wasn't always the smartest. It wasn't always the meanest, the most popular, or the most daring. The last man standing was always the one who had the most *belief*. Right or wrong didn't matter. It was always the one who *believed* he was doing the right thing, no matter how twisted that thing might be."

We listened to a train whistle in the distance.

"You seemed to have gained a lot of insight," I said.

"When you stand back and watch, it's amazing what you can learn. The guys I'm talking about, the survivors, they didn't all last very long. For some of them, victory went to their heads and they didn't get out when they should have. Some of them had truly evil intent to begin with and it ate away at them. Their beliefs, no matter how strong, couldn't save them in the end. But the ones who thought they were righteous. Those guys . . . well, they may have had some screwed-up values, but they could live with themselves. So, I guess we all have to ask ourselves, what are we prepared to live with? And if we can live with the evil we have done, what does that make us?"

Brent let out a long sigh, and took one more look at the city glowing from a setting sun.

"I better get back to the courts. Rixey's going to say I forfeited if I'm too late. And guys like us . . . never forfeit."

With that, Brent Lancaster retreated from the field and left me standing with a pair of running shoes dangling from my hand. My only company was a deranged steel icon and the most terrifying thing I have ever encountered—a clear conscience.